Slow Hand

©John Goodwin 2016

Published in 2016
by Anixe Publishing.

First Edition
ISBN 978-0-9574523-6-7

Cover Artwork enhancement by J Goodwin
Images courtesy of shutterstock.com

Acknowledgements

I would like to thank Detective Superintendent Michael Field QPM rtd, for his advice and guidance on police procedural matters which, I believe, lends authenticity to this story.

A special thanks to Teresa Elliot, whose help and enthusiasm have been invaluable.

Slow Hand

A Novel by
John Goodwin 2016

x

To my wife, Jean, whose faith and support continues to amaze me.

Contents

Chapter 1

Saturday 26th March

The negligee, held closed by her folded arms to cover her nakedness, told all; but I studied her eloquent face. Those hazel eyes, that once I thought were filled with love, now held nothing but contempt. Her mocking laugh taunted me as I moved closer. I held up the knife, eight inches of gleaming stainless steel.

'You wouldn't dare,' she sneered; but she took a small step back anyway.

I wanted to speak but no words would come. I wanted to tell her that I knew she had betrayed me, that the months of devotion and nights making love were spoilt now. She had shamed me and dirtied herself with that man. No utterance could express the pain I felt.

'Don't be stupid,' she said calmly. I advanced and she backed down the hall. Her expression betrayed her mounting nervousness. 'Let's have a drink . . . eh. For old times' sake?' Her eyes darted back and forth, looking for somewhere to bolt.

We had passed the foot of the stairs. Behind her, the kitchen door was closed. She backed up to it. I followed, my gaze locked on hers. Real fear began to show. I had never seen that look on her before and I liked it. I moved the knife towards her right ear, pushing her blond hair aside like a curtain, revealing her long white neck.

'Don't,' she whispered.

I felt a smile begin to grow on my lips as I touched the blade to a spot just below her ear lobe. A tiny jewel of red sprang from its razor sharp tip. She turned her head away, stretching the exposed flesh. I pinned her against the door with my left hand on her shoulder and slowly, sensuously, drew the blade across her throat. I felt it bite through her carotid artery. Her blood, warm and sticky, embraced my hand.

Her expression changed from beseeching to terror. Now she could not speak.

The blade slid smoothly through the soft tissue. God, I loved that feeling. After a brief frantic struggle, she slumped against the wooden panels. I thrust my knee between her legs to hold her up, not wanting it to end. I brought the blade down and found more yielding flesh above her groin, felt again the thrill as I cut smoothly upward until I reached the hard resistance of her sternum. I do not like that. I peered again into her eyes but there was nothing there; no fear, just blank. Her death had robbed me of that pleasure. I should not have cut her throat and let her die so quickly. It was a mistake. A mistake I would not make . . . next time.

On a good day, Detective Inspector Samuel Miller thought of himself as wiry and smart but this was not a good day. With nothing to do but sit at home and brood, he had come into the office to tie up

2

reports and brood over another case thrown out of court on a technicality, instead. Holidays were never the same since his wife died but he needed little excuse to dump the file back in his in tray and get down the pub. It is Easter weekend after all, he thought. As he shuffled the dog-eared sheets back into the folder ready for the off, his phone rang.

'Miller,' he said gruffly.

'Feel like a murder?' it was DCI Archer, Sam's immediate boss, from an outside line.

'It's better than a suicide.' *Like mine for instance,* his unspoken thought.

'A fire down in Colman Street, the Brigade found a body.'

'Foul play?'

'Very foul. SOCO are on their way

'Right, Sir, on our way.' This was better than a pub lunch to raise his spirits.

Chapter 2

The neat terrace of well-maintained two up, two down houses had, in recent years gained higher status than when Victorian builders had created the estate of artisan cottages. Occupied mostly by commuters from the City of London or Canary Wharf, they brought a hefty price on the Greenwich housing market. Corralled in blue tape it was obvious which house it was. The ground floor windows were surrounded by smoke stains and the first floor ones were missing except for some charred remnants of the wooden frames. Only one fire appliance remained at the scene blocking the narrow street. From it ran a small hose passing through the front doorway. Blackened water trickled down the steps and a couple of the fire crew were studiously sweeping debris into small piles in the kerb.

Miller had called round and dragged Mick Forest, his Detective Sergeant, away from his family and was still apologizing as they climbed from the car. A uniformed sergeant whose name Sam could not recall came to meet them.

'The area is secured Sir, but the fire crew are still in there damping down. Here's their boss now.' He nodded towards the front door.

A tall man wearing a London Fire Brigade cap and overalls emerged from the building. He looked pale and shaky.

Sam flashed his warrant card, 'DI Miller,' he said offering a handshake.

'Bill Turnbull. Watch Manager.' The hand was accepted absently. 'The Police Surgeon is over there in his car writing up his report.

'That the seat of the fire?' Miller gestured towards the gutted first floor.

'No actually it was in the kitchen . . . ground floor rear.'

'And the body?'

'Same place.'

'Can we go through?'

'It's safe enough, we're just damping down.' Turnbull led the way along the passage. The musty dank smell of charred wood rose from the littered floor at each step. A wisp of smoke rose from the stairs.

A fire-fighter gave the spot a burst from a mist spray then stopped to allow them to pass.

Miller looked ruefully down at the crud that was adhering to his previously gleaming Italian brogues. It had already splashed up onto the turnups of his dark blue herringbone suit. Squeezing past the all but destroyed kitchen door his elbow brushed the wall collecting a nasty brown stain. Another cleaning bill that will be knocked back from his expenses, he mused.

As they entered the back room, the burnt building smell was overpowered by the sickly sweet smell of death. To their left was what had once been a line of fitted kitchen units with a large gas hob set in the middle of the run. A granite worktop lay at an angle on top of the blackened and collapsed base units. On the other side of the range, it continued cracked but still horizontal. The afternoon light poured in through the remains of French doors in the end wall. It illuminated the motes of dust and vapour hanging in the still air and a blackened corpse.

'I've seen some gruesome sights in my time so I'm kind of immune to it, but this . . .' Turnbull looked away. Outside a bird was singing making the silence in the room more poignant. 'I guess it's because someone actually did that to the poor woman.' The fire officer stepped over the remains of the kitchen fitments and stood in the doorway to the small rear yard breathing deeply.

Sam could not blame him. The odour of burnt flesh and rendered fat was somewhat akin to a kebab shop's drains and the sight of the mutilated corpse was enough to make a statue heave.

'Did you find the body?' he said softly.

'No, it was a young fire-fighter, just out of probation. He's sitting in the crew cab. Pretty shook up I'm afraid.' Turnbull continued to gaze out across the debris-strewn back yard. The bird had stopped its song.

'Better bring him through, Mick.' The DS, who had followed his boss in, gladly returned to the street.

If Turnbull was pale, the young fire fighter was more like alabaster; this was gradually changing to light onyx as he confronted the corpse again.

'I won't keep you a minute, lad,' Sam said, 'Just a couple of questions and you can be on your way.' Mick had positioned himself behind the young man ready to catch him if he should faint. However, even the hard, sardonic detective sergeant avoided looking at the victim. 'Firstly, did you move the body?'

'I,' a gurgle choked the young man's throat. He swallowed 'Yes . . . It . . . I. . .' he swallowed again then the tears flowed and with them, the words tumbled out. 'It . . . she was half buried under the wall units; they had fallen down on top of her. I knew she couldn't be alive but I had to check didn't I? All I could see was her legs sticking out all burnt and bloated like.' He spoke rapidly as if trying to get it all out in one breath. 'When I got the stuff off she was on her side, I rolled her over onto her back. Oh, God my fingers went right into her arm. I shouldn't have touched

her should I? I wish I hadn't. Oh God, oh God. . .'
A new line of tears cut a clean trail down his smoke-smudged cheek.

'It's alright son, as long as we know.' Sam nodded at his Sergeant, who took the young man by the shoulders and guided him back the way he came.

'It was his first.' Turnbull had come back in and was clearly feeling better. 'They see videos, of course, but nothing prepares them for it.'

'I'd give him the afternoon off if I were you.' Sam squatted to examine the remains. In the silence that followed the sound of someone retching carried from the street triggering a response he found hard to control.

'SOCO are here,' Mick called from the front door, 'and the fire investigation officer.'

'Send them through.' Sam nodded at Turnbull. 'I suggest we leave them to it eh. Mick will take charge here.' The pair made a solemn exit as the Sergeant led a small crocodile of coverall-clad technicians into the building.

'I'll have a word with the doc and see you back at the office, Mick.' Sam turned to Turnbull, 'Could we have a joint meeting as soon as the reports are in . . . tomorrow afternoon?' Sam looked at his watch, 'say three? I'll set up an incident room at Greenwich nick.' The man nodded his assent.

Sam spotted PC Jackie King taking a statement from a large woman on the steps of the house next door. She looked over with a grim smile. Sam raised his hand in recognition and left her to it. She had been temporarily assigned as a trainee detective on his last case and he was pleased he now had a reason to keep her on. She had been the first person he called after Forest and responded without hesitation. Her Kawasaki Ninja was parked between the bumpers of two cars on the opposite side of the street. Sam wondered how such a slight woman handled such a heavy motorcycle.

He ambled over to one of them, a Renault estate; the doctor was sitting in its open door, writing in a black leather-bound folder.

'Hi doc, "What you hear? What you say?"' Sam leaned against rear door and squinted over the man's shoulder at the spidery writing that covered the foolscap page.

'What?' the Doctor looked up quizzically.

'James Cagney . . . Rocky Sullivan . . . Angels with Dirty Faces? 1938? Sam Shrugged and shook back his sleeves.

'Before my time.'

'OK, doc, I believe you. What have you got?'

'Called it at 08:15 "Life extinct at the scene." Cause of death, probably exsanguination. You saw the cut I assume.' The doctor sadly shook his head.

'I saw it,' Sam replied, 'What about time of death?'

'All I can say is more than two hours, the fire made anything else impossible at this stage.' The doctor closed his folder, 'The Home Office Pathologist is on the way. She will be of more help once she gets the poor woman on her slab.'

'Anything else you can tell me?'

'No, the fire took all the external evidence.'

'OK doc, thanks, I'll have to wait for the post mortem I suppose.'

'I'll get my report typed and faxed over.' The doctor swung his legs into his car tossing his folder onto the passenger seat ready to drive away.

Sam walked back across the road to where PC King was waiting on the pavement scrutinizing the departing Renault as it eased round the front wheel of her motorcycle.

'I've spoken to the neighbours on both sides, Guv. No one heard anything until the front windows blew out. Both put that at about five am, Her Sheffield accent reflecting the steely determination of her nature.

OK, Kingy, well done.'

Two more members of the squad had arrived and were stooging around, smoking and chatting

to the uniformed constable on security duty.'
Forest had reappeared at the door.

'Mick,' Sam waved his DS over and gestured
to the rest of the team to join the huddle.

'Mick will be my number two here. He'll
organize a house to house, uniform can do that.
But we'll need full statements from the
neighbours on either side and those three houses
opposite. We'd better do that ourselves and follow
up on anything uniform might pick up.

'According to the immediate neighbours, the
fire was blazing by five am so we are interested in
everything up to and including the time the fire
crew arrived. PC King can get the numbers of all
the cars in the street.' He turned to her, 'it will be
your job to trace the owners when we get back,
right?'

'Yes, Boss.' King grinned back.

'I'll see you all back there later, planning
meeting at four. No Easter holidays for us now.'
He tried to look sympathetic. The guys shrugged
and set off to carry out their tasks.

Sam scraped the crud from the instep of his
shoes on the kerb before returning to his car. *I
should have waited for some overshoes,* he
thought, *First job, go home and change.*

Sam, once again immaculately dressed,
sauntered past the large open plan squad room that

was his domain and poked his head round DCI Archer's half-glazed office door. 'George?'

'Come in Sam' Archer looked like an advert for Pringle. His golf clubs were standing in the corner behind his desk. 'I was just about to come down to Coleman Street. How is it?'

'Pretty bad, Mick Forest sorting out that end, I came back to set up the incident room. We can use the squad office I reckon. I'll make room for the HOLMES team at the back.'

'Do we need them? These things usually turn out to be a domestic anyway.'

'Maybe so, but it's pretty vicious.'

'Let's see what happens over the weekend. A good bit of old fashioned police work and you could have it cracked by Monday.'

'If you say so, Sir,' I knew that was coming, 'I've got fire and forensics lined up for a briefing tomorrow at three.'

'Right I'll get off down there.' Archer stood up and collected a garish plaid cap from the drawer of his filing cabinet. 'You're my deputy SIO on this one. Keep me informed. Text will do for now.'

'Fine, Sir. It's pretty mucky in there I'd get coveralls from forensic before you go in if I were you.'

'Thanks, I'll do that.'

Sam returned to his desk. There was a mail notification on the screen of his computer. He opened the Inbox.

"Confirmation of verbal instruction from DCI G. H. Archer. To DI Samuel C Miller appointed as Deputy Senior Investigating Officer in the case located at Coleman Street Greenwich." it was dated and timed with the crime number.

Probably the first thing he did when he came in, Sam thought.

Sunday 27th March Easter Sunday
Saturday Continued

I have often watched TV detective programs so I realised that it required something extreme to blot out traces of my DNA and such. Wearing a pair of Marigolds I found under her sink, I raided the drinks cabinet and found plenty of alcohol to act as what they call an accelerant.

Something like an adrenalin rush gripped me as I doused her body and the kitchen units. The plan seemed to form instantly in my mind. I recalled how once I had left the gas on under a chip pan and caused a fire that, if it was not for my prompt action with a damp tea towel, could have easily spread through my flat. It was easy to replicate that scenario supplementing it with half a bottle of vodka standing in the oil. By lighting the gas under the pan as I left, I figured I would get a good ten minutes before the oil caught.

14

Now for myself I was covered in her blood. No way could I walk through the streets like that. I stripped naked, right there in the kitchen. Soaking my clothes in a rather good single malt scotch, I left them in a heap on top of her body. My shoes and socks I kept. Upstairs I showered and put on a pair of zip at the side slacks. I found them in her bedroom together with a blouse and the wig she sometimes wore when her hair was a mess. There was no problem getting into her clothes, and now I had a fuller appreciation of how curvaceous her body was. There was plenty of alcohol left so as a precaution, I soaked her bed and wardrobe in brandy then ran a trail of Tequila and Sambuca to form a fuse cocktail back to the kitchen.

With one last look round I put on her favourite fur-trimmed duffel coat lit the gas under the pan of oil and, slipping the knife in the coat, pocket left.

A kind of post coital trepidation consumed me as I made my way back to my third floor flat. Two miles of sweating and shaking, trying not to run, keeping the hood up and my head down; I dreaded someone seeing through my disguise. Safely indoors, I heard the first of the sirens. After that, they seemed to be wailing on and off all day. I cannot wait to see what the papers have to say.

Sam glanced through the tall square paned windows of the first floor room in Greenwich Police Station. The Town Hall clock, across the way, showed it was ten past three. It was a large open plan office but the other half dozen occupants were clustered round a whiteboard at one end. He leaned a shoulder against the wall and returned his attention to Bill Turnbull who was summarising the Fire Investigation team's preliminary report.

'So there you have it, gentlemen. The fire was started in the kitchen and using flammables that were already present deliberately spread to the first floor bedroom.' Bill had asked to present his stuff first so that he could get way. It was after all no longer his case and he had other things to do on an Easter Sunday afternoon.

Sam thanked him with a nod and without waiting for him to make his exit, turned the meeting over to his sergeant.

'We believe that the victim is the householder, a thirty seven year old divorced woman named Sheila Delaney. We won't get confirmation until dental comparisons are done on Monday. From what we have gathered from the neighbours either side, she was a pleasant outgoing person, perhaps a little too friendly for their taste. Not exactly a hooker but a serial dater. Often disposed to entertain men younger than herself.' Mick turned to his DI. 'I have organised uniform to do CCTV trawl of the High Street as well as the house to house to see if there are any significant comings and goings in the last twenty-four hours.' He glanced at Sam who nodded approvingly. Forest went on, 'we have not as yet been able to find a photograph but apparently she was a tall woman with long blond hair and greenish or brown eyes. There is still no sign of the weapon. SOCO are still going through the debris but it will take time.'

Sam nudged himself off from the wall and hands in the pockets of his grey mohair suit strolled to the front.

'First of all thanks for coming in. I'm sorry to ruin your long weekend but this is a particularly nasty one and we can't afford to waste any time on it.' He gave them what he hoped was a sympathetic smile before going on. 'Now. The Pathologist says that death was quickly brought about by a cut across the throat with an extremely sharp instrument.' He gave an almost imperceptible nod to his DS.

Forest, taking this as his cue, extracted a photograph of the injury from a folder at his side and pinned it to the board with a small round magnet.

'The rather gory abdominal wound,' Sam paused while a second picture was displayed and the murmured reaction died down, 'It had minimal local bleeding so was almost certainly post mortem. There were only the two precise incisions

17

with no ripping, stabbing or sawing action, which leads the pathologist to conclude this was not a frenzied attack. The victim would not have known anything about the second cut so what was the motive for it? Perhaps a ritual or to send a signal? If so to who? We need to find out what she was in to and trace her movements over the last few days. So, full victimology report is a priority. Also I want all relatives, boyfriends, partners, work colleagues . . . anyone who knew her traced and interviewed. Mick will give you your assignments.

Monday 28th April Bank Holiday

The report of the fire made the London News on TV but with only a passing reference to a woman's body being found in the building. I was disappointed. They must have realised how she had met her fate.

I popped down to the minimarket bought a beef dinner for one and a bottle of Barolo. I toyed with the idea of spending the night in but Monday night was one of my dance nights. It would look suspicious if I changed my habits.

The venue was in Welling and the most direct route passed the end of her road. As I approached, I was so tempted to make a loop round the block into Colman Street, just to see what was happening. I found myself tensing as I joined the queue at the traffic lights. My neck felt like it was in a splint and, although we shuffled slowly past, I did no more than swivel

18

my eyes in that direction. All I saw was the market trader packing up his stall on the corner.

At the Jive night, no one made the connection between the body in the fire and Sheila so I played along. I even managed to ask, "Has anyone seen Sheila?"

"he was at Greenwich Town Hall on Friday." Maureen, replied, "She said she'd be here tonight."

"Oh I wonder what happened to her then." I said, faking faint interest.

Chapter 3

Rain lashed the windows of the incident room the running water distorting Sam's view of the commuters scuttling towards the station in the street below. He drifted over to his desk passing the whiteboard he picked up an eight by four photographs from a table. The lab had blown it up from a snapshot that SOCO had recovered from a singed and sooty photo album in the burnt out house.

The face, so different to the one he had viewed in the mortuary, smiled at something out of shot. Her eyes sparkling, lips full and pink, hair cascading with abandoned elegance onto bare tanned shoulders, all frozen by the lens, in the act of turning. A picture of life . . . a life that someone ended in such an horrific manner. What motive would anyone have to do that to her?

Turning to secure it to the board his toe brushed against the waste paper bin beside his desk. He drew back and kicked it with all his might across the room. The metal tub clanged and clattered against the window and, for a moment, he thought the glass might break.

Rosie, their civilian secretary burst through the door, raincoat half off her shoulder, dripping on the parquet floor. 'You all right Sam?'

Sam shrugged, 'Get me a coffee would you.' The anger in his voice was apparent even to him, so he added, 'when you've got your coat off.' As he fixed the picture to the board, he could not help overhearing a hushed conversation as the woman retreated into the corridor.

'Keep your head down,' Rosie hissed.

'Bad?' Mick Forest's voice.

'About a three,' she replied.

Sam knew that his team had a scoring system for his mood swings, "1" being suicidal and "10" being intolerably manic. "3" was not too bad but he knew that if he did not get some immediate progress he would soon be approaching "2".

Sam walked over to retrieve the bin. 'What time d'you call this,' he snapped as he heard his DS come in.

'I call it eight am British Summer Time, O-700 Zulu if you prefer.'

'Shut up.' Sam tried his best not to be in the mood for levity; but they were in Greenwich after all.

It was going to be a long day, waiting for information to trickle in about the victim. Maybe a relative would pop up, probably demanding to know why they had not caught the killer yet.

There were the reports from the house to house to go through, enough to drive a man to drink. Sam called a meeting for three o'clock, 1400 Zulu to go over the progress.

The heavy rain had stopped but this was worse. Thick dark clouds lay low in the sky oozing a fine drizzle onto the already wet street. *Typical holiday weather,* Sam thought. *British Summer time be-damned.* He looked up at his team from his accustomed position by the window and nodded to Mick who opened the briefing.

'Our victim's name is confirmed as Sheila Delaney a former showgirl, dancer and entertainer. Had a bit of a career working on cruise ships and a spell at Butlins but her last employment was working in a florist shop in Charlton.'

'I've spoken to the owner who says that she was an open and friendly woman and as you can see from this picture quite attractive.' He tapped the board alongside him, 'She had any number of male admirers but as far as we can find out not anyone significant at this time. One thing she was known for was her ongoing love of dancing. Ballroom, Jazz, Rock-and-Roll you name it she did it. Out to some dance venue or other three or four times a week.

'As a matter of fact she had been at a dance right across the road from here on the night she died.'

Sam glanced down to where the cantilevered canopy of the Town Hall covered the side entrance that led to the function room where the Easter dance had been held. Right on his doorstep.

'Any luck with the dance organizers?' Sam asked.

'Not yet, Guv. They are some sort of amateurs, only hold about three or four dances a year . . . Something called "Modern Jive." I only have an address and a home number, no answer, but I expect we'll be able to contact them this evening.' Mick went on, 'From the house-to-house we gather that Delaney inherited the property from her mother and has no siblings or in fact any close relatives.

'The Pathologists report confirmed cause of death as massive and rapid blood loss brought about by the cut to the throat, severing the artery here.' He pointed to the pictures taken at the scene. 'The weapon, still not recovered, is a long high quality blade, extremely sharp like a butchers or chef's knife. It seems to have been wielded with a certain amount of skill, cutting just deep enough to open the epidermis especially the lower cut,' he pointed to the blow up of the lower torso, 'these were inflicted post mortem.'

Sam strode to the front of the group. 'Right, for now, follow up on the house-to-house. Anyone who might have seen her on Friday night going off to the dance or coming back. Was she alone when she left home? Did she walk or maybe get a cab? And I want the area searched again, find that knife. Also, the killer would have been covered in blood. How did they leave the scene? Someone check the traffic cameras.

'Coordinate through Mick. I'll follow up on the dance connection myself. Does anyone know anything about this "Modern Jive"?'

'I do Guv' Rosie raised her hand, 'I have a friend who does it, apparently it's like rock and roll but you don't have to learn any formal steps and everyone dances with each other as well as if they were regular partners. Thousands of people belong to clubs all over the country.'

'If you say so, Rosie.' Sam wondered if there was some kind of dance rivalry as a motive.

Gloria Wallace, the woman who organized the dance, lived in a private block of flats way over in Ealing, West London. She was not exactly pretty but had a pleasant look for someone who obviously worked out in excess. Her slim build and tight musculature betrayed her obsession with the physical. She showed Sam into her small sitting room.

'This was such a shock,' she began, 'Oh sorry, would you like a cup of tea?'

'Not just now thank you.' Sam looked around the room. A narrow mantelpiece was adorned with dance trophies and the opposite wall was smothered in framed photographs of Gloria with various dance partners. In the majority of them she seemed to be airborne.

'Did you know Sheila well?' he asked.

'We met often at various venues, that tends to happen you know. We'd chat sometimes but I can't say I know her well. Danced with her once or twice, she was good.'

'Danced with her?'

'Yes women often dance together. In the clubs there is often a shortage of men so sometimes we swap roles just to get some practice in. Sheila was a better partner than most men I know. We love to dance . . . nothing more.'

'And you saw her on Friday?'

'Oh yes. She was with her usual crowd mostly. They all come from Ceroc Charlton.'

'Ceroc?'

'Yes it's a dance style, a franchise business actually. They meet every Wednesday. They have a nice venue in back of the Charlton Working Men's Club. I've been there once or twice.'

'And did she leave with them?'

'I don't know. I didn't see. We had two hundred people there that night and I was busy at the end sorting out the D.J. and stuff.'

'Would you have a list of everyone who attended the dance?'

'Like I said there were two hundred, but I could probably put together a list of those who bought tickets. They tended to buy two or more at a time but if that would help . . .'

'That would be most useful,' Sam said, 'perhaps you could email it to me.'

'It might take a while some paid by credit card and I'll have a record of that but most paid cash when I saw them at other venues and that will be only from memory.'

'Well do your best. Is there anything else you can tell me about Sheila or that night?'

'I can't think of anything off hand . . . sorry.'

'Well if anything comes to mind,' Sam fished in his jacket pocket and found a business card. He quickly scribbled on the back, 'This is the incident room number, call me there any time' He showed her the card then flipped it over 'My email is here, OK?'

She took the card, wedged it under one of the trophies above the fireplace, and showed him to the door. She paused as she turned the latch, 'There is one thing,' she said, 'It may be nothing but . . . she danced a lot with someone I'd not seen before . . . not a Modern Jiver.'

'How do you mean?'

'Well, most styles of modern Jive, Ceroc, Le Roc, Le Jive and so on are interchangeable but he was clearly a ballroom jiver. Very big on steps, you know?'

Sam did not, but he said, 'Can you describe him?'

'Tall, middle aged, well, fiftyish, fair thinning hair, good tan. He wore a nice suit and really expensive dance shoes. Black patent leather.'

'Would you recognize him if you saw him again?'

'Yes I think so . . . quite handsome really. . . Oh you don't think . . .'

'Probably not. But at this stage we need to speak to anyone who saw her that night. Would you mind coming in and describing him with one of our Identikit people?'

'Not at all. Anything I can do . . .'

'Thank you, Miss Wallace you have been very helpful, we'll be in touch.'

On his way back, Sam called his DS on the hands free and filled him in. At last, there was something to go on. Sam was up to a six.

Chapter 4

By the time Wednesday evening came around, Sam's impatience was beginning to show. Greenwich, being astride several of London's main arteries had plenty of traffic cameras but without knowing what they were looking for, the search of the tapes was pointless. Sheila was well known at the local minicab office but had not used a cab from them that night. She was a familiar figure in the local shops friendly and chatty but the dozens of interviews did not reveal anything significant. Only the local branch of Boots had CCTV and nothing significant showed up on it.

The several days of rain had lifted and the evening sky was streaked with high cirrus clouds dyed pale pink by the late afternoon sun. Sam drove his Saab Aero to Charlton arriving at a quarter to seven. Mick had already assembled the team in the small concert hall at the back of the CIU club. The marked cars had been parked discreetly a block away for fear that their presence might panic their quarry. Anyone arriving for the dance night would be politely invited to stay until interviewed.

If the change in the weather had been reflected in his mood, Sam would have been pleased. As it was, he was all too aware that the more time that passed the chance that they would catch the killer diminished. Furthermore, without a clear motive, could it be that they would kill again.

The main entrance was by way of a small lobby, with doorways to male and female toilets on either side. Just inside the double doors to the auditorium, an arch to the right led to a small bar. A barman, employed by the proprietor, was already being interviewed by a young DC. The Hall was about twenty-five-metres by ten, laid out with a line of bench tables to each side; folding type chairs were set around them. There was a raised stage at the farthest end where a young man fussed with cables connected to speakers set on tripod stands and a music consol.

A half a metre lower on the polished wood main floor Mick was talking to a young woman. When he saw Sam in the entrance, he took her by the elbow and guided her towards him.

Next to Mick's hulking great frame the woman looked quite petit but, as Sam got her into perspective, he realized that she was quite shapely in a chunky way. Not particularly tall, she took long, confident strides to match Forest. The diminutive, flared skirt swayed with every step and her full bosom bounced under a lose sweatshirt that hung off one shoulder. However, it was her iridescent blue eyes that drew Sam's attention.

'This is Julie Button, Guv. She runs the club. I've told her what we are proposing to do here tonight.'

'Good evening Miss.' Sam tried to sound formal. 'I'm Detective Inspector Miller. You understand this is a murder enquiry?'

'Yes. It's terrible . . . she was a lovely girl. Why would anyone want to kill her?' Moisture began to fill her eyes making the blue orbs sparkle even more. 'I thought about cancelling this week's session, out of respect, but it would not be what she would want. She loved dancing.' Her focus flicked to the entrance as a door began to open.

'OK Mick you get on I'll interview Miss Button.' Sam guided her to one of the tables where PC King sat with notebook in hand. 'This is not a formal interview. We just want to establish Miss Delaney's movements last Friday night. Did you go to the dance at Greenwich Town Hall?'

'Yes, quite a lot of us did.'

'And you saw her there?'

'She sat at our table a lot of the time . . . when she wasn't dancing. But she was with someone . . . a partner.'

'Do you know him?'

'Not really. She introduced him as David. I'd never seen him before. Seemed like a nice guy. Not a Cerocer though.'

'Ceroc, that's Modern Jive, right?'

'Yes, it's what I teach here. There are other kinds but he was strictly Ballroom. Quite good though.'

There was a background hum as, in twos and threes, the dancers started to trickle in. They were ushered to the tables where officers were waiting to take their statements.

Sam posed the burning question, 'did they leave together?'

'Yes, I saw them drive away in a big silver car, Mercedes, I think. Or maybe a Bentley'

'I don't suppose you got the number?'

'No reason to. Do you think it was him?'

'We just need to trace him at this stage. Did you talk to him?'

'We had a chat while Sheila was off dancing with one of the guys.'

'Did he seem put-out by her dancing with someone else?'

'Not at all. It is normal. We all dance with each other, there's nothing in it.'

'Did he say where he was from or anything?'

'No nothing like that. Although I gathered he was a doctor.'

'GP or hospital?'

'Don't know, I'm afraid.'

'Is there anything else you remember about him?'

'Seemed very well off. Nice clothes, proper pumps, like I said, Ballroom. Oh and I think he was married.'

'Why d'you say that.'

'Gold ring, third finger left hand . . . like yours.'

'Not definitive evidence but it helps.'

'You're not married then?'

'Not any more. No.' That was the first time he had admitted that out loud since his wife died. He wondered, why now. 'Would you be able to identify him if you saw him again?'

'I think so.'

'Good. Just one more thing, do you have a list of members handy? We need to be sure we speak to everyone who knew her.'

'That will be a long job she belonged to a lot of dance groups and she was very popular.'

'Were there other groups at the dance on Friday?'

'Yes, most of them in the area. I know she went to another Modern Jive club at Woolwich on Mondays. She told me she also did Jazz, Zumba and Ballroom classes. That was probably where she picked up her doctor.'

'Do you know where that was?'

'Somewhere in town I think. She didn't say . . . perhaps one of the others . . .'

'We'll ask. Now if you have that list we can see who is here tonight. Perhaps you can mark up all those that were at the Town Hall for me, Constable, make sure they all know to ask about that, right?'

'So, what is this Modern Jive all about?' Sam asked Julie as they walked across to the corner of the stage where she had left the box file with her paperwork.

'In its simplest form it is a formula and set of signals that enables strangers to dance with each other in a similar way that regular partners would.' She turned to face him, 'Here, give me your hand,'

'No, no . . . I'm no dancer,' he stammered.

'But you could be.' she picked up his hand and hooked her fingers over his. 'No, don't grip . . . now spin me.' Reluctantly, he pushed her hand to one side; she pirouetted on the spot and returned to face him in the blink of an eye. 'There,' she said, 'you're dancing.' The intoxicating perfume of her long blond hair wafted over him. Thoughts he considered long forgotten flashed into his head. He felt his face redden and was suddenly aware that many of his team were watching him. Most looked away at his glance but

Mick just grinned. Sam lip-read across the room "seven."

It took less than an hour to process the twenty or so dancers that turned up that night. Half a dozen had been at the Town Hall but they could not furnish any more information about the mysterious doctor than had Julie. There were a couple of absentees to follow up and they knew their names and addresses. Tomorrow they would re-run the CCTV footage. This time they were looking for a silver Mercedes or Bentley. The team bustled out leaving Mick and Sam to have a quick beer at the bar.

'It has to be him, Guv,' Mick said raising his voice as the music started in the hall, 'he obviously drove her home, probably hoping to get his end away.'

'He did, the pathologist found evidence of recent sexual activity . . . consensual as far as she could tell.' Sam sipped at his lager, 'No useable trace of semen so far. The fire took care of that.

'We'll find him tomorrow no problem. You can't get out of Greenwich without being picked up on the traffic cameras these days.' Mick downed his beer in one. 'If you don't mind, Guv, I'd like to get off home for a bit.' He glanced at the clock above the bar, 'Too late to tuck the kids in but the wife will be pleased that I tried.'

'Off you go Mick; I'll just finish this then be off to my bed too.' In truth, Sam was considering ordering a scotch.

'Good night, Sergeant,' Julie called after him as Archer made a hasty exit. She had donned a headband microphone, which pulled her hair back from her face. 'Inspector, how would you like to continue your jive lesson, I am about to start the beginners class.'

'No I don't think so . . .'

'Oh come on, you're off duty now aren't you?' She looked deep into his eyes as she took his hand again. 'Come on it will be fun.'

Powerless to resist he allowed himself to be dragged out onto the floor where a line of five men faced a line of seven women. 'We need you to make the numbers up.' She whispered. Reaching behind her back, she threw a switch on the small radio transmitter. 'Everybody,' her voice boomed from the speakers, 'this is,' she covered the black bulb of the microphone that was suspended on an arm in front of her full lips, What's your first name, inspector?'

'Samuel but . . .'

'This is Sam. First time tonight so try and help him out, right ladies?'

Sam almost walked out when he realized that he would not be dancing with Julie but he was handed over into the firm grip of a large woman with tattoos and multiple piercings who introduced herself as Carol. She took him into custody to practice the first move. Julie leapt onto the stage and shed her t-shirt to reveal a sporty crop top and, with the aid of the DJ as a partner, danced a short sequence of moves that she proposed to teach in the session.

Tantalizing glimpses of thick but firm thighs fascinated Sam enough to keep his interest as she broke the dance down stage by stage. Sure enough, he did not need to learn any steps. Just hold his hand in a certain way and push or pull as appropriate.

At the end of each set of instructions Julie chimed, 'One lady on please' and he was presented with a different partner. By the time they had gone through the whole sequence he had met and danced with every one of them. He was back with the painted juggernaut that he had started with. A new record was put on and they were left to practice the four basic moves on their own.

Mercifully, the record came to an end and Sam excused himself to make a dash for the bar before another track started.

Julie joined him there. He offered her a drink; she flashed him a dazzling smile and asked for a bottle of mineral water.

'Can't I tempt you to anything stronger?' Sam downed his Scotch and added a larger to his order.

'Not while I'm on duty,' she grinned. 'But you can buy me a vodka at the end if you like.'

Sam knew it was a trap but stayed. He watched with interest as the others demonstrated their dancing prowess. Some were busy practicing basic moves, while others showed a remarkable array of complex contortions. Julie moved among them giving tips here, demonstrating there. He was impressed.

Several women asked him to dance during the course of the next hour or so. He managed to decline all, except for when Julie took him to practice his four moves. He hardly noticed when she slipped in another one which he took in his stride and in all he quite enjoyed the experience. How much because of his vivacious partner he could not be sure. He fervently hoped that the Modern Jive element of the case would not prove significant.

The intrusion of a ballroom dancing doctor had to be the answer. He was definitely at "seven."

Wednesday 30th March
The police were at Charlton interviewing everybody. They were interested in the doctor. Serves him right. They took down my details

then lost interest because I had not been at the Town Hall on Friday. Later, the detective in charge stayed on and made a prat of himself in the beginners' line. I joined in myself just for the fun of it.

I was surprised how easy it was to brazen it out. After the half hour beginner's class, I sat chatting with some of the more advanced dancers.

I joined in the intermediate class, perfecting a complicated cross-armed manoeuvre with which I had previously struggled. In the free dance session that followed, I asked Julie to go over it again with me, working it into a new routine. She was wearing a Nike top with a bare midriff and a flared skirt which showed flashes of her knickers when she spun. Although I enjoyed dancing with her, I could not help imagining how her ever-smiling expression would change as my blade sliced slowly through her dimpled navel.

Chapter 5

It is amazing how many Silver Mercedes cars pass through Greenwich on a Friday night. Only one Bentley, but that was green. They were looking for any owned by a doctor but came up with none.

Sam's mood was slipping. 'Have you traced the ex husband? Sam shot a glance at Mike who was talking to PC King by the door. 'He's on a cruise in the Caribbean,'

'Lucky him,'

'He's working. Cruise Director or something.'

'Better check it out, make sure he's actually on board.' Sam knew that in many cases husbands, especially ex-husbands, had a hand in this kind of crime.

'I've traced some relatives, Guv.' Rosie called from across the incident room.

'Good, send someone round to break the news and bring them in for a formal ID.' 'Perhaps they might know this man.'

'Maybe not,' Rosie responded, 'they're in Australia.'

'Shit . . . OK. Get the details off to their local police; let them break the news . . . Where abouts are they?'

'Canberra, Guv,'

'Do the honours Rosie. Make sure they ask about recent boyfriends.'

'I'll email them the pictures now, Guv. The Identikit picture has just come through from Acton, Shall I send that too?' She nodded towards a printer that was humming its way through a new sheet of A4.

'Can't do any harm.' Sam studied the image of a handsome, well groomed man, in his early forties, a first hint of grey at his temples. Dark brown eyes looked back at him without any hint of malice. Could this be the killer? He handed it to Forest and stood with him as he stuck it onto the board.

'Priority,' Sam said to the office in general, 'Find this man.' Check it out with those we know saw him make sure it's accurate. If we don't find him by morning I'll get the boss to put out a TV appeal.' Printers hummed as his team ran off extra copies.

'Now,' Sam placed a hand on Forest's shoulder, 'Sheila belonged to several other dance groups. Let's get round to them. Do we know where they are?'

'Mostly local, Guv. The Zumba class is on at Greenwich Baths this afternoon it's more a fitness thing,' the DS checked his notes, 'Jazz at the college tomorrow night and another Modern Jive on Mondays. We're still looking for a ballroom connection; it could be one of hundreds.'

'OK, the ballroom connection is the key to finding the man. He could have been lying about being a doctor. Keep going with the car trace, I want all the owners interviewed.'

'We're on it, Guv.'

'Come on Mike, let's get down to the Baths, Kingy can drive.'

They could hear the Zumba class as soon as they entered the building. The assault on the eardrums as they entered the room almost had Sam turning back.

'Do they always have it this loud?' He bellowed at Mike.

King was already waving at the instructor, a slim dark haired woman in a bright green leotard, trying to get her to stop the class. The woman waved back but continued to call encouragement to the assemblage of sweating women in front of her.

Sam marched down the side of the room, found where the amplifier was plugged in and turned it off. Warrant card in hand, he stepped up to the instructor, smiled without humour and said, 'Sorry to interrupt your . . . er . . .'

The woman glared at him. 'I'm holding a class here . . .'

'I won't keep you long.' He scanned her class, they stared back, some with malice but the majority, it seemed to him, with relief. 'We are looking for anyone who knew this woman,' he held up a copy of the picture.

'Knew?' said the instructor.

'I am sorry to tell you,' he composed his face, 'she was found dead earlier this week. We need to establish her movements. I understand she was a member of this group.'

'It's Sheila. Sheila Delaney.' The colour drained from the woman's face making her look gaunt and old. 'What happened?'

'Murdered, I'm afraid. We are particularly looking for a recent boyfriend, possibly a doctor?' He handed her the Identikit.

'I gathered she had quite a few male friends but I never met any of them and she didn't mention a doctor.' The instructor picked up a towel from a plastic chair beside the wall wiped her face and swigged from a bottle of water. 'I can't believe anyone would hurt her she was a lovely girl, very fit.'

Sam sat on a chair beside her and watched the interviews going on in front of them. Mike and PC King were moving among the class taking details occasional shaking of the head in Sam's direction, indicated that this visit was fruitless. 'Do you know of a ballroom dancing class she might have gone to?' he asked.

'She did mention that she had taken it up. She loved to dance.' A tear ran down the woman's cheek. She dabbed her eyes with the towel, 'It was her new thing,'

'Do you happen to know where she went?'

'Not really, but I think it was across the river because she was on about the traffic in the tunnel.'

'Nothing else?'

'No, not that I can think of. We didn't talk much; she always had to rush off after the session.'

Back in the incident room, Sam refocused the search for the Ballroom dancing class to those north of the river. There were two tunnels she might have taken, the Blackwall that led to Newham and Canary Wharf, and Rotherhithe to Tower Hamlets and the City. Even in that limited catchment area, there were more than thirty dance organizations. With the exception of Rosie and PC King, Sam set his team off trawling around them, armed with Sheila's picture and the Identikit picture of the Doctor. Resources were short so Sam decided to take on the remaining Modern Jive club himself. He called Julie Button and asked her if she would accompany him. To his delight she agreed. All he had to do was keep busy over the weekend until their date on Monday night. He set about making a nuisance of himself among the other lines of enquiry but only succeeded in allowing the frustration to drive down his mood. By Monday afternoon, he was a depressed four.

Julie Button lived in a mews cottage in Bexley; about a twenty-minute drive from Greenwich. Sam had phoned ahead and arranged to pick her up, so when the police car slid to a stop outside the house, effectively blocking the lane, she appeared almost instantly at the door. She was wearing a knee length, summery print dress and looked stunning. Behind her, an older woman stood half in shadow, holding a toddler by the hand. Sam jumped out from the front passenger seat and opened the rear door.

Julie turned and kissed the child, 'Thanks Mum,' she said, 'I won't be late . . . will I Sam?'

'What time does she have to be in by, Mrs Button?' Sam almost put his hand on Julie's head to guide her into the car before checking the autonomic response. Closing the door after her, he leapt back into the front and swivelled in his seat to look into her eyes; noting in passing the smirk on his trainee's face.

'You know PC King?'

'Yes we met at Charlton,' Julie smiled.

'It's Jackie.' King grinned.

'Before we go take a look at this picture,' Sam Showed Julie the Identikit. Is that the man Sheila was with at the Town Hall?'

'Yes that's him.'

'Good, Jackie put that in the system as a confirmed identity.' Sam swivelled back to face Julie, 'If it's alright with you, Jackie will drop us off, we'll get a cab back.' Sam wished he could be in the back with her but protocol prevented that. Of course there was the ride home to look forward to.

The club referred to as Woolwich was, in fact, located in the function room of a large pub in nearby Welling. Apparently, the group had moved there when the original venue had closed down. Sam was relieved as the Woolwich area had become depressingly shabby. Most of the decent shops, in the formerly bustling town centre, had moved out leaving it to tacky pound shops and boarded up frontages. He did not want anything to spoil his mood.

King dropped them off in the already crowded car park and quickly drove away. By contrast to the Zumba place, the music was playing softly in the background. A man and woman were practicing some moves in one corner of the dance-floor, while two young women danced enthusiastically in front of the large speakers set up on the low stage at the far end. Everyone else seemed to be gathered round the bar near the entrance. The buzz of conversation dropped dramatically as they pushed through the double doors.

A tall, athletic looking, man of about thirty detached himself from the knot of people and came over to greet Julie. He gave her a hug and murmured, 'I heard about Sheila . . . so sorry she was a good friend of yours . . . of all of us.'

Julie turned to Sam, 'This is Tony Russell, he runs this venue. Tony this is Detective Inspector Miller.' They shook hands.

'Did you know Sheila well?'

'We used to dance together, came second in the national championships last year.'

'And when did you last see her?'

'At the dance, Friday before last,' Tony frowned, 'she was with this bloke.'

'Did you know him?'

'No . . . he wasn't a modern jiver.'

'Well did you speak to him? We need to locate him urgently.'

'No. Not a word. He stayed with the Greenwich crowd mostly.'

'Did you see him leave?'

'Yes, he took Sheila home.'

'Did you see his car?

'Yes . . . Big flash S-Class Merc''

'Are you sure it was an S-Class?'

'Yes, silver, nearly new, worth a small fortune.'

'Thank you, that is most helpful. Would you do me one favour . . . If I could use your microphone to talk to your group.

'Sure, fine, we're about to start. Let me tell them what is going on, OK.' He set off towards the stage.

'What he didn't mention,' Julie whispered in Sam's ear, 'is that he and Shirley were once an item.'

Distracted by the tingle that ran down his spine, Sam did not immediately take in what she said.

'One. One, two,' Tony tested his headset microphone, 'Right . . . before we start . . . you will all know about the tragic death of Sheila. She was a regular here and at Charlton could we perhaps have a minute's silence in her memory, after that Detective Miller would like a word before we get under way.' He gestured to the DJ who had taken up position behind the consol at the edge of the stage who abruptly cut off the music that had, up to that moment, continued to play in the background.

It was an awkward silence that followed, the odd whispered comment hissed among the crowd at the bar and an unfortunate giggle had heads turning just before the end.

'Thank you,' said Tony at last, 'Detective Miller, would you care to . . .' he handed Sam his microphone unit, its pick up wired to a transmitter that he plucked from his belt. Sam did not bother fitting the thing to his head, speaking directly into the black foam rubber bulb on its curved arm held up on front of his face.

'Ahem . . . I won't delay you long. I know you are keen to get on with the dancing but this is a murder enquiry and we would like to hear from anyone who knew Miss Delaney well. We need to trace anyone who had contact with her over the previous week especially those who went to the dance at Greenwich Town Hall on Friday the 5th. In particular, we are interested in tracing this man,' he held up a copy of the Identikit, 'her dancing partner for most of that night. The man who gave her a lift home. Also if anyone knows where she went for ballroom dancing lessons . . . I know that some of you were interviewed at Charlton last Wednesday but I will be over there,' he gestured to a table by the door, 'if you have anything to add.' The music restarted as soon as he handed back the microphone. The floor became crowded with gyrating bodies even before he reached his table.

Julie was sitting behind the table, talking to a woman with a bright red quiff that flopped over one eye; the rest of her hair was short and black. Sam remembered seeing her before.

'Sam, this is Gilda,' Julie said, 'she was at Charlton last week,'

'Yes, I recognize the . . . er' he waved his hand vaguely at his forehead 'Do you have any new information for me?'

'Well.' She flicked her head to dislodge the hair from her heavily made up eyes, 'I was interviewed but they were only looking for people that were at the Town Hall, I wasn't,' she scowled, 'I was away when Julie ordered tickets for the group, and when we applied later they had sold out.'

'We?'

'Yes, Maureen and me. She didn't know if she could go until the last minute. So we tried for cancelations but no good. They'd all gone to Gloria's local group.'

'Anyway, Sheila had a spare but she'd already promised it this man she met at Ballroom, Dave, his name was Dave.

'Dave,' said Sam, 'do you know his surname?'

'She only mentioned it once. What was it now? It began with "S" oh yeah, Sykes, that was it, like the bad guy in Oliver.'

'Do you know anything else about him? Was he a regular boyfriend?'

'Nah. She'd only jus' met him.'

'Is that him?' He spun the Photocopy in front of her.

'Never actually met him . . . actually.'

'But Sheila told you about him?'

'Yeah, we was mates . . . see. She said he was a doctor or something.'

'Do you know anything about her ballroom classes?'

'Yeah, that's where they met. She'd only just started.'

'Do you know where it is?'

'Some posh place in the City, not sure where exactly, but I know it's on Tuesdays.' She'd dance every night of the week if she could, our Sheila . . . used to.'

Sam looked, between the fronds of hair that had dropped down again, into the girl's eyes. He could not quite make out what he saw there but it was not the remorse he would expect from a good friend of the deceased. 'Is there anything else you can tell me?'

'No, I think that's all.'

Sam made a quick note of Gilda's address and telephone number and thanked her for her time. He took a seat behind the table as Julie and the woman got up to join the dancers as a new record began. He watched them as they went into a routine, Gilda taking the man's role sending Julie into an exhausting looking series of spins. Although they were the same height they struck him as remarkably different. Julie's curvaceous body, moved with elegant grace under a welter of flowing blond hair. Gilda's pear shape, seeming stiff and awkward as her short spiky black mop by comparison. However, their synchronization was faultless.

The music was louder now and the buzz of conversation among the dancers rose. Sam wondered how they still had the breath. He slid from his seat and stepped out into the car park to call Mike and bring him up to date. When he returned, a beginner's class was in progress.

Tony was on the stage, demonstrating the moves with a stunning supermodel type brunette; he interrupted the chant, which accompanied each movement, without stopping the dance to call out, 'Inspector. Would you care to join in?' Sam shook his head.

'Come on, Sam, I'll be your partner.' The Tattooed Juggernaut from Charlton was at his elbow, which she took in a vice like grip, and propelled him into the line. He found himself next to a grey haired wiry man in light grey slacks and a Hawaiian shirt. The man had to be well over fifty but Sam was immediately jealous, as his partner was Julie.

Relief came at the end of the sequence when the ubiquitous chime of "one lady on please" meant that Carol thanked him and left the floor to be replaced by Julie. Despite being separated from her several times, Sam stuck it out, learning four more moves. When the tuition was over; he sought out Julie and dragged her to the bar for a well-earned drink. With the drinks in hand, a beer for him and Julie's usual mineral water they returned to their table by the door. Before he could ask the question that was bothering him throughout the lesson, Tony whisked her away to dance in the free dance session that followed. Gloomily Sam watched, but could not help being impressed by the practiced ease at which they strung the moves together.

While he sat, feeling more and more like a wallflower, a few people came over to offer snippets of information but none added anything to what they had not already gathered. The session seemed to go on forever, with Julie barely having time to snatch a gulp or two from her bottle of Evian before being dragged back into the fray. Sam was looking seriously for an excuse to leave when, in a brief lull between tracks, Julie flopped down in the chair at his side.

'You all right Sam?' she trilled, her bosom heaving to regain her breath. The dress was sticking to her body here and there but she still smelled wonderful.

'I really should go.'

'Oh not yet, Sam. You haven't practiced your new moves yet. Come on lets go through them.' She clutched his hand and all the resistance he had planned was lost. He was soon going through his paces. She laughed as the tempo of the music increased; he could not help a grin of his own. Now, to his surprise, he felt it was over all too soon.

Aware of the level of perspiration the frantic nature of the dance had engendered, Sam felt compelled to apologise for the sweat stained state of his shirt.

'Most men bring a spare or two,' she said. 'The demand for a male partner barely gives them a break in the free dance sessions.'

When the group broke up Sam called for a minicab and, as they stood sweaty and chill in the late evening air, he noticed she was shivering and wrapped his arm around her shoulders. Something he had not done to a woman for years. She snuggled in and it felt so good.

Monday 4th April

She only brought that stupid policeman to Welling, the silly cow. He must still be

55

*convinced there is a Modern Jive connection. I
really want to do it to Julie but it will convince
him that it is one of us. Perhaps if there were
another killing somewhere unconnected he
would leave us alone.*

The minicab, when it arrived, was an old
Mercedes diesel with rear seats adequate for three.
Shunning the seatbelts, Sam yearned to cross the
central divide to feel the proximity of her thigh, to
smell her natural fragrance above the pervading
smell of old leather, engine oil and disinfectant.
However, this nasty old down-market model of
the car they were trying to trace, brought his
thoughts back to the case in hand. The consensus
was that Sheila's companion that night was a
doctor in his late forties or early fifties and had
access to a seventy grand car. Something rarely
afforded to all but top consultants or high end
private practice specialists. Therefore, he probably
lied about being a doctor.

Sam glanced across at his companion, her
profile picked out sporadically in the light of shop
fronts as they cruised along. Welling High Street
slid by as they headed for Bexleyheath. She turned
towards him. Aware that he was staring, he started
to look away but caught her smile from the corner
of his eye.

Sliding over he murmured, 'Julie . . .'

'Sam . . .' she looked into his eyes, her own twinkled turquoise in the flickering sodium streetlights.

'Ah . . . I've been meaning to ask you . . .'

'Yes, Sam?'

'It was something you said earlier.' Their bodies rolled together as the driver negotiated the roundabout at Danson interchange. Her thigh against his, his slightly clammy upper arm against her yielding breast, he wanted to stay there forever. However, they were almost at her house and he had a case to solve.

'You said that Tony and Sheila were once an "item."'

Julie frowned at him; it was obviously not the question she was hoping for. She turned to face forward, 'Next turning on the left driver.'

Sam eased away. *Trust me to spoil the moment,* he thought as he asked, 'when did they break up?'

'Just here, please.' She turned back to Sam. 'Quite recently, actually.'

'Do you know why?'

'Something about Sheila not wanting to go in for the Championships again this year, I think. You don't think that . . .'

'Just gathering facts . . . Thanks for your help this evening . . . I did enjoy the dancing.'

'So did I, Sam . . . Will you take it up?'

57

'Maybe . . . If you'll be my teacher.'

She smiled and kissed him gently on the cheek, 'Good Night Sam.'

A light came on in the front room of the house as she got out of the car. Sam directed the driver to take him home.

Chapter 6

Sam was reading through the Post Mortem report again, not on paper but in his mind. Leaning back in his chair, eyes closed, he visualized ". . . some evidence of recent sexual activity, probably consensual." He allowed his backrest to swing him upright and looked at the DNA analysis on his desk. "Conclusion: White male of predominantly Anglo Saxon descent. Insufficient for a positive match due to degradation in the fire." That pretty much includes everyone.

Across the incident room, the situation board had been updated. Suspect #1 Dr David Sykes — Motive — pervert? Had been joined by Suspect #2 Anthony John Russell — Motive — Sexual/Professional jealousy.

DS Forest had been dispatched to bring Russell in for interview while the rest of the team were trying to trace the mysterious doctor. The board was still dominated by the beautiful face of the victim. Sam had removed the lurid images of her burned and mutilated body more for his own sensibilities than those of the younger members of his team.

'Got a hit on a Doctor David Sykes, Guv,' Rosie called across the room.

'Does he drive a silver Merc'?'

'No, Guv.' Rosie hit a few keys and scrutinized her screen, 'DVLA have only a blue, Alpha Romeo Gulietta, registered to him.'

'OK, let's have him in anyway.'

'Mick's just arrived with Mr Russell'

'Fine, we'll do his interview first. Get someone to track down Sykes so we can pick him up this afternoon.'

The interview room was cold. It's off white walls and stark metal framed furniture offered no comfort. That's how it was supposed to be.

'Detective Inspector Miller has entered the room,' Mike stated for the tape.

'Ah Sam,' Russell smiled like a smug crocodile, 'Will you tell this . . . officer . . .'

'Thank you for coming in, Sir,' Sam used his most formal tone.

'I didn't have a choice . . . this . . . Am I under arrest?'

'No Sir, Sam's voice soft and deliberate, it barely twitched the needle on the voice recorder at the end of the table. PC King stood up to allow Sam to take over her seat alongside Mike, opposite their suspect. She took up a position between them and the door.

'Thank you Jackie . . . Would you get our guest a cup of tea?' Sam turned his cold, blue eyes on Russell and smiled, equally crocodilian. "You would like a cup of tea wouldn't you Mr Russell?'

'I don't want your hospitality; I have to get to work. I haven't done anything. Why have you brought me here?'

'You're helping us with our enquiries, Sir.'

'I told you all I know last night,'

'However you were not exactly forthright about your relationship with Miss Delaney were you, Sir.'

'I don't know what you mean.'

'Did you forget to tell me that you and our unfortunate victim were, what I understand they call, an item?'

'What . . . No . . . That was ages ago. I didn't . . .'

'That's right you didn't.' Sam snapped.

'Could it be that you were upset at being dumped?'

'No I wasn't . . . I . . .'

'Could it be that you were jealous of her new dancing partner with his flash car? Could it be that you followed her home, had sex with her one last time, then killed her?' Sam's voice was getting progressively louder.

'No I didn't,' Russell's normally confident voice had become a whine. 'I'm innocent.'

'Then you won't mind giving a DNA sample will you?'

'But I went home with Stella. You can ask her.'

'Oh we will.' Sam watched Russell for a moment. There was a hint of Latin in his dark and swarthy good looks. This was not the Anglo Saxon of Sheila's last stand, but that did not mean he was not the killer. Despite the cool of the room, a trickle of sweat ran down from the man's forehead to be absorbed by his thick black eyebrows. 'Get the details Mike.' Sam rose to leave. 'Oh and a DNA sample. If that's all right with you, Tony, purely for elimination purposes of course.' He smirked at Russell a grin that left his face the moment he turned away.

Sykes was sitting exactly where Russell had been the previous day. He had not been at his North London home so it was not until dawn on Wednesday that Forest had picked him up from his west end surgery. At first he denied knowing Sheila Delaney or that he took her home from the Town Hall Dance. Now he sat flushed and sweating despite the chill of the room. Nevertheless, he was still one of the few to enter nick better dressed than Miller. His eyes followed the black line of the emergency call strip that formed a dado to the off-white walls; anything to avoid the penetrating gaze of the detective sitting opposite him.

Forest slid the buff coloured file in front of his boss and pressed the button on the recorder. The machine bleeped once, the sound echoing off the bare walls. Forest recited the standard advice to suspects ending with, 'Please state your full name for the tape.'

Sykes leaned in towards the machine and in a hoarse but loud voice stated, 'David Richard Sykes.'

Sam picked up the folder and thumbed through the scant contents. His silence held more menace than any uttered threat possibly could.

'Do you own a silver Mercedes, Mr Sykes?'

'No.'

'No?' Sam slammed the folder down on the table and thrust forward into the other man's face, Sykes recoiled as if he had been punched. 'But you drove one on Friday night. Was it stolen?'

'No . . . is that what this is about?'

Sam returned to perusing the folder. 'I understand you deny knowing Sheila Delaney. Do you wish to maintain that position?' Sam did not look up as he spoke softly again.

Sykes gulped but did not reply.

'Now come on,' Sam dropped an intense gaze on his suspect. 'You spent the evening with her and her friends in that Town Hall out there.' he waved his arm at the blank west wall of the room. 'Then you took her home in a Silver Mercedes S class.'

'Y-you don't understand . . .'

'Well you're going to have to make me understand.'

'I'm a married man, Inspector, your bully boys came into my office asking all these questions in front of my patients and my secretary. I . . .'

'Does your wife know about your dancing?'

'Only the Ballroom.'

'That's where you met Miss Delaney.'

'Yes.'

'And you took her to the Greenwich dance on Friday?'

'Yes,' Sykes hung his head.

'And . . . Look at me . . . and you took her home in a silver Mercedes.'

Sykes met his stare only long enough to say 'Yes.' His head dropped again as he muttered, 'But I don't know anything about the fire. It must have happened after I dropped her off.'

'You are a doctor, aren't you, Mr Sykes, Harley Street practice?'

'Devonshire Place actually.'

'A specialist? What's your specialty, Doctor?'

'It's Mr, I'm a Plastic Surgeon.'

'Then you'll know all about this then.' Sam threw the close up picture of the slash across Sheila's charred neck in front of him. 'And this,' he threw a second picture down.'

Sykes convulsed, his hand flew to his mouth, vomit appeared between his fingers and began to drip. His face white, he slumped down onto the table.

Forest jumped up and grabbed the man by the lapels sat him back in the chair and made sure he was not choking.

Sam strolled to the door, opened it and called to the constable waiting outside, 'Quick, lad bring some water for our guest,' and as the officer turned, 'and some stuff to clean this lot up.'

It was a while before Sykes was able to speak again. After a drink of water and a trip to the bathroom, he was returned to the interview room, which now smelled of strong disinfectant that did not quite hide the odour of puke.

The pictures had been wiped clean but remained on the table. Sykes glanced briefly at them before turning away. He was still shaking when he said, 'I think I should speak to a lawyer.'

'Do you, Mr Sykes, do you?' Sam, who had been leaning against the far wall walked to the door, 'Get him a solicitor, Mick, let's make this official.'

'Right Guv.' Forest shuffled the documents back into the file and reached for the post mortem photographs.

Sam looked back from the corridor, 'No, leave them,' he said, 'it will give him something to look at while he's waiting for his Brief.'

Sykes accepted the offer of the duty solicitor, although he could clearly afford a more high-powered legal team. It was almost six pm when the interview resumed.

'My client would like to make a statement,' Emanuel Okeke, spoke with a slight Nigerian accent. He was young, bright eyed and clearly excited at being involved in such a dramatic case. With a glance at his client seated to his right, he pushed his heavy rimmed glasses up into his tight-cropped hair and began to read from his notes.

'Mr Sykes admits that he knew Miss Delaney and he did accompany her to the dance at Greenwich Town Hall on Friday 29th March. He denies any involvement in her subsequent death.

'They left the dance at approximately one fifteen on Saturday morning and he took her home to her house in Colman St. He was invited in and, after several drinks; Miss Delaney invited him into her bed where they made love. He left the premises at approximately three am and made his way home. Miss Delaney was asleep in bed when

66

he left and there was no sign of a fire. Mr Sykes arrived at his home in Highgate at three-fifty-five am and went straight to bed.' He slid the statement across the table. Sam fielded it before it slid off the edge and looked down at the large but neat handwriting of the Solicitor. 'If you would like to have it typed up,' Okeke went on, 'my client will sign it and then we will go.'

'Not so fast, Mr Okeke, I still have a few questions for Dr Sykes.'

'My client will be happy to cooperate but it is getting late and he has appointments this evening.'

'Perhaps he would prefer to resume in the morning then.' Sam snapped. 'Take him back to his cell, Mick.' He stood up to leave.

'No wait, I have to meet my wife at Heathrow at nine.' It was the first time Sykes had spoken since entering the room. 'If we do this now can I go?'

'I sincerely doubt it,' Sam smiled, 'you admit being the last person to see that girl alive and we have your DNA to prove it.'

'The DNA is inconclusive All that shows is that it was a white man.' Okeke's voice rose to match Sam's.

'But your client admits having sex with her.'

'I used a condom,' Sykes murmured.

'So are you saying someone else happened to arrive after you left, had his way with her and murdered her, then set the place alight?'

'It's possible.' Tears were forming in Sykes eyes.

'Did you see anybody? Someone lurking around or perhaps forming an orderly queue outside her door?'

'No, but . . .'

'I've had enough of this,' Sam stood again, 'David Sykes I am holding you on suspicion of the murder of Sheila Delany, you will remain in custody pending further enquiries.' Sam strode to the door then turned. 'What about the car?'

'What?'

'The Mercedes car, the one you denied owning and were driving that night.' Sam grinned at Forest, 'Charge him with taking and driving away and drunk in charge, Mick.'

'It's my wife's car,' Sykes blurted out. 'I'm allowed to drive it.'

'And where is it now?'

'I don't know.'

'Were you that drunk, you don't know where you left the car?'

'No . . . I know where I left it. I had too much to drink and I went home by cab. I left the car at the corner of her road. When I came back to get it on Sunday it had gone.'

'Did you report it stolen?'

'It belongs to her company. I got them to do it.'

'Really!' Sam walked out. 'Lock him up, Mick,' he called over his shoulder, 'we can check on it later. I'm going home.'

Back in the incident room, Sam organised a new search for the Mercedes, based on lost or stolen, and left a note for Rosie to arrange for a search team for Sykes home and office, before he left.

Chapter 7

Sam ignored the five-mile per hour limit in the marina and his tyres skidded on the wet cobbles as he came to a hasty stop in his parking space. Leaping out of the Saab, he stifled a laugh as he glanced at his front bumper that was hanging nine inches over the edge of the dock wall. He just had time to shower and change before heading off to Charlton.

The converted Dutch Barge had been his home for two years. After his wife died, he could not face the big house they had shared in Loughton and moved into the boat he had been fixing up for the previous five years. At that time it lacked amenities and sat on the hard standing alongside the River Lee. He had it craned in and motored down to South Dock Marina when he was transferred to Greenwich. It was convenient for work and saved him house hunting. Now it had state of the art houseboat facilities and, being moored alongside the old stone wall, had need of only a short flight of wooden steps for access.

The rain had stopped when he re-emerged and the sky was clear except for a few orange clouds out to the west. He tossed his umbrella back into the wheelhouse before locking its sliding door. His team would say he was a "two", and why not. He had Sheila's killer in custody and was off to have another go at jiving.

The hall was already familiar territory, the barman gave a nod of recognition as he walked past the arch to the bar alcove. However, Sam was focused on the stage, where Julie was in deep conversation with her DJ. She looked up as he perched on the edge of the raised platform.

'Sam.' Her smile was captivating, 'you've come back for more punishment . . . or is this business?' She frowned at the thought.

'No-no, strictly for the dancing,' he replied.

Wednesday 6th April

That damn policeman was at Charlton again. He was all over Julie when she was not teaching. Disgusting. I am so looking forward to sliding my knife through her flesh. This morning, I took it out of the dishwasher for the first time since that day. Three full cycles, Pick the DNA out of that, forensic team. I put it back in the block with the others of my professional set. The gap looked suspicious otherwise.

Sam had hung around nursing a pint of lager, his second of the night, while Julie and Dave, her DJ, cleared up their equipment. He offered her a lift but she declined saying that she had her own car. He thought about following her home but realised that would appear a bit creepy, so he wished them both good night and went home alone. He might have slipped down to a "four" but the recollection of the fleeting contact with her twirling body kept him at "five". To his surprise, he had been able to, more or less, keep up with many of the moves and had even danced with one or two of the several women that asked him. For the others, his excuse of being close to exhaustion was not far off the truth. For the first time in years, he had had a good night out.

The success of that night only served to exacerbate the comedown that awaited him at the office.

'We found the car, Guv.' Forest's demeanour was far from jubilant.

'And?' Sam went from "five" to "three" in that one word.

'It was towed away at seven am on the Saturday morning. That's why the traffic cameras didn't pick it up.'

'I've always said the auto search system fell short of the mark. Get forensics down to the pound. Even if the knife is not still in it, there could be trace. He would have been covered in blood.'

'Too late, Guv, the company,' Forest looked down at his notebook, 'Global Advertising and Media, paid the fine and picked it up on Monday.

'Get someone over to them and bring it in.'

'It gets worse. I've spoken to G.A.M, the first thing they did when they collected the car was get it valeted. I doubt if there is anything to find.'

'Damn,' Sam was heading into the low numbers. 'Do it anyway, we may get lucky.'

The search of Sykes' office proved fruitless and the only thing the simultaneous hunt through his home produced was a violent confrontation with his wife.

A formidable woman in all respects, her diminutive frame hid a raging bull. She had a team of corporate lawyers at the house within half an hour. A set of chefs knives were found in a kitchen drawer and taken away for forensic examination. However, it was the consensus that, although they were a good make, they were too blunt to inflict the clean cuts the body bore.

By the time they returned to Greenwich, a company solicitor, with enough paperwork to keep them tied up for a week, was already seeking his client's immediate release.

Sam managed to get a quick meeting with the CPS solicitor, but was unable to obtain permission to charge Sykes and, much to his disgust, had to let the man go.

'The only consolation,' Forest said, as they watched from the incident room windows as

Sykes was driven away, 'is the thought of Sykes explaining to his wife what had happened.'

'Yes, I'd like to be a fly on the wall for that one.' It did nothing to raise Sam's mood.

Thursday 7th April

I decided to make a chicken casserole in the slow cooker for the weekend. I took one out of the freezer before work. In the evening, I chopped the vegetables and jointed the bird ready to put it on when I left on Friday.

I used the same knife as I had on Sheila. It slid effortlessly through the skin, a pleasure to feel its exquisite sharpness and see the flesh part but not the same thrill. I really need to experience that again soon. I miss her; I will miss her more tomorrow it was our regular evening together. I would cook; we would open a good bottle of wine and watch TV until bedtime and then — So good.

Chapter 8

The examination of the Mercedes proved fruitless, Sam knew it would, but the report in black and white still drove his mood deeper into the low numbers.

It fell to Forest to add to the pain. 'So far Sykes' story holds up, Guv.' They were standing by the board where Sam had replaced the pictures of the dead girl. 'The vehicle had a state of the art tracking system which records all movements and operations within the car's systems.' He unfolded a digital printout of the GPS log.

'Go on,' Sam sounded resigned to more bad news.

'01:20 Engine start, Royal Hill, Greenwich, Forest droned out like a broken gramophone record:

'01:25 in motion, Royal Hill, Greenwich, SE10.

'01:35 in motion west, A206 Greenwich, SE10.

'01:37 Stationary Colman St Greenwich, SE10.

'01:38 Engine off Colman St Greenwich, SE10.

'01:38 Interior light on Colman St Greenwich, SE10.

'01:39 Interior light on Colman St Greenwich, SE10.

'02:45 Interior light on Colman St Greenwich, SE10.

'02:46 Interior light off Colman St Greenwich, SE10.

'08:12, Alarm triggered. That's when Parking Services picked it up and from there it went straight to the pound, tracked all the way. Sykes said he stopped by the car on the way home to pick up his notebook from the glove compartment. So I guess it all fits.'

'But who's to say he didn't go back to the house and kill her then. He'll have to produce a witness, the cab driver who drove him home for instance, otherwise he's still in the frame.'

'We're looking into that now, Guv.'

'Yes, well, I suppose you'd better track his mobile phone too. But he could have already set the fire by then anyway.'

'That's a long delay, Guv.'

'Hmm . . .' Sam crossed the room to his desk, picked up the phone and punched some numbers as if he was beating a suspect.

'Bill . . . Sam Miller. Can I pick your brains on the fire at Colman Street . . . Yes . . . I'm trying to pin down the timing. The alarm was raised at four-thirty? How long before that do you reckon the fire started . . . as quick as that?' Sam made some notes on his desk blotter. 'And how much of a delay would the source of ignition give it? . . . Yes I know it is only an estimate but . . . and that's the best you can do?' Sam scribbled some more. 'OK . . . yes thanks, Bill, thanks. He slammed his finger down on the cradle and immediately dialled again.

The Pathologist's office, please.' Sam snapped his fingers and looked quizzically at Forest.

'Dr Gordon,' Mick offered, 'Melanie.'

Sam waited impatiently tapping his pen on the desk stopping only to slurp some coffee from his "Man of the Moment" inscribed mug. It was cold; he turned the cup round and read "Mug of the Moment" on the other side.

'Doctor Gordon?' Sam stopped tapping, 'Oh sorry, Professor . . . Melanie, Sam Miller, here . . . Yes, our Miss Delaney. I was wondering if you could pin down the exact time of death. Yes, I know . . . the fire . . . OK, He added to his notes and, with hasty thanks, hung up. He grabbed the blotter, almost overturning his mug that was perched partly on its edge. He did a double take but luckily no spillage. Clutching the blotter, he marched up to the board. 'Right, Mick let's get this laid out.'

Forest attempted a graphic as Sam read out the significant facts.

- Delaney seen leaving with Sykes   01:30
- Pathology earliest time of death   01:30
- Sykes alone with Delaney   01:30 — 02:40
- Arrival at House   01:39 — 01:42
- Earliest Fire set   02.30
- Sykes car door opened   02:45 — 02:46
- Pathology latest time of death   03:30
- Latest Fire Set   04:15
- Fire alarm raised   04:31

'So we have a Schrödinger's Cat situation.' Sam took the marker from his sergeant and traced a rough bracket to the left of the list. 'Between, say, One-Forty and Three-Thirty the unfortunate Miss Delaney may be considered both alive and dead until proved otherwise.'

He moved to the other side of the board and started another bracket. 'From the data in the Mercedes tracker system,' he traced the new bracket as he spoke, 'Sykes was with her from One-Thirty to Two-Forty. This gives a window of opportunity of one hour, ten minutes.'

'Not much time to get drunk, take her to bed, have sex, clean the blood off himself set the fire and get to the car.' Mick shrugged.

'Unless,' said Sam with a sardonic grin, 'unless he went to the car, having had his way then, having second thoughts, went back and killed her. That gives a second window of another almost two hours.' Sam slashed another crescent on the board. 'Plenty of time and anyway how do we know he wasn't over the limit when he left the dance. So, time for a large scotch and then straight at it.'

'We need to find the cabby that picked him up.'

'No. He needs to find the cabby.' Sam fleeting smile did not reach his eyes, 'We've motive,' he held up one finger, 'Sexual perversion and-stroke-or to keep his wife from finding out. Opportunity,' he held up a second digit and slapped the board with the back of his hand. 'And means. He's a plastic surgeon for God's sake. Come on people he's slipping through our fingers. Find the knife.'

Sam knew that with what they had, a jury would have reasonable doubt. He slouched back to his desk to go over the reports one more time. His eyes were not focused on the page in front of him when Rosie put a fresh cup of coffee on his desk. He did not acknowledge her or the cup. He was considering going to the pub and almost knocked the cup over when he turned his arm to look at his watch. Steam was still rising from the inky black liquid. He drank deeply, enjoyed the slight burn to his mouth and the bitterness that matched his mood.

The caffeine hit, galvanised him into action. 'Come on, Mick, there's nothing we can do here, let's take another look at the scene.'

PC King turned the car into Colman Street. Of the three market stalls lined up on the right the first, selling fruit and vegetables was the busiest, with customers spilling out onto the road.

'Drop me off here.' Sam tapped King on the arm. 'Which stallholder reported the Merc?'

'The fruit and veg man, Guv.' She swung the car to the side at the end of the yellow lines but it still partly blocked the road.

'OK, go and find somewhere to park and we'll meet you outside the house. Come on Mike.'

They crossed the road to where the trader was busy charming his customers. 'There you go, Luv, two-pound of the juiciest apples this side of Covent Garden. Anything else?' The woman shook her head, 'That's a quid exactly.' He took the money and dropped it with a clink into a pouch in his leather apron.

Forest touched him on the shoulder.

'Just a minute guv'nor, 'the trader glanced over his shoulders, 'this lady's next.'

Forest held his warrant card in front of the man's nose.

He half turned then looked back at his customers. 'Sorry folks, it's the rozzers. What can I do you for, Constable?' He grinned.

'Sergeant Forest and this is Detective Inspector Miller.'

'Ooo, pardon me,' his smile quickly faded, 'is it about Sheila.'

'You knew her?' Forest asked.

'Yeah . . . lovely girl . . . she used to come here all the time.'

'When did you last see her?' Sam's question was autonomic.

'The day before. She bought apples too.'

'I gather you reported the car parked in your spot.'

'Yeah, it was halfway over two pitches. I was here first so I called enforcement. It's always happening. I got their number in me-phone. Hour-an'-a-half it took, hour-an'-half!'

'Did you see anyone around when you arrived or while you were waiting?'

'Only the usual, you know, people going to the station an' that. I could've been sellin' them stuff, you know.'

Sam walked away.

Forest looked up at the little knot of customers listening intently on the pavement, thanked the stallholder and hurried after his boss.

The council workers still had not cleared away the debris from the fire and cars were parked on it where it lay strewn along the kerb, after it had been sieved through by the SOCO team. Inside, the house was lit only by shafts of light from the cracks in the shutters nailed over the windows. Dust motes still drifted in their beams. As their eyes got used to the gloom, they could see that it was in even more of a shambles than when they were last there. In the kitchen, Sam closed his eyes and conjured up the scene. The burnt body at his feet, the cupboards, then half collapsed, were now stacked like their original flat packs against the wall. The search had been thorough, he knew that, but he wanted to re-motivate his senses. The pervading smell now was just damp but he had no difficulty recalling the smell of death.

They picked their way through each room, their shoes crunching on the debris that had formed a more or less even coating on the floor. Both men were glad to get out front again.

Forest was locking the sheet-metal door that replaced the broken down original when King strode up.

'I had to park in the next street,' she said breathlessly.

'Well you can go and get it now,' Sam snapped.

As she turned on her heel, Sam caught the reproving look on Forest's face, and called after the retreating PC, 'Hang on, we'll walk with you.'

Back at the incident room, over another cup of coffee, Sam checked for further developments. There were none. This time the caffeine only made him itchy. He needed a proper drink. He considered the pub again but it would now be full of office workers, all jolly and looking forward to the weekend. Not his scene. The prospect of nothing to do for two days sent him plummeting into a three. He left them to it and drove slowly home.

Ten pm and a bottle Bush Mills had passed when Sam fumbled through his wallet and found the scrap of paper on which he'd written Julie's home number. He dialled with exaggerated care and listened to the ring tone for an interminably long time. Just as he was about to give up he was rewarded by a sleepy female voice.

'Hello?'

'Julie?'

'Yes,' she sounded wary.

This was not a good idea but he pressed on. 'It's Sam,'

'Who?'

'Sam Miller, er . . . did I wake you?'

'Oh Sam, sorry . . . I was in bed.'

Images flooded his brain, 'Sorry I . . . Julie. Sorry I'll call you back on Monday.'

'No it's all right Sam,' her tone had softened, 'I'm awake now, what was it?'

'I was wondering about this Modern Jive Movement. I need to fill in some background. He took a deep breath to replace the alcohol fuelled courage that was waning. 'Perhaps over dinner? Tomorrow?' He listened to the long silence, only her faint breathing indicating she was still there.

'Oh, Sam, that would be very nice but I have Jody. I can't ask mum to babysit again she has him daytime all week and three evenings.'

'Oh.' It was all he could think of.

'I'm free during the day though,' she threw him a lifeline.

'Oh, well how about we take Jody out to the park and maybe some lunch?'

'That sounds perfect.'

'Good that's . . . settled.' He was going to say "a date," but checked back. 'See you tomorrow then.' He started to hang up when he heard a faint question.

'Er . . . What time.'

He slammed the handset against his ear again, 'About twelve, is that alright?'

'Great.'

'Good . . . Goodnight, Julie, good night.' He

slowly brought the handset away from his ear and

pressed the hang up button. He went to bed a

comfortable six.

Chapter 9

Sam was awake by five am. Flat light from a hazy sky promised a fine day. He sat on deck, wearing just his boxer shorts, relishing the chill morning air and each sip of his Blue Mountain coffee. He wondered, as he often did on good days, if caffeine could possibly take the place of alcohol in his life. However, this was not a day for philosophy. He poured another mug full from the cafetiere and pondered getting a larger one in case of guests, well one guest in particular. He did not even know if she drank coffee. With a smile he settled on getting smaller mugs. He had cups and saucers somewhere on board still packed and stacked for a trip he never made.

The morning dragged by. He selected beige chinos and a bright red polo shirt all fresh from the laundry service and still wrapped in plastic. He had a washing machine on board that he used for his socks and underwear but anything that needed ironing went to the cleaners. A crisp, wrinkle free shirt, he joked to himself, must be the ultimate irony.

Pottering around, achieving nothing was making his teeth itch. Under other circumstances, he would take a drink, even though it was only nine in the morning. A fried breakfast with another half litre of coffee seemed to take less time to prepare and eat than usual. Wired as he was, he decided to pop into the office and check up on any developments. Donning his tan Gucci loafers at the gangplank, he walked purposefully to the car and opened it with the remote. A thought crossed his mind; his breath must smell of bacon and coffee, so he dashed back to brush his teeth again, committing the ultimate sacrilege of walking on his teak deck in street shoes. At least it passed another five minutes.

His team were taking advantage of the current ban on overtime so, in a deserted office, Sam shuffled through the few reports on his desk, all negative. A quick check of his voice mail revealed only a gruff summons from his DCI to see him first thing Monday morning. Sam knew that meant ten o'clock. Archer was not what you might call an early riser, another half a day wasted. Sam felt himself sliding into the low numbers; he needed a drink. Purposely avoiding looking at the whiteboard as he left, he went for a drive instead.

Taking the back roads up to Blackheath, he turned left to avoid the frustration of the inevitable heavy traffic heading into town and found himself drifting towards Bexley.

It was only eleven thirty when he turned into the mews. Parking opposite the house, he turned off the engine, rolled down his window and settled back to wait. He watched the house as if on obbo. Minutes later the door opened and Julie appeared. She was wearing a blue full-length dressing gown of some silky material, which she hugged to her as she trotted over.

'Sam, you're early.'

Sam shrugged and grinned bashfully but could not think of a reply.

'Well don't sit there, come in, I won't be long.' Julie turned and hurried back. Sam hurried after her. She had left the front door open for him. He closed it quietly behind him, and followed the glimpse of her trailing robe into the small lounge. The room was almost filled by an overstuffed three-piece-suite in floral patterned fabric, on the floor in front of which sat her, curly haired, three-year-old son.

'Jodi.' Julie raised her voice, 'Jodi.' The boy reluctantly turned his big dark eyes away from the thirty-two-inch TV that looked huge mounted above the fireplace.

'Jodi, this is Mr Miller, he's a policeman.' The boy's eyes widened a little. 'Sam, this is Jodi.'

'Hello Jodi,' Sam had no experience with children but he pressed on. 'That is a nice name . .

. do you like it?' Sam sat in one of the armchairs to be nearer to the boy's eye line.

The boy shrugged. Eyes riveted on Sam's.

'Say hello, Jodi.'

'lo,'

'My friends call me Sam,' Sam was withering under the uncompromising gaze.

'I . . . I'll leave you two to get acquainted,' Julie said as she headed for the door, 'I'll just get dressed.'

Sam found himself alone with only a toddler and a trace of her perfume.

'Where's your proper clothes?' The boy's sudden outburst made Sam jump.

'Proper clothes . . . What proper clothes?'

'Your policeman clothes . . . where's your policeman clothes?'

'Oh . . . my uniform . . . I don't wear a uniform much . . . I'm a detective.'

'Have you got a gun?' The lad's freshly scrubbed, chubby little face was the colour of caramel toffees. It maintained a grave and thoughtful expression throughout their encounter.

'No I don't have a gun.'

'Show me some ID,' a stern demand.

Sam reached into his hip pocket and brought out his warrant card and flashed it at his young inquisitor.

'Where's your badge?'

'English policemen don't have a badge. We have a warrant card with a photo . . . see?' he opened the wallet again.

'Let me see,' the boy climbed up onto the arm of the chair and held on to the edge of the wallet.

'You see, that's a picture of me, and that says Detective Inspector Samuel Miller.'

Jodi looked at the image then up at Sam's face, did a double take and said 'you've got gray hair.'

'Well . . . I'm a bit older now.' He had not realised how much he had aged since his promotion. Nevertheless, he was warming to this pint-sized interrogator. 'What are you watching on TV?' he asked, trying to change the subject.

'I'm three.'

'Really . . . you are a big boy.'

'How old are you?'

'I'm forty.'

'I'll be forty soon.'

'Yes . . . one day.'

'Ready,' Julie declared from the foot of the stairs. She was wearing blue jeans and a pink knitted v-necked sweater that clung to her curves. Her hair, pulled back in a ponytail made her look impossibly young. *Seven years is not too big an age gap,* he thought, *is it?*

Jodi loved the Saab, despite the disappointment that it did not have blues and twos. At Julie's insistence, they had transferred the child safety seat from her little Fiat and the boy had clambered in it as soon as it was secured, eager to be off. He chattered all the way on the short journey to Danson Park. Once they had parked and passed through the gates, he ran excitedly around making siren noises, American rather than English.

'He watches too much TV,' Julie remarked as they strolled after him, 'It's his granny, she's hooked on American cop shows.'

'Does he like boats?' Sam nodded towards the lake.

'He's not been on them but he often watches, when I bring him here. I worry about him falling in while I'm rowing.'

'Come on then, I'll row and you can keep hold of him.'

With Jodi togged out in a bright orange life-jacket, Sam took them on several circuits of the lake. The boy, despite his mother's firm grip on the back of his jacket, hung over the side pointing at every piece of weed or half-submerged crisp packet, demanding to know what kind of fish it was. In truth he did spot a couple of live ones which Sam identified, rightly or wrongly, as Perch or Bream until his repertoire of freshwater breeds failed him, and he settled on a tiddler. This made Jodi laugh and laugh, though Sam did not know why.

Once safely ashore, they walked over to the restaurant 'Jodi seemed to like the boat ride,' Sam watched as the boy walked backwards in front of them making a rowing motion with his hands. 'I'm glad, because I live on one.'

'Jodi, watch where you're going,' Julie cautioned her son then turned to Sam, 'You live on a boat? Where?'

'South Dock, it's not far. I'll take you there sometime.'

'I'd like that, Sam.'

Tucked away in a leafy dell in the centre of the park, the restaurant was a converted stable taken up by one of the carvery chains to serve good pub grub. They all had worked up a remarkable appetite and, to Sam's surprise, the one beer he had allowed himself did not lead to a craving for another.

They waited for the bill, sipping a rather disgusting filter coffee, while Jodi demolished the last of his giant ice-cream-sundae and then made their way slowly back to the car. What actually made Sam's day was, as he walked hand in hand with Julie, another little set of fingers slid into his free one.

Jodi was asleep before they reached Julies house and Sam carried him to the door while Julie unlocked it. Reluctantly he handed over his charge and returned to recover the child seat, which he brought in and deposited in the hall.

'Did you want me to fix it back in your car?' he asked as Julie reappeared at the top of the stairs.

She shook her head, touched a finger to her lips and waved him into the sitting room. Closing the door behind her, she said softly, 'with a little luck he'll be out for at least an hour, so now we can talk.' With a sigh she collapsed onto the sofa, 'that was a lovely day, Sam; Jodi seems to be quite taken with you.' She patted the seat next to her. 'You wanted to know more about Ceroc, we didn't get a chance over lunch.'

Sam realised he had been standing gawping at her and, with an effort, closed his mouth and joined her. He felt her cool skin against his as their bare arms touched. His internal organs were doing gymnastics for which his frame had long since lost the capacity. His gaze fixed straight ahead he croaked, 'I was too busy talking to Jodi,' He cleared his throat and turned. She was staring hard at him. From inches away, her eyes were big and brilliant blue. The policeman in him noted that her pupils were dilated but he guessed that his were too.

He thought they were going to kiss and tilted his head a little but suddenly she turned away.

Her face fell serious and, leaning forward in her seat, she said, 'I don't want to fall for you, Sam.'

'But . . .'

'Not if I am just a part of your investigation.'

'You're not . . .'

'Let me finish, Sam, please. I fell in love once before and ended up with Jodi. He's my life now and I wouldn't go back but he needs a father, not a string of uncles. Do you understand?' She turned looking deep into his eyes. 'Sam?'

'Julie . . . because we met during an investigation, I am . . . was a little restricted by my job, but that is not what today was about. I used the excuse of researching Modern Jive just to see you again and if Jodi needs a father well . . .'

Julie put a finger to his lips, 'Let's take it slow then,' she smiled, 'and believe me, it's killing me to ask this.'

'Perhaps I should go.' He got to his feet. She came with him and he realised they were holding hands.

At the front door, she stood on tiptoes and kissed him gently on the lips. 'Good night, Sam,' she whispered.

'Good night Julie,' he gave her a quick hug and crossed the road to the car then looked back.

She was still standing in the doorway. 'When can I see you again?' he asked.

'There's a Ceroc meet at Woolwich on Monday if you're game.' Her eyes twinkled with the reflected streetlight.

'OK . . . I'm game.'

'Pick me up about half seven?'

Sam nodded.

Saturday 9th April

I need a distraction I phoned Julie this morning she told me that she had a date with that policeman. If he makes the connection to Jive Clubs, he will not be able to carry on seeing her. Moreover, I know just the candidate, that cow who told me she had run out of tickets for the Greenwich bash. If I had been there, Sheila would never have gone with that disgusting old man.

Chapter 10

Sunday was interminable. Caffeined to the eyeballs, fighting the urge to open a new bottle of Bushmills and drink himself into oblivion, Sam went over the events of the previous day. Time and again he recalled the touch of her skin, the feel of her body in the hug, and that parting kiss. He tried reading, watching TV, even the Sunday Times crossword, but he could not concentrate. Somehow, he survived, went to bed too early and after a fitful night's sleep arrived, still wired, at the office at six am.

Sunday 10th April

It was easy to get her into bed. I just turned up on her doorstep at ten pm rang the bell and when she looked through the peephole I stood casually dangling a pair of fur lined handcuffs in one hand and a bottle of Champagne in the other. She was wearing her nightclothes, pink boxer shorts and a sleeveless white top. They did not meet and I was drawn to her belly button. "Wish I Didn't Miss You" by Angie Stone was playing on her stereo. We danced into the sitting room. It was on a compilation album, we let it run while she got some glasses. The tablet I dissolved in her first drink might have been unnecessary as, before it could possibly take effect, she suggested we take the wine into the bedroom. I turned the player up so that we could hear it from there.

She had a bedside draw full of stuff. Handcuffing her to the bed frame had her giggling with delight and she laughed out loud when I tied her ankles to complete the spread eagle effect. She even joked that I had forgotten to take her knickers off. That is when I got the knife from my bag. I asked if it was all right, as I slid the blade under vest. She said to go ahead as it was only an old thing. Before I did I found a rubber gag and thrust it between her teeth.

I made the cold, blunt spine of the blade run against her skin as it parted the material to reveal her tiny breasts and erect nipples like a pair of prunes on caramel blancmange. When I reversed the process, parted her elastic waistband and moved slowly downwards, her clitoris stroked the side of the blade. I let her enjoy the moment while I stripped naked myself. Her eyes never left me as I deposited the neat pile of clothes on a chair at the far side of the room. She even grinned when she saw the knife was still in my hand when I returned to the bedside. I lay the sharp edge across her taut stomach. It broke the skin easily and she wriggled with masochistic pleasure as I drew the blade across under its own weight leaving a thin red line an inch above her navel. She was enjoying this more than I was. I pushed the handle between her legs and slipped it into her moist opening. Then as she arched her back and moved rhythmically against it removed it and *made a second cut across this time just below her navel. She tapped her hand on the bedpost to signal enough but I ignored it.*

Without any subcutaneous fat, there was no pleasure in the passage of the blade I made two more cuts vertically to make a grid. Her face was a picture. lips curled back as she struggled to scream. Her eyes filled with the fear I craved to see. I touched the blade to her throat and slowly made the final cut then watched until life had gone from those dark, Arabic eyes.

There was blood all over her, the bed and me. I needed a shower and to clean my knife before leaving. Before I did, I looked down at the pattern on her abdomen and had an idea. Wiping it with the remains of her vest and treating her navel as the first turn, I cut a neat cross in the left hand bottom segment then stuck the point to make a round dot in the bottom right.

Your move, Detective Inspector Miller. That will give you something to think about.

I put another album on while I cleaned up. Pulling the fitted sheet out from under her like that trick with a table cloth, I used it to wipe the blood off her so that only the cuts were bright red. I bundled it into her washing machine with all the other stained sheets, set a long wash with the soap trays fully loaded then showered. Just to be safe, I found a pair of blue Marigolds in the kitchen and thoroughly cleaned everywhere I had been. Strangely enough, I do not mind housework. The last track on the album was playing as I left, Baby Face and Des're had just started singing "Fire". Not this time I think.

There was a woman in the DCI's office so Sam knocked and waited, watching through the glass panel of the door, for a signal to enter. Archer broke off his conversation and waved Sam in.

'Ah, Sam, this is Dr Fielding, she is a criminal psychologist. I've asked her in to consider the significance of the ritual cutting on the victim's abdomen.' He turned to Fielding and said, 'Dr Fielding, Detective Inspector Miller.'

'She stood and extended a long fingered hand, 'Elisabeth' she said, her voice soft and cultured to match her elegant image. She was tall with dark brown hair tied back in a bun, wearing just enough makeup to soften the harsh lines of her high cheekbones, and an unfortunately crooked and over long nose. She smiled, revealing small white teeth almost too even to be real.

'Sam,' Sam replied taking her hand, aware of her fingers crossing over under his grip, he released it immediately.

She resumed her seat, crossing her long legs, allowing the split in the grey, wrap around skirt of her smart suit to reveal a considerable length of golden thigh before readjusting it demurely.

'Have you seen the body?' Sam asked.

'A picture.'

'And?'

102

'It is most unusual.'

'Perhaps,' Archer interrupted, 'you would like to take Dr Fielding to a conference room and talk her through what you have so far.'

'Of course,' Sam, always glad of an early exit from the DCI's office, stood and held the door open for his guest.

He left her perusing the whiteboard while he returned to his desk and gathered up the files he had been going over for the tenth time that morning. He asked Rosie to fish out the interview tapes of Sykes and Russell then led the way to interview room number 3. They did not have a conference room per se, and the recorder was a dead giveaway, but nothing seemed to elicit any reaction from the psychologist, not even the gory images on the board.

Settled side by side at the table, he spread the main case file in front of her and said, 'Perhaps you would like some time to read through this first.'

'Why don't you talk me through it, Sam, I can always look at the notes later.'

'OK . . .' she made him nervous but he did not know why. 'You know about the fire and how we came to be called in,' he began.

She nodded.

A knock on the door heralded Rosie's arrival; Sam was relieved to see a friendly face. She was carrying a tray with two mugs of coffee with a small cup of milk and a few paper tubes of sugar. On the side, secured by her thumb, were the tape cassettes. 'I didn't know how you took it ma'am so I'll leave you to help yourself.' She put the tray down and left quickly, leaving the door ajar.

Fuelled by coffee, Elizabeth also took it black, Sam gave an abbreviated account of their investigation so far. She listened attentively skeletal fingers steepled in front of her, sometimes with her eyes closed, interrupting only to ask to see the relevant picture in the file and to ask to play the tape when Sam mentioned the dance instructors interview.

When the tape ended she said, 'You sounded angry, Sam.'

'It's a technique,' he replied, 'A bit of shock to break down the suspect's resistance . . . What do you . . .'

'Do you get angry easily, Sam?'

'No,' he snapped, 'What about Russell?'

She looked into Sam's face for a long time without saying anything. He stared back, imagining her as a hostile witness. At last, she said softly 'He's hiding something . . . but I don't think it's about the killing. What do you think, Sam?'

He was getting fed up with hearing his name at the end of each sentence. From her it sounded so patronising, and always a question. 'I agree, Elizabeth. I agree . . . Shall I go on?'

'Liz,' she said, 'my friends call me Liz.'

He took a defensive sip of his coffee; it was stone cold. Grimacing he said, would you like a break . . . Liz? Perhaps lunch in the pub over the road, the food's quite good.'

She looked at her watch. 'A bit late for lunch wouldn't you say, Sam?'

A glance at his Omega Seamaster revealed Four-thirty already. He recalled he had a hot date and that raised his mood, he smiled. 'Sorry,' he said, 'doesn't time fly when you're having fun?'

'But perhaps, Dinner?' she left it hanging, like a hand-grenade on a string.

'Liz . . . I'm afraid I'm tied up tonight, but ...'

'Then maybe some more coffee?'

'I'll organise it,' he said and picked up the tray; at the door he handed it to uniformed constable, he found lurking in the hall, with instructions for both to be black and returned to his seat.

'Why didn't you use the call button?' she asked, 'that is a call system I take it.' She gestured to the black strip along the wall.

He laughed, 'one press on that and a couple of burly PC's with a straight jacket will be in here in seconds and to be honest I'm not sure which one of us they'd put it on.'

She laughed; a tinkling sound that belied her stern countenance. She returned to the pictures in the file, a sobering influence for them both. When the coffee arrived, Sam started to tell her about their prime suspect but she stopped him.

'I think we had better pick this up again in the morning, Sam. We'll only have to go over it again then.' She sat back in her chair and sipped the hot brew.

The hard plastic must be murder on her bony behind, Sam thought. His own bum was getting numb too.

'So what about you, Sam, do you usually take a pub lunch?'

'Occasionally. Just a beer and a sandwich, you know?'

'Hmm,' her reply sounded judgemental to him.

He decided to wind things up and gulped back his coffee, although it burned the back of his tongue. 'Would you like a copy of anything from the file?' he asked, as he rose to his feet.

'Not just now, Sam, but perhaps we could start a little earlier tomorrow?' it sounded like she was apportioning blame.

'Eight o'clock, Suit you?' He snapped.

'Sam . . . Nine would be fine. A girl needs her beauty sleep you know.'

Some more than others, he thought. Retrieving the tape from the machine and gathering the files, he ushered her back into the incident room. 'You know your way out,' he stated as he crossed to Rosie's desk and dumped the bundle on it. She had already gone for the night but they would do there until morning. When he looked up the Psychologist had gone too.

Chapter 11

Sam's anger at the psychologist quickly abated at the thought of his date with Julie. By the time he had showered and changed, his focus was on remembering the dance moves she had taught him. The case was stalled anyway.

At Julie's house, he met her mother; a short round woman in her early sixties with dyed black hair and a stern expression, as she answered the door. She regarded him suspiciously, arms folded in a, they shall not pass, stance, showing no hint of welcome until her daughter's voice carried from upstairs.

'If that's Sam, ask him in, Mother.'

The woman backed against the passage wall to allow him to pass but her expression softened when Jodi, with a cry of 'Sam - Sam,' raced from the sitting room and clattered into his legs. He clung there until he was picked up and carried in to be dumped from a height onto the sofa. He continued to chatter about boats and fishes as he bounced up and down on the upholstery. Sam sat alongside him as Julies mother came in and muted the TV.

'Oh, Nan! We was watching that,' Jodi scowled, 'wasn't we, Sam?'

'Weren't we, Sam,' she corrected automatically, 'I'm Julies mother.'

'Pleased to meet you, Mrs Button,' Sam stood and offered a hand. She took it in a surprisingly strong grip for such podgy fingers and regarded him in thoughtful silence.

Eventually she said, 'Margret, son, you can call me Margret.' She was about to say something else when Julie burst into the room. She looked stunning in her black and gold dance outfit.

'Ta-da,' she pirouetted for inspection, making the short skirt flare out and lighting a fire in Sam's loins that was hard to ignore. She bounced over, pushed his chin up where his mouth had fallen open and pecked him lightly on the lips. Then she turned, scooped up her son, hugged and kissed the protesting little boy and handed him over to his grandmother.

'I'm going dancing with Sam now,' she said, 'say goodnight.'

'But we was watching, Nemo.'

'Sam will watch Nemo with you another night.'

Sam nodded and grinned inanely.

'Awe.' the boy buried his head in Margret's shoulder.

'Come on Sam.' Julie picked up a light raincoat from the back of a chair and took Sam's arm. Margret carried Jodi to the door to wave them off.

'Night Sam,' came a little voice as Sam clicked the car remote.

'Goodnight, Jodi, see you soon.' Sam replied and returned the wave.

Settling Julie in the car, he hastened to join her and with one last glance at the pair, still waving from the doorstep drove slowly off.

'I don't think it's going to rain,' Sam said, as they turned toward Welling.

'Oh you mean this,' Julie laughed, lifting the cream coat off her knees a fraction. 'Purely for mum's benefit. She thinks my dance outfit is . . . too provocative to be seen on the street. She twisted and tossed the offending garment onto the back seat, revealing all of her tantalising thighs.

Sam so wanted to skip the dance and divert to his place but dare not suggest it. Instead, he just looked and grinned.

They arrived at the venue with time for a drink before the beginners class began. Russell looked down from the stage and smiled widely when Julie entered, this quickly became a frown when he saw Sam appear behind her. He turned his back and returned to rehearsing with his partner.

Sam went to the bar while Julie was greeting friends at a table not far from the door. He had just put the drinks down when Russell stormed over.

Ignoring Sam, he snapped at Julie, 'Is he a member?'

'You mean is Sam a member of Ceroc?' Julie fished in her clutch bag and came out with a small membership card. 'Here Sam, I meant to give you this earlier.' She handed it over to questioning looks from her date.

Russell, his face like a cauldron, turned on his heel and stormed off towards the gents.

'I'll be back in a minute,' Sam followed the retreating figure.

Russell had turned on a tap and was leaning heavily on the edge of a washbasin. From the look on his face, reflected in the large wall mounted mirrors, he was still seething.

Sam stood alongside and addressed the mirror image, 'Tony . . .'

'Have you come here to disrupt my session again,' Russell literally spat out the words, 'am I still a suspect?'

'No, Tony, you are not part of my investigation at the moment and the only disruption to your class will be from my clumsy dancing.'

Russell grunted and started vigorously washing his hands but his face was returning to its normal colour.

Sam went on, 'I'm sorry I gave you such a hard time at the interview, but this is a very distressing case and I was only doing my job.'

Russell grunted again and turned to the air hand-dryer on the end wall. He punched the button as if it was Sam's face.

'Tonight I'm only here for the dancing,' Sam said over the whine of the machine, 'so ... are we good?'

Russell nodded imperceptibly.

Satisfied he had done his best, Sam returned to the group at the table and downed his half of lager in one.

'Is he OK, Sam?' Julie asked.

'He will be fine,'

Russell came past, walking purposefully towards the stage.

'I think you know everyone,' Julie guided Sam into a seat beside her.

'Only in passing or in the beginners' line,' Sam smiled, 'we've not been formally introduced.'

'Well in that case, I'm Carol O'Connor,' the tattooed Juggernaut extended a mighty mitt, and this is Maureen.' A skinny young woman with a boyish haircut, nodded curtly in response. Wreathed in smiles Carol continued the introductions, 'Ted,' a stocky man in his forties, 'Patrick,' a slim good-looking black man, 'Gilda,' a pear shaped young woman with a blood coloured quiff in her otherwise short, black hair, 'and Roger,' a skinny bespectacled twenty something who smiled shyly. 'Everyone, this is Sam, he's a policeman.'

'No, no, not tonight,' Sam replied, 'Tonight I'm here to learn to dance.'

'Actually,' Julie corrected, 'Sam's here as my date, so hands off girls.'

'Sod that,' said Carol, with a grin. She lunged at Sam's hand. 'Come on, Sam, let's see what you've got.' With that, she dragged him onto the floor to join the half a dozen couples already dancing. The DJ was playing "Brown Eyed Girl," a moderate paced favourite of modern Jivers and, despite himself, he found he had enough moves to enjoy it.

When the music changed, to Kylies "Spinning Around," Julie came to his rescue, cutting in with a cheery, 'mine I think.' However, his delight at being able to dance with her was short lived as Russell called the class to form two lines, men on the left women on the right and already worn out and desperate for a drink, Sam was plunged into the lesson.

Tuesday 12th April

They were at Welling last night. Obviously, he has not made the connection. There was nothing in the papers about Gloria, so maybe she has

not been found yet. I put the restraints and gag
in the dishwasher with my knife. It really ruined
the fur on the handcuffs but they may still come
in useful. I cannot wait to get my hands on Julie,
and I see an opportunity coming up, but first
things first.

The night had been a great success, although he did not have the exclusive attention of Julie he had hoped for. It seemed that she spent an inordinately large part of the final free dance session with Tony Russell. Despite himself, he had to admire the way they moved. He could see the attraction but he did not have to like it.

In the end, it was Sam who took her home and their kiss on her doorstep was too long and passionate to be platonic. He promised to meet her at Charlton on Wednesday night and made up his mind to invite her back to his boat the first chance he got.

For once a dreamless full night's sleep, which he put down to the unaccustomed cardio workout at the dance club, found him sharp and eager in the morning. He could even face another session with the Psych Witch. In the office he retrieved the files and tapes from where he had left them and organised a flask of coffee from the canteen before making his way to the interview room. He was on his second cup, fourth of the day, when Dr Fielding arrived.

Sam looked at his watch as he stood to greet her, 'Ah, Elizabeth, right on time,' he smiled, determined to do his best to get on with her, 'get enough beauty sleep did you?' However, he could neither resist nor hide the sarcasm in his voice.

She took off her coat and placed it with her briefcase on the spare chair. She was wearing an identical outfit to the previous day but to Sam's eidetic memory it was clearly different.

'Yes thank you, Samuel, and you?' her response was similarly tinged. 'Out on the town, were you?'

Sam did not bite, 'I've set up the Sykes tape, would you like to start with that?'

'Fine. Do you have the transcript?'

'In the file in front of you. Coffee?' he did not wait for an answer and pumped a mug full from the flask, and then leaning across her and pressed the play button.

She listened in silence, following each word on the paper in front of her. At the end of the first recording she said, 'Was that outburst interview technique too?'

'Of course.'

'You made the man sick!'

'Well he makes me sick.' Sam snapped back.

116

'I sec.' She studied the notes, 'And these,' she fished out the crime scene photographs, 'do they make you sick?'

'No . . . well yes . . . of course but . . . not physically . . . I . . .' he decided to say no more on the subject. 'Shall we go on?' His hand was shaking a little as he changed the tape.

When it had run its course Sam pressed the eject button and said. 'Well?'

'Hmm,' she tapped the side of her nose with the eraser end of the pencil she had used to underline occasional sentences in the transcript.

Sam summoned all his patience in order to let her think. Eventually he could hold it no more. 'Come on, Doc, all I need to know is, is he capable of carrying out such a perverted act. 'cos if he is I'll have him brought back in here this very day.'

She pushed back her chair, turning it slightly towards him leaned back, crossed her legs and looked seriously at him. 'You think it was him, do you, Sam?'

'Yes I do . . . but I know what I think. What I want to know is what you think!'

'It would help if I could see the body language of course, but . . . What do you put his motive down as?'

'Covering up that he'd been unfaithful.'

'But then why the post mortem cuts?'

'You tell me, you're the expert.'

'From the forensic reports all the cuts were slow and deliberate, right?'

Sam nodded.

'That rules out frenzy.'

'Frenzy with a slow hand?'

'Unlikely, so that leaves us with some form of deliberate act.'

'To put us off the scent? You know, send us chasing around looking for some kind of fetishist.'

'Possibly both suspects are capable of concocting such a scheme but . . .' her response was interrupted by a knock on the partially open door.

Rosie poked her head round. 'Mr Archer wants to see you in his office right now, Sam. You too Dr Fielding.'

They followed Rosie upstairs and entered the DCI's office without knocking.

'We've just had a call from Ealing; they have a murder on their hands.' Archer did not wait on formalities. 'They found one of your cards at the scene, Sam.'

'Gloria Wallace.' Sam was visibly shaken.

'They have forensic on site but on first impression it sounds like the same killer. Throat cut with a very sharp instrument and other cuts as well. They are emailing pictures.'

Sam could hear the printer in the outer office start to whine as it churned out a high-resolution image. He rushed over and watched as line by line the photograph emerged from the slot. Dr Fielding was looking over his shoulder as he pulled the paper out of the roller, rather than wait until it dropped into the tray.

Together they studied the image, probably taken on a cheap digital camera it was not the quality of the ones a forensic team would produce. However it was clear enough to make out the red lines of some fine incisions on the abdomen of the young woman spread-eagled naked on the mattress. 'What do you make of that, Elizabeth?' Sam held the picture out for her to see.

'The pattern of cuts is different but I think we have, potentially, a serial killer on our hands.'

'I'm going over there,' Sam looked around the incident room, 'Mick, get a car organised,' he shouted at his Sergeant, then turned to the psychologist and said, 'I have to go, Dr Fielding. Could you get your report to me as soon as you can.'

Before he could walk away she said, 'Wait, I'll come with you.'

'No,' he said taking his first stride.

'It would be helpful if I could see the actual scene.' She stayed at his elbow.

'The living may reveal many things to you, Dr Fielding, but the dead only speak to the pathologist.'

'I have a medical degree,' she protested.

'I tell you what, Elizabeth, you can come with us when we go and confront Sykes about his movements, all right?' He clattered down the stairs in pursuit of Forest and PC King before she could reply.

'You had better include Russell in your enquiries as well' she yelled after him, 'he's a better fit now.' Her voice tailed off as the detective pushed through the door to the front desk area. 'Pig,' she said loudly with the half hope that he would hear.

He did, it made him smile.

Chapter 12

The search had been widened to the surrounding area, with overalled officers scouring the communal rubbish bins and picking through the scrubby hedge that surrounded the block.

Sam showed his ID to the young constable on the front door and led Forest up the three flights to Gloria's apartment. They were met on the landing by a short, swarthy old timer, in a shabby, grey suite, who introduced himself as DI Owen Jones.

'I think this is one for the Murder Squad' he said, a residue of a Welsh accent in his soft voice. 'I'm retiring next month and we haven't got a replacement lined up at Ealing. The last thing I want is to be called back from Spain as a witness in a long murder trial.'

'If I'm right, this is linked to the murder - arson case that I've been on for a fortnight now. Can we go in?'

'Be my guest, boy,' Jones lifted one side of the blue crime scene tape that criss-crossed the doorway, 'but there's no sign of fire here,' he said as he followed them in.

'Phew this place stinks of bleach.' Sam fanned his nose as he followed it into the bedroom.

'Smells better than the last one,' muttered Forest, as he followed.

'SOCO said the whole place had been thoroughly cleaned; even washed the sheets. They were still in the machine. There's plenty of stains to work with though.'

'Who found the body?'

'Victim's mother, poor soul. We had her taken home. She was in a terrible state . . . well . . . seeing your daughter like that . . .' He glanced at the bed where a plastic sheet hugged the star shaped outline of the corpse. 'The pathologist wants it as soon as you've done.'

'Time of death?' Sam nodded at his DS and one on each side they peeled the cover back.

'He says more than a day, maybe two.'

'What do you make of that?' Sam squatted to examine the scratches on the abdomen.

'Looks like they were playing noughts and crosses, Boy.'

'It does, doesn't it. I wonder who was noughts and who was crosses,' said Forest.

'If we knew that, we could all go down the pub to celebrate.' Sam dropped his corner of the sheet. Forest flicked it back up to cover the face that stared up at them.

Impatient for a definitive time of death, they decided to camp out at Ealing police station, which was just round the corner from the mortuary.

They were in the canteen munching bacon sandwiches when DI Jones came to find them. 'My boys are writing up their reports now. We will send the over to you soon as and the pathologist puts the time of death at either late Saturday night or early Sunday morning if that's any help.

'Well, that's something to go on.' Sam stood and placed a friendly hand on the little man's shoulder 'Do you mind if we take the lead on this one, Owen? I'm sure it's related to our case.'

'Help yourself, boyo. Glad to be shot of it. Just let me know if you need anything,' he grinned and added, 'before the end of the month that is.'

'Thanks. I'll buy you a beer at your leaving do,' Sam grabbed the remains of his sandwich and turned for the door, 'Come on Mick, we've a suspect to interview. Where's the car, Jackie?'

PC King gulped back her tea, 'In the yard, Guv.'

'Lead on McKing.' Sam grinned.

King secretly signalled a one to the Detective Sergeant. He shook his head imperceptibly and signalled back with two fingers. King rolled her eyes and headed for the stairs.

The north circular was packed with rush hour traffic. More to pass the time than anything, Sam called his DCI to tell him what was happening. The call elicited a warning to tread carefully. 'Everything by the book,' he said, 'I'm going to refer this upstairs.'

Even with the judicious use of her siren, the eight-mile journey took close to twenty minutes. Sam opened the door of the unmarked, Ford Focus before King could bring it to a stop across the gated drive of the impressive nineteen-fifties mansion in the leafy enclave, north of Hampstead Heath. He chased round the back of the car and pressed the button on the entry phone. Seconds later, he pressed again. The presence of the Mercedes S, class parked across the porticoed entrance, indicated that there should be someone in. Sam looked at his watch, five-fifteen. He put his finger back on the button and held it there. Still no response.

Forest had walked the frontage examining the eight-foot tall railings as best he could through the dense, neatly trimmed, privet hedge that matched it for height. 'No other way in, Guv. As far as I can see the fence goes all the way down both boundaries.'

'Oh I'm fed up with this. Jackie hit the twos.' Was Sam's response

King touched the button allowing the shortest of whoops to escape from the siren.

'Come on, that's no good.' Sam stormed over and reaching through the open window flipped the switch, keeping it on until it had run through its full repertoire of sounds. Along the avenue curtains were twitching and people were appearing in their driveways. 'Loud isn't it?' Sam said in the general direction of a woman across the road that was standing cross-armed and looking daggers at him.

'There's someone coming out,' Forest was peering through the gates. A male head could be seen moving behind the bulk of the Mercedes. 'Oi, you!' Forest held out his warrant card, his arm extending through the wrought iron bars of the gate. 'Police,'

The man appeared in full carrying a large leather suitcase and proceeded to lift it into the boot that had slowly opened as he approached. At a further shout from Forest he looked up raised a hand in cursory acknowledgement and ambled towards them.

Sam joined Forest at the barrier. 'Police,' he said.

'I never would have guessed.' The man, wearing the typical grey wool suit of a chauffeur, was two yards away. 'What do you want?'

Mike flashed his card again. 'Detective Sergeant Forest, Detective Inspector Miller, we want to speak to Mr Sykes.'

'He's not here.'

'Well Mrs Sykes then.' Sam snapped. 'Open these bloody gates.'

The man turned and slowly walked back towards the house, leaving the pair fuming on the pavement. A woman appeared, triggering a sharp increase of pace from the driver. She handed him a small valise as he opened the car's rear door for her. He placed it in the boot, which immediately began to close and hastened into the driver's seat.

The gates slowly began to open as the Limo swung around in the drive and headed towards them. Forest and Miller held position in the opening.

The driver pressed his horn.

Leaving Forest blocking the way, Sam strolled to the side of the car and tapped on the rear passenger window. 'Mrs Sykes?'

The woman opened it an inch. 'Will you get out of my way, Sergeant?' Sam knew the mistake was deliberate and refused to bite. 'I am on my way to the airport.'

'We are looking for your husband,'

'He's not here.'

'You won't mind us verifying that, will you.'

'I don't have the time.'

'Just let us in and you can be on your way, Madam.'

'Do you have a warrant?'

'No, but I can get one.'

'Then come back when you do. Now kindly remove that vehicle. If you make me miss my flight your Chief Constable will hear about it I assure you.'

'One question, Madam, if your husband is not in the house, do you know where he is?'

'You should have asked that question first, Inspector.'

'Well?'

'No. Try his office.' There was a hint of a smile as she rolled the window back up signalling the end of the conversation.

Exasperated, Sam waved Forest aside and, as soon as Jackie rolled the Focus out of the way, the Mercedes swept out. Almost simultaneously, a silver Jaguar XKR swooped to a stop in the vacated space. The driver was the Psych Witch and she was not amused.

The gates were closing and Sam had to hurry out in order not to be trapped. He hoped she did not read his haste as for her benefit.

'Elizabeth.' He smiled, 'what brings you here?'

'You agreed I would attend any interview with the suspects.'

'We were just passing and . . .'

'Mr Archer told me you were coming here.'

'Well you haven't missed anything. He's not here.'

'Do you know where he's gone?'

'We'll try his office next.'

'I'll follow you then.'

The Psychologist kept up with them surprisingly well and, when they parked on a yellow line in Devonshire place, Sam wondered whether it would be too much to issue a speeding ticket.

Sykes' surgery was closed for the night and a call through to the house in Highgate was answered eventually by their housekeeper who said that she was not expecting him home that evening. They had to call it a day. With a promise to Elizabeth Fielding that they would call her as soon as they had tracked him down, they went their separate ways.

It took a complex property search, running late into the night, to discover that Sykes had a small apartment in the attic three storeys above his first floor consulting rooms. He had probably been there, laughing at their futile ringing of his office doorbell, before they gave up and went away.

The tall Georgian terraced house had the benefit of a honeycomb-gated lift in the well of the stairs so they only had to walk up one flight. Despite the fact that it was only a little after dawn, he let them in quite readily. The apartment door was open and at their foot falls on the hardwood floor of the landing, Sykes voice called out. 'Come in, Inspector, I'll be right with you.'

The door led straight into the lounge, with two dormer windows facing the street sculpturing the slope of the ceiling. It was painted plain white and furnished with simple, well designed, items, a little upmarket to be IKEA. Maybe Conran, Sam thought.

To their left was a recess fitted out as a kitchen and one other door, probably the bedroom.

'I assume your wife told you we were coming,' Sam opened the conversation.

The door opened and Sykes appeared, wiping his hands on a towel. 'No, Bill our driver, actually. My wife and I are not . . . talking at the moment, but she must have told him to. They were on the way to the airport.' He turned and tossed the towel onto the corner of the bed, just visible behind him, came out and closed the door. 'So what's the urgency, Inspector Miller, am I still a suspect?'

'You didn't tell us about this place, when we last came to your office, Sir.' Sam looked slowly round the room. Forest was wandering around, looking at the few items of objet-d'art that were the only thing to break the functionality of the room. The Psychologist was perched on the arm of a dark blue leather sofa, studying their suspect closely through narrowed eyes.

'Should I have? You didn't ask.' Sykes ambled towards her, 'I don't think we have been introduced.' He held out a hand.

She took it. 'Dr Elizabeth Fielding. I am assisting the police in this enquiry.'

'Hmm,' he smiled, 'that's what they told me too.'

'You still are, Mr Sykes. Tell me, do you know this young woman?' Sam thrust a copy of an ID photograph of the second victim in front of him.

'No. I don't think so.'

'Gloria Wallace. She was the one who organised that dance at Greenwich . . . perhaps you remember her better like this.' He showed the crime scene photograph.

Sykes collapsed back into an armchair that was fortunately close enough behind him to break his fall. 'My God, another one.'

'Where were you Saturday night between ten pm and say two Sunday morning?' Sam stood over the man who had slid slowly to the floor.

'I . . . I don't know.'

'Come on, it was only three days ago! Where were you?'

'H-here, I think . . . Yes, here from midnight anyway.'

'Alone?'

Sykes nodded.

'And before that?'

'Dinner at Quaglinos.'

'What times.'

'About nine until half past eleven, I suppose. Then I walked home.'

'Alone?'

'Er. Yes.'

'Can you prove that?'

'I have the receipt in my wallet.' As he clambered to his feet, beads of sweat glistened on his brow. 'In the bedroom.' He pointed.

'Go with him Mike,' Sam nodded towards the door. Then shot a quizzical look at Elizabeth. She stood up and came closer to murmur. 'Do you always have to do that?'

'What?' Sam exclaimed.

'You almost made him faint.'

'Never mind that, Is he telling the truth.'

She glared at him for a moment before saying, 'He's hiding something, but I don't think he did the killing.'

Forest returned carrying the restaurant bill and a credit card receipt. 'Payment timed at twenty-three-thirty two, Guv.'

'There's still time for him to drive over to Ealing by two though.'

Sykes reappeared, wiping his face with the towel. He had taken the opportunity to splash his face with cold water in the small en-suite. 'I didn't do it, Inspector. Really I didn't.' He looked utterly pathetic. 'Why should I? I have never even spoken to her.'

'Do you mind if we have a look round.' Sam asked.

'Do what you like,' Sykes sank down in the armchair as if his legs would no longer keep him up.

The search, mostly of the kitchen and bedroom, turned up nothing significant. They had possible opportunity but no tangible motive or means. With a warning not to leave town they left him where he still sat, somewhat traumatised. Sam hoped so anyway.

'I don't think he spends many nights alone here,' Elisabeth said, as the lift made its stately way to the ground floor.

'You mean the smell in the bedroom.'

'"Chanel", I think. "Coco" if I am not mistaken, not cheap.'

'I suppose you have a nose for these things,' said Sam, glancing at the great hook that mutilated her long thin face, and looking away quickly when she met his gaze.

'Not the scent of choice by ladies of the night.' Forest smothered a smile at Sam's wink.

'It was on the pillow, I know that,' said Sam, thinking, I'll buy some for Julie.

'Whoever she is, she must be an early riser,' Forest offered, 'it's only half seven now.'

'Do we have time to interview Russell?' Elizabeth clearly had chosen to ignore Sam's tactless joke. 'I think he is a more likely candidate than this guy.'

'Right then,' said Sam, 'do you want to leave your car here and ride with us or follow.'

'I'll follow,' she replied, looking with distain at the white Ford. She clicked the remote on the Jaguar.

'Did you see the way she looked down her nose at our car,' Sam quipped as he took his usual front seat.

'She can still hear you,' Forest laughed.

Chapter 13

Russell worked as an estate agent in Dartford so they decided to call in at the office on the way. Rush hour traffic was at its height and it was a slow, frustrating drive back to Greenwich. Sam found his mind wandering to the planned evening dancing with Julie rather than concentrating on the poor girl so brutally mutilated. With some effort, he forced himself to review the two crimes.

Swivelling in the front passenger seat to face his Sergeant, who was starting to doze off in the back, he said 'So, Mike . . . It seems we have a serial killer.'

'Yes Guv.' Forest blinked back at him.

'Let's review the similarities.'

'OK, there's the obvious one. Both women had their throats cut with a very sharp blade, like a scalpel.'

'Or a chef's knife. Don't try to make the facts fit the suspect, Mike.'

'Well, it's sharper than any knife I have in my kitchen.'

'Or mine, but I could still cut my throat with one or two of them. What else?'

'There's the cut's on the abdomen, why there?'

'You mean why not other places? The breasts for instance.'

'Maybe he likes breasts. Most blokes do.'

'And some women,' PC King giggled.

'You just concentrate on your driving, Kingy.' Sam grinned at her. 'Any way, poor little Gloria hardly had any. So why these two particular women? They were nothing like each other. On one hand, you have a tall, curvaceous blond and on the other a dusky, athletic type. My God she had a six-pack a boxer would be proud of. So what puts these two on the list?

Forest thought for a moment. 'There was no sign of forced entry at Gloria's flat, so we can assume it was someone she knew.'

'We can't tell if it was the same in Sheila's case because of the fire and the brigade smashed the bloody door down . . . but assume it was.' Sam's neck was getting sore and he turned back to stare unseeingly out of the windscreen. 'At least someone they both knew well enough to let into their homes late at night . . . Lovers?'

'Well, Sykes admitted making love to Sheila. But why Gloria?'

'Misdirection,' said Miller, flatly.

'Then why another dancer? If he'd picked someone at random it would be more distracting.'

'You're right. It has to be a connected to the dancing.'

136

'This Ceroc, you mean?'

'Well Modern Jive at least. They were from different . . . factions of Modern Jive. I think we can rule out ballroom.' Sam's thoughts drifted back to the Charlton jive club and chilled at the realisation. If someone was targeting dancers, Julie could easily be in serious danger.

When they arrived at Greenwich, the incident room was in chaos. Desks had been shunted forward to make room for half a dozen more. IT techs were running cables through flat tracks stuck to the parquet floor to service the batch of computer terminals that were being installed on them. They were immediately directed to the DCI's office. He was demanding a full report. Sam asked Rosie to make an appointment with Russell for eleven o'clock. There would be no point in driving out there if he was off estate agenting somewhere.

'I see you've brought in a Holmes team,' Sam said by way of greeting.

'Yes. You should have done that right from the start.' Archer admonished.

Bloody liberty you told me not to, Sam's unspoken protest. He let it go.

'Holmes?' Fielding queried.

'Home Office Large Major Enquiry System.' Archer explained, 'It uses a computer program to cross reference all the data for a crime or series of crimes.

'They couldn't find the right words to make Sherlock an acronym,' Sam quipped.

'Be that as it may,' Archer scowled, 'make sure they have all the data so far they have a hell of a backlog to input already.'

'Well I did . . .'

'Now until it's all up and running,' Archer cut across Sam's response, 'bring me up to date with Ealing.'

A frustrating hour was spent going over what Sam had already reviewed in the car. The only productive moment was when they broached the subject of the cuts to the abdomen of the victims.

It was on the pattern and depth of the cuts that Elizabeth offered some insight.

'Do you have the forensic photographs of the abdomen of both women to hand?' she asked Sam.

He handed her one of the two files he had been nursing on his lap, 'That's Sheila's. You'll find the pictures at the back.' He flicked through the manila folder he retained and withdrew an eight by four close-up print and placed it on the edge of his DCI's uncluttered desk.

Elizabeth placed a similar print alongside it. 'You notice . . .' she began.

Archer reached across and drew the pictures towards him. Sam and Elizabeth had to scoot round the desk and peer over his shoulders.

'You notice,' Elizabeth tried again, 'how in the first case the cut is deeper and, in the case of the vertical one, far longer than any on the second.'

'Yes.' said Archer thoughtfully.

'If you look at the second, Gloria's case, the cuts as well as being shallower are more precisely oriented horizontally, with the abdominal muscles, and vertically, at almost perfect right angles.'

'With the navel exactly in the middle,' Sam added.

'Exactly . . . precision and, apart from a few minor wiggles, quite straight.' Elizabeth straightened and stretched her back. 'Gentlemen, I think that in the first case the cuts were made by touch, either in the dark or unsighted in some way. You see how they curve.'

'Could it be,' said Sam returning to his seat, 'that it is just the difference in physique of the two victims; Sheila, although hardly tubby, had a generous layer of body fat, whereas Gloria's stomach was like a cobbled path.'

'You mean a different canvas makes different strokes,' Archer slid the pictures back across the table.

'Something like that,' said Sam retrieving the folder from Elizabeth's chair, allowing her to sit back down. He put the pictures back in place. 'I'd like to get our pathologist to look over the body at Ealing. Perhaps between the two of them they will come up with something more . . .'

'Good idea, Sam, arrange it. Is there anything else?'

'We were just on our way to have another chat with Mr Russell. Dr Fielding here would like to take a gander at his body language.'

'OK, But the Holmes receiver will need your written report as soon as possible, Doctor. Sam, keep me appraised.'

Forest was waiting in the incident room when they came out of the meeting. He had set up a second whiteboard in the now cramped space at the front and had started to pin up duplicate pictures from the second crime scene. 'Should I combine the files now, Guv?' he asked as Sam walked in.

'No. We'll let the Holmes team do that. We can run them in parallel for the moment but get someone to make a duplicate with all the most important documents from both cases in it.'

'Fine, what shall I call it, "Noughts and Crosses"?'

'That doesn't apply to the first case,' said Elizabeth, dogging Sam's heels.

'So what do you think the case should be called, Doctor?'

'What was that you said at our first meeting, "Frenzy with a slow hand"?' Elizabeth smiled her crocodile smile, 'it's the only firm common denominator.'

'Except for dancing,' Sam smiled back but his thoughts flashed to Julie and the danger she might be in, bringing a sudden increase in his heart rate. 'Oh, what does it matter? Call it "Slow Hand," Mick.'

Before leaving for Dartford, Sam contacted the two pathologists and scheduled a meeting for late in the day at the Ealing mortuary. Elizabeth Fielding even condescended to travel in the police car out to Russell's office.

Tony Russell's workaday clothing made him look like a sixties Mafia Godfather. He sat, feet up on his modest desk, at the rear of the agency shop reading the property section of "Horse and Hounds." As Miller and Fielding approached, he swung to his feet, 'I was just about to give up on you and go to lunch,' he greeted them.

On the way over, Elizabeth had suggested that Sam should hold back on telling the suspect of her function if possible. "Sometimes the knowledge that they are being appraised could set up a false positive result." She had said. Sam avoided any introductions and, as Russell turned on the charm, taking her hand with a questioning look on his face, she offered, 'Elizabeth Fielding; Mr Russell?'

'It's Tony, call me Tony.' He was completely unabashed by her unfortunate looks and treated her as if he was addressing a film star.

'Liz,' she said, 'er, Tony.'

There was one other occupant in the shop front office, a petite woman with a deep mahogany tan and a face that looked as if it had been slept in. She had a telephone handset to her ear but had paused in the act of dialling to tune in on their conversation.

'Is there somewhere private we can talk? Er. Tony,' Sam butted in before his specialist melted and they went off to get a room by themselves.

Russell made a show of dragging his attention away to reply, 'Yes, Mr Miller, right this way.' He led them through a door to a small windowless room similar to one in a police interview suite, except that the end wall was adorned with a thirty-two-inch flat screen TV. In addition to the central table and four chairs, there was a small drinks cabinet in the corner. An empty wine cooler on a stand stood at its side.

'Can I offer you a drink?' Russell addressed them both but he was looking at Elizabeth.

'No thank you,' said Sam, sternly, as he took out a notebook and unclipped its attached pen.'

'Then how can I help you?'

'We would just like to go over your movements again, if you don't mind, Mr Russell.' They had agreed that if Sam conducted a fairly lengthy conversation, the Psychologist could obtain a representative base line before revealing anything of the new case.

Sam made him go over the entire week surrounding Sheila Delaney's death while Elisabeth adopted her usual pose, crossing her long legs to reveal a distracting length of thigh, easily her best asset, and smiled attentively at her subject.

'And would you say that was a typical week?' Sam asked when Russell had finished.

'Well, apart from the dance at Greenwich, I suppose so.' Russell was looking confused. 'My life is pretty routine, Inspector. Work, eat, sleep, dancing once or twice a week, that is about it.'

'So, apart from the Friday night dance, say . . . last week was pretty much the same as that one?'

'Yes, pretty much.'

'So on Saturday night you did the same,' Sam looked at his notebook, 'Cinema, supper in Nando's and home to bed.'

'Yes, except this week I went to a noodle bar. I'm a creature of habit but not a slave to it.'

'And can anyone corroborate that?'

'Do I need to?' for the first time he let his annoyance show, 'As an innocent man, I don't need to spend every day setting up an alibi, you know.'

'So you were alone all Saturday night?'

'If you like,' He shrugged and looked defiantly from one to the other of them.

Elizabeth nodded at Sam.

'In that case, sir, we'll not take up any more of your valuable time.' Sam stood and marched out.

Elizabeth paused long enough to say 'Thank you, Tony. You have been most helpful,' and followed. She waited until they were driving away before she said, 'He didn't do the Ealing job.'

Sam swung round in his seat. 'You're sure of that, are you?' He grinned, 'Perhaps he just charmed you into thinking he's just an innocent, lonely, single guy. For a minute there I thought you were going to get a room.'

'I am well aware of the way I look, Samuel. He was turning on the old machismo for me, probably out of force of habit. Although he may be single, he's far from innocent and I suspect, rarely lonely at night. He was lying about that. In a way it's rather chivalrous.'

'So you do . . . admire him.'

'Fancy him? She thought for a moment, 'maybe I do, but I can't rule him out for the first murder.'

'Then why the second?'

'When you asked him about last weekend, he was curious but put up no barriers. If he knew anything of it, he would have turned into a hedgehog.

'That means if he is still in the frame for the first one, we have two killers . . . a copycat?'

'Let's think on about that. How about some lunch, I'm starving.'

Sam had Jackie swing by the Central Criminal Court in London to pick up Melanie Gordon. She had spent the whole day waiting to present evidence in a nasty gang rape case that had at last come up for trial.

'How did you get on?' Sam asked, as he held the back door of the Focus open for her.

'Bloody frustrating! They kept me hanging around for half the day, then the defence barely bothered to cross examine.'

'Result?'

'Should be. It'll drag on for another week yet. God I'm bushed. That's much more tiring than slaving over a hot autopsy table all day.'

'I thought autopsy tables were cold,' PC King remarked as she waited for a gap in traffic to pull out of Old Bailey into Ludgate Hill.

'Oi, I'll do the jokes, Kingy.' Sam winked at her then turned back to Melanie, 'Sorry to drag you all the way over to Ealing at this time of day, Mel . . . you too Jackie. It's going to be another late night I think.'

'No worries Guv, I need the overtime.' The trainee detective was first to respond.

'Just sign my chit,' said Melanie, 'actually I'm looking forward to it. Eric Larsen and I go back a long way. I haven't seen him in over a year . . . and the case is interesting of course.' She smiled but Sam could see the familiar tiredness in her eyes. He knew her department was under staffed and underfunded.

Chapter 14

The District Mortuary was attached to Ealing General Hospital. As PC King guided the Ford past the main entrance to the staff parking area at the back, Sam spotted Elizabeth Fielding leaning on the wing of her Jaguar, a mobile phone pressed to her ear. He smiled and considered leaving her there, until the police work had been done, but rejected the idea. She would only have him go over it all again. As soon as they were parked, he sent Jackie King to find the woman.

DI Jones met them at the door of the sub-basement. From there he guided them through the rabbit warren of passages, essential to the behind the scenes running of a modern healthcare establishment.

Dr Eric Larsen was a tall man with a ruddy face, dominated by a substantial handlebar moustache; apparently as compensation for his completely bald head. He greeted the delegation with a warm smile, which widened dramatically when he saw Melanie. After a quick hug, she made the introductions and they all followed him to the small staff lounge that was to serve as a meeting room. Waiting there was a thin, bespectacled young man in a white lab coat; he handed over a green cardboard folder to Larsen then left.

'I asked the lab to send their results down as soon as they were ready.' He opened the file and perused the contents.

'Quicker than we thought,' he muttered absently. He made a soft snorting noise and held it for Melanie to see pointing to a particular passage. The others arranged themselves, seated round a table.

'What is it?' Sam demanded.

'Tox-screen,' Melanie replied, 'Alcohol 72 milligrams per 100 mls' not even over the limit for driving.'

'We found an empty champagne bottle at the scene,' said DI Jones.

'Any prints?' asked Sam.

'No such luck, boy. It was in the dishwasher.'

'Whoever did this knew how to cover up alright.'

'I blame the telly.' Jones shrugged, 'All those crime scene programs it's like an education, man.'

'Anything else significant in there?' Sam could see that Melanie was itching to tell them more.

'Flunitrazepam,' she said, taking the printout from the file and handing it to Sam. He scanned it to find the key word looked up and raised a quizzical eyebrow.

'Rohypnol to you. Quite a big dose too.'

'Date rape drug. That explains why there was no sign of a struggle.'

'That and ligature marks on the ankles,' Larsen offered, 'perhaps we should go on to the Post Mortem report.' He put the folder he was holding down on the table and withdrew another, pink this time, from a capacious pocket of his lab coat. 'Or would you rather take a look at the body yourself, Mel.'

'Maybe after, Eric.' She glanced at Sam for confirmation.

'Yes, Dr Larsen if you could give us the gist . . . in layman's terms. You and Miss Gordon can compare notes later.'

At that moment, PC King appeared at the door. 'Ah, here they are,' she sang and signalled down the passage.

Elizabeth Fielding, face like thunder, stormed in. 'You might have told me where you were,' she blustered. 'This place is like a maze.'

'Well you insisted on making your own way.' Sam replied.

'I got directions from reception, Guv. They weren't very accurate.'

'All right, Jackie, go and get yourself a cup of tea. I'll call you when we're ready to go.' Jackie returned his grin and disappeared into the labyrinth. Sam indicated a spare chair to the

149

Psychologist, introduced her to Dr Larsen and went on. 'Now you're here and to bring you up to speed the lab results for Gloria indicated the presence of alcohol and Rohypnol.'

'Quite a lot of Rohypnol,' Melanie added, 'at least a double dose, although some had not been absorbed into the blood stream, indicating that death occurred within about half an hour of it being administered. Probably in the champagne.'

'Thanks, Mel.' Sam looked around the room. 'This confirms that Gloria knew her attacker. She let him in and accepted drinks from him in the comfort of her own home. Now if you would go on with your report Dr Larsen.'

Larsen outlined his findings: Cause of death, exsanguination due to a cut passing across the throat and severing the carotid artery. The fatal cut was in all senses the same as that of the first victim. However, the ancillary wounds differed in as much as they were made antimortem.

'So the poor girl was tortured before she was killed.' Sam mused, 'she must have been in agony.'

'Not as bad as you might think,' Larsen replied, 'the cuts barely broke the epidermal layer. Similar to one you might get while shaving, inspector. On a larger scale of course. In addition, the drug and alcohol would have had a deadening

150

effect. Once again, there was no tearing. This suggests controlled, gentle pressure.'

'Slow hand,' Sam muttered, then louder, 'Was there indication of sexual activity?'

'There was some tearing of the vagina and a little bruising of the area. So, penetration? Yes, DNA no.' the pathologist referred to his files again. 'There were faint ligature marks on the ankles but, strangely, none on the wrists so if these were held it must have been by something soft like, say, a scarf or pillow case. We found a fibre that,' he consulted the path lab file, 'has been sent to the police forensic team for identification. Apart from that, the body had been wiped down with domestic bleach. Would you like to go through and take a look for yourselves now?'

Sam nodded reluctantly.

The body, laid out on the stainless steel autopsy table, was discreetly hidden by a thin green cover. Sam and Elizabeth stood well back while the two pathologists lowered the sheet, for the moment folding it above the pubic area. Jones declined to enter, claiming it would put him off his dinner. Sam wished he could do the same but he stepped shoulder to shoulder with Elizabeth when they were beckoned forward.

They gravely studied the pattern carved on the girls abdomen for what seemed like an age until Sam, having had enough, put a hand on

Elizabeth's shoulder and saying, 'have you seen enough?' guided her away. She remained deep in thought as they rejoined Jones in the small waiting area to the Mortuary Suite.

'Do you know where the canteen is, Owen? I think she needs a cup of tea.' At Jones' nod, he returned to stand against the wall of the autopsy room to observe the post mortem process.

The light and bright, self-service restaurant was busy with patients' visitors and a few uniformed hospital staff. The psychologist was sitting with PC King at corner table. Jones was retrieving a sandwich at the counter.

'Can I get you anything?' the DI enquired.

'Just black coffee, no sugar thanks.' Sam joined the others, 'Mel and Eric will be up soon they are just closing up.'

'Are you OK?' Sam murmured to Elizabeth as he pulled up a chair.

'I'm fine but I have a problem.'

'What do you mean?'

'I think we should wait until DI Jones joins us. You see I have doubt that this is the same killer.'

Sam was taken aback by this bombshell. 'But . . .' He spotted Jones, tray in hand scanning the room stood up and waved to get his attention. Holding on to his patience he allowed the man to hand out the drinks before bursting out, 'Now say that again, Elizabeth!'

'It's the nature of the cuts, the pattern and size. They may have been administered by a different perpetrator.'

'Oh don't say that, woman. I don't want this falling back in my lap.'

'But the fatal wound is identical, slow cut right to left with a very sharp blade.' Sam took up the cause. 'The same weapon made the other cuts too . . . As far as we can tell.'

'As far as you can tell,' Elizabeth responded, 'but in the first case, the cuts were long, deep and free flowing; instinctive if you like. In the second, they were controlled, precise and planned; like sending a message. At the very least the motive is different.'

'I can go along with that, man.' Jones said with relief.

'Don't worry, Owen, I'm not handing this back.'

'So what motive have you come up with?' Elizabeth demanded.

'Well it's easy, isn't it,' Jones smiled, 'Gloria discovers who killed your girl puts the squeeze on and gets killed for it. Simple.'

'Possible,' said Sam.

'Not impossible,' Elizabeth acknowledged, 'but why the cut pattern, noughts and crosses.'

'He's playing with you,' PC King said, without looking up from the empty cup in front of her.

The arrival of the two pathologists at the far side of the room brought the table's contemplative silence to an end.

'Quick, Kingy, get their teas in while we see what they have to say, then we can get back south of the river.' He handed his aid a five-pound-note and stood up to attract Melanie's attention. His mind strayed to the Charlton venue and thoughts of Julie Button. He looked at his watch, a quarter-past-eight.

Gordon and Larson confirmed that all the, incisions despite the difference in depth and length were from the same instrument. Melanie's demonstration on Larson of how the fatal cut to Sheila was administered, using a teaspoon as the murder weapon, created a momentary lull in the hubbub that inevitably provided a background to their conversation.

'You had better see this, Guv.' PC King lowered the tray she was carrying carefully onto the edge of the table and released the folded newspaper trapped under her arm into her bosses lap.

It was the evening edition of the local rag. The headline read "NOUGHTS AND CROSSES KILLER AT LARGE IN EALING". Mercifully the accompanying photograph only showed Gloria's head, the rest too graphic to print the article said.

Sam looked across at Jones. 'Did you give them the whole image, Owen?' He had recognised it as part of the one the Ealing DI had sent by phone.

'Of course not, boy. I edited it down to head and shoulders. He pulled out his smart phone and showed the, head and shoulders, cropped version of Gloria.

'I wish you hadn't.' Sam looked around the table. 'I suppose it had to come out sometime but let me make this clear. No more details of the cuts to get out, understand? The last thing we want is a copycat out there too. If we can keep the link between the two quiet for as long as possible, that might keep the nationals from going into a feeding frenzy. Owen, you can take the flack from the press, keep me out of it, right?'

'Right,' was all Jones could sheepishly reply.

Chapter 15

It was almost nine-thirty when PC King dropped Sam at the front of the Charlton CIU. He told her to call it a night and pick him up at his boat at eight in the morning. By the time, she had the Ford in gear; Sam was halfway down the side passage that led to the hall. The strains of "Hero" by Enrique Iglesias met him in the lobby.

He pushed through the inner double doors and spotted Julie immediately. She was in the process of taking off her headset microphone while stepping down from the stage. By the time he skirted the dance floor, Maureen Duffy had started dancing with her. Neither of them saw him approach. He had not quite got a handle on women dancing together, despite realising that the men were outnumbered two to one.

Maureen was leading; he tapped her on the shoulder and said, 'Can I cut in?'

The venomous look she gave him, as she whirled to see who it was, almost carried a physical impact.

'Sam!' Julies face lit up, 'you made it.' She continued to dance one more spin with Maureen then without breaking her rhythm, caught Sam's hand and for a moment took the lead, spinning the girl while she drew Sam into her.

'I'll leave you lovebirds to it,' Maureen said as she completed her spin and disappeared into the throng.

Sam decided not to mention Gloria's death while they were with the dance crowd. He did not want to reveal his involvement in case the killer was present. Both the beginners and advanced classes had finished but Julie happily showed him a couple of new moves in the free dance session. Later, while she gave some of the advanced students pointers, Sam nursed a small beer sitting at a table which had been co opted by Julies friends that he'd met at Welling, dancers who he couldn't help thinking of as, "the usual suspects".

This time he did not refuse to dance with the other women that asked him and their tolerance even gave him the confidence to ask the still disgruntled Miss Duffy to join him on the floor for a song called "Regular Joe". She declined, but at least he had tried.

At the end, he helped Julie and her DJ pack up their gear and put it in their cars and when she realised he was not encumbered by his Saab Julie offered to drive him home. The highly appropriate last track of the night echoed in his head "How Lucky Can One Guy Be," by Indigo Swing.

Sam directed Julie into his allocated parking space and invited her in for coffee. While he was unlocking the boat, she called her mother on her mobile phone, to let her know she would be late.

'Mum worries,' she said as Sam took her hand to guide her over the gangplank, 'now she knows I'm with you, she'll go to bed happy.'

'Oh, she stays the night then?'

'Yes, she doesn't like driving at night so she usually sleeps with me, on dance nights.'

Sam was humming "How lucky can one guy be," as he loaded the cafetiere, but realised the version in his head was the line from the more familiar to him "Aint That a Kick in the Head." He smiled at Dean Martin's next line, "I kissed her and she kissed me,' and hoped he wouldn't get to that bit, 'Aint that a hole in the boat.'

Julie was roaming the surprisingly spacious cabin space of the Andrea, running her fingers over the polished wood and brass fittings, clearly delighted with its uncluttered but traditional design. With the coffee made, he joined her as she paused at the open door to his sleeping compartment. The foot of the bed that almost filled the space, was all that was visible by the low light from the salon. Sam reached in and turned on the light. She turned to face him, her hand followed his arm to locate the switch. She kissed him at the same time as she flicked it off.

They made love rapaciously at first, clothes discarded as they went. As the night passed, they found out how to better please each other and apart from a few short naps did not get to any kind of deep sleep until dawn threatened to break the spell.

In fact, it was PC King's urgent honking that did the job of an early morning call. Sam pulled on his boxers and staggered up on deck. King had pulled the Ford across the back of Julie's Fiat and was walking towards him an inane grin on her face.

'I'll see you in the office at nine, Kingy,' Sam called to her.

She waved acknowledgement, turned on her heel and left without a word.

The buzz in the incident room dropped noticeably when Sam entered. At least one of his squad of highly trained investigators would no doubt have observed Julie dropping him at the front entrance just before nine. Jackie King was sure to have given a full briefing in the interim.

The signals round the office were all sevens and eights until Forest, doing a great job of keeping a straight face approached his boss. 'Have you seen the papers, Guv?' He handed over the morning edition. It was only a column heading but in bold letters, "Tic-Tac-Toe killer strikes in

W5". It went on, "Killer carves noughts and crosses on his victim's abdomen." It ended with "Police baffled." *Well at least they got that right,* Sam thought.

Laid out on his desk were the full pathology and forensic reports. He checked his email and found a summary from "Elizabeth Fielding MD C.Psychol AFBPsS." It simply said, "Please find attached." Sam speed-read the psychobabble of medical jargon in the file, extracting the essential inconclusive conclusion. The killer could possibly be the same in each case. However, the motive could not be. Indications of a crime of passion and a sexual motive in the first would not carry to the second although the victim was, according to the pathologists', violated in the same way. Expert Opinion: Not a serial killer as such but cases could be related.

There was no CC. to the file so Sam forwarded it to DCI Archer, in the hope that it would keep him quiet. He needed time to think. Two suspects without, as yet, corroborated alibis, plus around two hundred others who had attended the Town Hall dance, that was the main connection between the victims.

A second email was from DCI Owen Jones. It also carried an attachment.

"Sam. Sorry about the press last night, I've kept your team's interest out of it and plan to keep a low profile myself from now on.

My boys found this on Ms Wallace's computer. It appears to be intended for you."

Sam opened the file, named, "List.docx". It was headed, "Detective Miller — Purchasers of Tickets" then, "Credit Card Sales"

A few down from the top he found: Button J — 8; two lines further on Delaney S — 2 and close to the bottom was Russell A — 2. None of the others on the sixteen line list struck a chord so he passed it on to Rosie to run down. Clearly, the Gloria had made a start but had not got around to adding in the cash purchases. *She'll never do that now, Sam* thought. Without any other data, it meant cross-referencing the list with her bank records and that would take a while.

He brought DS Forest up to speed including the new option. What if Gloria was killed to prevent her completing the list? Sam left him to organise discreet interviews to be carried out as each name and address came up. Dull, dull, dull; but what else could he do apart from feel guilty. He may have been the catalyst that caused Gloria's death. *Somehow the killer must have figured out the direction of my investigation*, he thought, *our perpetrator must be on Gloria's list.*

Thursday 14th April

I suppose I knew from the first little jewel of blood that this would become addictive; that they would call me a serial killer

Tic-Tac-Toe. It is in the papers at last. Not just local either, the Nationals have it. It would be so great if I could tell someone it was me. Just one someone but I have no one like that anymore. I so miss Sheila. Still, she did betray me so maybe she would not be the right one to tell anyway.

For the first time since this case started, Sam went to the pub for lunch. A quick pint with Mike Forest savoured as they mulled over the case but broke no new ground. Rosie called Forest on his mobile to say she had tracked down a bunch of the names on the list. Downing the last of his Guinness, Forest rushed back across the road to organise the interviews.

'If they are in Ealing, get Jones to deal with them,' was Sam's parting remark. He looked at the half inch of lager in the bottom of his glass, ordered another before finishing it and followed it with a third. Heading into the low numbers again, he was well over the limit when he drove home. It seemed a long time until he would see Julie again.

Chapter 16

The act of dumping the empty bottles jangled every nerve in his body. He had run out of Bushmills at about ten pm and resorted to scotch. He must have passed out by midnight but was awake at two. He got precious little sleep after that. Fretting mostly over the fact that, in the heat of the previous night's passion, or was it lust driven self-interest, he had forgotten to warn Julie about the killer.

There was a little man with a big hammer inside Sam's head adding emphasis to every road hump and pothole as he drove to work. Even through the combination of morning coffee, toothpaste and Listerine, he could still smell the booze. It must be coming out of his pores. This would never have happened if he had not lain off for such a long time. Lost his immunity.

Forest had the routine enquiries well in hand so Sam could do no more than go over the files once again. His stomach rumbled a reminder that he had not had anything to eat since breakfast the day before. The canteen did not offer fresh cooked food until lunch so he dragged his aching carcass out to the greasy spoon on Greenwich High Street. A big fry up: two eggs, bacon, sausages, mushrooms, tomatoes, beans, fried bread, followed by toast and marmalade and two cups of possibly the worst coffee in South London, brought some semblance of sanity to his innards. Wiping his mouth on a paper napkin, he dislodged a sliver of toilet paper he had used to stop a razor cut that must have been on display all morning. No one had said anything. What a state to be in.

Feeling better, he decided not to go back to the office. Instead, he collected his car from the yard without going up stairs and drove off towards Bexley. The best he could do was to warn Julie to be careful about letting anyone into her home.

Julie opened the door with a smile that lit the darkest recesses of his soul. Over coffee, remarkably good for instant, he told her of Gloria's death. She had already seen it in the papers and admonished him for not breaking it to her before it was splashed all over the news.

'I meant to, Julie, honest I did but the night was so special. I got carried away and . . . well, you know what happened in the morning.'

'Well, you could have told me then,' her frown was manufactured for effect only, 'but I forgive you.' She smiled coquettishly and sipped her coffee. 'Can you stay a while? Jodi's at nursery school.'

'I wish I could but I have to get back to work.'

'Catching Sheila's killer?'

'I'm trying.' Sam got up to leave.

'Well off you go then. Get on with it,' she stood to kiss his cheek, 'When will I see you again?'

'How about Sunday, we could bring Jodi over to see the boat.'

'Oh he'd love that.'

'What time shall I pick you up?'

'Why don't I drive over to you, say about eleven?'

'Fine, I'll cook lunch.'

'And you cook?' She had her hand on the door latch to let him out.

'You'll have to wait and see about that.' He drew her to him and kissed her gently. Was that a wrinkling of her nose as they parted. Did he still smell of whisky? 'One thing, 'It was Sam's turn to frown, 'The thing I came to talk to you about.' He stood back to give her room to open the door in the narrow passage. 'Be careful about letting people into your house. We expect the second killing was the end of it but both women were killed in their own homes and they were both connected to Modern Jive.'

'I'm always careful, Sam,'

'Use this,' he flicked the door chain. 'Also, when you're out, don't leave your drink unattended. You know what I'm saying?'

'Alright, Sam, I'll be careful, I'm not expecting any visitors, except for Tony.'

'Tony?'

'Yes, Tony Russell. You met him at Welling.'

'He's coming here?'

She nodded. 'This evening; he wants to talk to me about the World Ceroc Championships. He wants me to be his partner.'

'Julie' He tried to pick his words carefully, 'I don't think . . .'

'Are you jealous, Sam?'

'It's not that . . .'

'You are, aren't you? It's just dancing. Nothing else.'

'No, it's,' Sam blustered, 'With the case . . .'

'Oh, he's not a suspect is he?'

'Let's just say we've talked to him.'

'OK, I'll put him off if you think . . .'

'Don't tell him what I've said. Find some excuse.'

'OK, Sam, I'll do what you say.'

'Good. Call me if you have any problems.' They kissed again and he left.

Forest was at the board when Sam strode into the incident room.

'Archer wants to see you,' he rolled his eyes, 'and he's got the witch with him.'

168

Fired with a new determination to get this killer out of circulation, Sam went in ready for battle. 'You wanted me Boss?'

'Yes, Sam, we've been waiting for you. Are you alright?'

'Yes fine, thanks. What was it, only I've got . . .'

'Liz and I have been going over her assessment.'

'Yes, I've read it.'

'Frankly, I'm thinking of handing it over to the Serious Crime Unit.'

'What! Why?'

'Elizabeth, Doctor Fielding, feels that you are not coping well with . . . you have become emotionally involved . . .'

'Of course I'm emotionally involved. There are two young women in the morgue brutally mutilated and, in one case, tortured.' Sam exploded, 'what other reaction do you expect?'

'See what I mean?' Fielding murmured. Her chair was drawn to the side of the DCI's desk where they had been pouring over her report.

'I thought more resources would take the pressure off. After all, the case is quite stalled.'

'Stalled! I have two suspects in the frame and the second case is only a few days old.'

'According to Forest, you have another two-hundred suspects. And if this is a serial killer . . .'

'According to Dr Fielding, it's not.'

'I said it was unlikely,' Elizabeth said, 'but the fact is, you are clearly upset by the nature of the crime.'

'No one asked for your opinion on my state of mind,' Sam snapped.

The other two exchanged glances.

'So that is what this is about, is it?' Well bring in whoever you want but you'll be doing it without me.' Sam stormed out. If there was a condition called manically depressed, Sam had it.

Sam woke at about three in the morning, wondering if he had resigned or not. The familiar fogged feeling that followed a bender shrouded his memory. Most of the dialogue after he had left Archer's office was gone but he recalled the scene in image form like a silent movie but in full colour. Automatically he went into his practiced routine, one he thought he had left behind when he stopped drinking. Coffee - half a gallon, toast - six slices, throw up, empty bowels and bladder, shower, more coffee, shave if hands stopped shaking, (if not, more coffee and toast) shave, clean teeth, mouthwash, dress in a good suit, freshly laundered shirt, check hair, always short and spiky nowadays, ready. It had successfully covered up for him when this was as regular occurrence, five days a week at its peak - the other two were spent comatosed.

But that was then. Had it been three years already? For the first six months after his wife died, he had fallen apart. It was his routine that kept him in his job then; could it do it again now?

Memory was coming back to him. Forest was trying to tell him something as he stormed through the incident room. Something about a fibre. Sitting on deck, allowing the cool morning air to work its magic, Sam brought to mind the image. Forest was at the board, a piece of paper in his left hand, a blue board marker in his right. He had started to write something. "Fib", something referred to in the white printout he was holding. The paper was curling back at the corners he could make out the part of the, upside down, heading and inverted it in his mind. "...ic Repo" Forensic Report.

In the red mist of the moment, Sam had ignored everyone and everything. He returned to his desk, although he did not know why and then barged his way out of the building, passing the board en route. He brought up that fleeting glimpse. Forest was following him by then, asking what was going on but he had finished the note. "Fibre . . . white faux fur does not match anything in Gloria's wardrobe." A clue. What day is it? He looked at his watch Saturday. Five to six. Pausing only to survey the mess his normally immaculate salon was in and lock the door on it, he set off for the office.

His car was parked diagonally across two bays, evidence of his condition when he drove home. Sam hoped that was the only thing. Inside it smelt like a distillery. This was mostly due to the, not quite empty, scotch bottle, jammed with its top off, into the door pocket. He hurled it into the dock, where it bobbed on its own ripples, refusing to sink. He decided to do the same.

A bored constable on the desk looked up from his newspaper and recognised Sam. 'You're early, Sir, no one's in upstairs yet.'

'Good,' Sam replied, as he waited for the rookie to buzz him in.

On the other side of the door, the duty sergeant ambled out to meet him. 'Sam, I thought you were on leave.'

So that's the story is it, I didn't jack it all in then, Sam thought. 'Just a long weekend, Harry. I just need to check out something so as I can relax. How's the wife?'

'All the happier for having me on the night shift I recon.'

'Fair enough.' Sam was not really listening.

The stacks of files that normally adorned Sam's desk were conspicuous by their absence. He eventually found them, stacked haphazardly on a filing cabinet, in the DCI's office. He humped them back to his own domain and, dumping them on the floor, started to go through them, one by one, sorting them into places on his desk that suited his personal system. The forensic reports were half way down. He placed them side by side on his blotter but could not concentrate until all the others were in their proper place.

"Fibres," Sam wrote on fresh sheet of paper. "Fun fur?"

"Why no other fibres? Hair for instance?"

The fire would account for that but not in the second case; no amount of cleaning would remove every trace of hair, pubic or otherwise. Some must be the killers.

Sam dialled DI Jones' mobile. It eventually went to voice mail. Sam dialled again. It was engaged. The third attempt elicited a grumpy 'What?'

'Owen . . . it's Sam.'

'Sam, it's seven o'clock.'

'I know.'

'On a Saturday.'

'I know . . . Did I wake you?'

'Oh no,' was the sarcastic reply.

'Did your forensic team discover any pubes?'

'What?'

'Pubic hair. Was there any in Gloria's bed?'

'Wasn't it in the report?'

173

'No.'

'Then they didn't find any. The bed was stripped, remember.'

'OK. What about in the washing machine? That's where the sheets ended up isn't it?'

'I'll check,'

'Get them to check the filter too.'

'OK, is that all?'

'For now . . . sorry to have woken you, Owen.' Sam went to hang up.

'Sam. Where are you?'

'In the office.'

'I thought you were on leave.'

'Who told you that?'

'Your DCI.'

'Well I'm back.' *He's wasting no time,* Sam thought.

'Thank God, boy . . . Duw; I thought I was getting the whole mess back in my lap.'

'Not if I can help it. Did he say anything else?'

'Only that he'd call me Monday.'

'Well, get your guys on that for me and ring me on my mobile any time.'

'Right-o.' They broke the connection together.

Sam spent the rest of the morning going through the files and making notes. None of his team had turned up by eleven so he sent an

174

internal email request for a SOCO officer to meet him at Coleman St on Monday morning, CC.ing Forest and Archer. Suddenly overcome by fatigue and nausea, he drove slowly home.

Chapter 17

Confronting the mess in his salon did not come easily. All he wanted to do was sleep. Collapsing onto his he bed closed his eyes and let the cabin spin around him. The image of dumped clothes, empty bottles, spillages and stains of various substances that it would take a forensic expert to identify, denied him any rest. Changing into jeans and a polo shirt, he was compelled to clear up. It took him two hours working in short bursts, interspersed with coffee and fresh air on deck, to restore order. Setting the washing machine to work on his bed linen seemed like a good idea but once it started on the first of several rinse and spin cycles he had to escape.

Two suits and half a dozen shirts, dumped in a bin liner, were festering up on deck. They were destined for the cleaners, although he suspected one of the former was so impregnated with vomit and curry sauce as to be beyond recovery. He decided to take them now; he was out of coffee anyway.

The car, no longer sanitised by whisky fumes, smelled like a Bengal Lancer's jockstrap so driving with all the windows open he made his first call at the cleaners then dumped the Saab at the hand carwash for a full valet and walked back to Marks and Spencer's food hall.

Two packs of Blue Mountain lay in the bottom of the capacious depths of his trolley and he was considering buying a ready meal, when a thought trickled through his still recovering synapses. Tomorrow is Sunday and Julie was coming to lunch, he said he would cook?

The four, overloaded, plastic shopping bag were threatening to amputate his fingers by the time he reached the carwash. Sitting in the waiting area the bags leaning against his leg he kneaded life back into his hands and watched the final detailing being carried out on his car.

Contemplating the menu his impromptu shopping trip would provide he realised he should have compiled a list first. Cooking had been one of his pleasures even when Andrea was alive it took his mind off the stresses of work. Unfortunately, he had never had the pleasure of cooking for a toddler. He glanced down at the tin of spaghetti hoops threatening to escape from the top of one of the bags. He would use them only as a last resort, as he would the fish fingers. After all, Coquille St Jacques' was mostly mashed potato anyway.

Sunday dawned clear and bright. What little cloud there was, raced across the sky but there was no more than a strong breeze at ground level. Sam watched a keen group of dinghy sailors setting up their masts and rigging near the slipway on the far side of the marina. He hoped they would still be about when little Jodi arrived, it would give them something to talk about. Distracted from preparing the vegetables for lunch, he allowed his Eversharp Chef's knife to nick his finger. The blade barely touched his skin but still it drew a fair bit of blood. It tasted metallic as he sucked the offended digit. Once sealed with a skin coloured plaster, he did not have any blue ones, he washed the blood off the potatoes and the offending knife. It was a seven-inch blade in high carbon steel. A compromise, sharp enough for an amateur and never needing honing. For a professional, far too dull, or was that just cheffy machismo. *Sharp enough to inflict those fatal wounds?* He thought. *Probably. I must ask about that.*

Sam had set up a table in the spacious well-deck area behind his wheel-house and, satisfied all was under control in the galley, had been enjoying a coffee, only his third of the day, when he spotted the little red car pull in.

Julie arrived right on time. Looking radiant in a pale blue summer dress, she climbed out of the Fiat and reached back in through the open door to release the harness on her son's child seat in the back. Sam was already on the dockside and hastening to help. He was rewarded with a view of thigh that reset his pulse to a Salsa rhythm.

As he strode towards them, Jodi, released from his bonds, skirted his mother's leg and ran arms wide and with an extended cry of 'Saaam' at Sam's legs. Fearing another head butt in his "gentleman's region," Sam crouched down and accepted the onslaught on the chest, scooping the boy up and stood grinning at his mother.

Words tumbled from the boy like a waterfall, 'Look at all them boats. Can we go on one? Where's your boat, Sam? Is it that big one? I'm going to get a boat soon. When I'm gown up. When I'm six, I'll have boat like that one.' Clinging with one arm round Sam's neck his other hand pointed in all directions. 'Can we go on your boat now, Sam?'

'Wait for Mummy.' Sam continued towards Julie who had retrieved a large holdall from the front passenger seat and was locking the car. She turned and ran, over hugging the pair of them together. For the briefest of moments, her lips brushed Sam's. *I need more*, Sam thought, delighting in her touch. She shouldered her bag and took Sam's arm as he guided her onboard.

Jodi was wriggling in Sam's arms, his bronze curls bouncing, as he looked excitedly this way and that. Carefully, Sam set him down.

180

'Jodi, remember what I told you.' Julie warned. 'Do you remember?'

The boy's chubby little legs were going like pistons on the spot. 'Yes Mum.'

'What was it?' Julie dumped her bag on the bench that occupied the rear of the well area.

'No running . . .'

'And?'

'Don't go near the water.'

'OK.'

Sam closed the gate that completed the enclosure to the well. 'Do you want to see where I steer the boat, Jodi?'

The boy nodded repeatedly too excited to speak.

Sam opened the wheelhouse door. The delicious smell of roasting chicken wafted out to greet them. Jodi ran to the wheel, which was taller than he was, and Sam lifted him onto the swivel seated conning stool so that he could see out of the windows.

The boy was full of questions, 'Where shall we go? What is this for? What is that? What does this do?' and so on.

Patiently Sam explained all the controls. Jodi was soon into his own little world, off finding Nemo. With a warning to be careful climbing down from the high seat, which no doubt did not get through, Sam turned back to the deck. Julie, her face lit up, was standing in the doorway. At last they could embrace properly.

Lost in her scent and the feel of her body crushed against his, Sam would have been happy to stand there for the rest of his life. However, they had to come up for air.

'Dinner smells wonderful,' she breathed.

'So do you,' he kissed her again.

'I smell chicken,'

'Are you hungry?'

'Famished.'

'Me too,' he ticked her waist.

'Food first,' she demanded.

'Coming up,' reluctantly he broke the clinch, 'Go and relax on deck, I'll bring some drinks first.' He backed into the companionway, 'Would you like a drink, Jodi?'

'Yes please,' the boy was gripping the wheel, which was too heavy for him to turn so he swivelled in the seat instead. He went back to making foghorn and powerboat noises. Sam shot a quizzical glance at Julie.

'Orange squash?'

Sam gave the thumbs up as he reached the bottom of the companion way, his head now level with the deck. He could see her smiling down at him.

Despite having all its ports open, the small galley was like a furnace itself. Methodically Sam drained the parboiled potatoes, arranged them in the tray of smoking goose fat from the oven and put it back in. He made Jodi's drink in a plastic beaker, adding ice and a straw then retrieved the ice bucket he had stashed in his bedroom. Two champagne flutes nestled in the, partly melted, crushed ice alongside the bottle of Moet. He was sweating profusely when he clambered back on deck.

Jodi, sucking on his straw, watched through the wheelhouse window as the Champagne cork sailed out into the dock. He squealed with delight. 'Do it again Sam' he yelled as he clambered down from his high seat.

'I'm afraid that's a onetime shot,' Sam laughed, then whispered in to Julie, 'I've got another bottle in the fridge.'

'Save it for later,' she murmured. They clinked their glasses together.

'I had better get the starters ready,' Sam started back inside.

'Can I come?' Jodi asked.

'It's too hot in there, son,' Sam replied. 'After dinner I'll show you around inside.'

'Is there anything I can do?' Julie asked.

'You could lay the table; everything is on a tray under that seat.' Sam was nothing if not prepared.

'Starters,' Sam declared as he appeared with two dishes, 'I took the precaution of making spaghetti hoops in case Jodi doesn't like scallops.'

As it turned out, all three of them found Coquille St Jacques and Spaghetti in tomato sauce delicious.

How Jodi found room for even the small portion of the roast dinner that followed was a source of amazement to them. However, his mother spotted the full sign in his eyes and she settled him at her side on the bench in the certain knowledge that he would soon be asleep.

It was a perfect afternoon. Jodi, now stretched out across the bench under the shade of a sun umbrella, Sam and Julie, consigned to a pile of cushions on the deck. Their backs against the wheelhouse, they sipped champagne and munched strawberries that Sam had intended to serve with ice cream for dessert. They talked a little but mostly they just listened to the gentle lapping of the water on the hull and revelled in the proximity of each other.

The timing could not be better. Jodi woke and sat up rubbing his eyes, just as the first of the dinghy sailors returned through the lock that separated the marina from the Thames. Fascinated, he watched as they tacked around, waiting their turn to use the slipway to slide their trailers under their hulls and drag them onto the hard. Sam volunteered to walk Jodi round the harbour wall for a closer look. Julie decided to stay where she was.

When Sam returned, carrying Jodi by then, she had dealt with the washing up and was sitting on the bench with a cafetiere of Blue Mountain in front of her. Jodi told her of his adventures with the dinghy sailors, over a bowl of ice cream, then remembered Sam's promise of a tour inside his floating home.

Aft of the main salon and galley was the master suite, now smelling only slightly of roasting chicken, and infinitely better than the night before. Forward of the salon were two small cabins, one with double bunks and another with a single berth.

'Would you like to sleep here tonight, Jodi?' Sam looked to Julie for approval. She smiled back.

'In there.' Jodi pointed to the top bunk.

'I think not young man,' his mother replied.

'Oh . . .'

'This is a nice cabin,' Sam offered, 'it's where the captain usually sleeps.' That made all the difference.

'Come on let's get you into your jim-jams.' Julie took him by the hand and, back up on deck, recovered her tote bag. As she fished out his pyjamas from its copious interior, Sam was delighted to glimpse the lacy edge of her change of underwear.

Jodi was asleep almost before his head touched the pillow. Sam watched as Julie tucked him in then led the way back on deck. The second bottle of champagne was waiting in the last of his crushed ice but they did not bother to open it. Instead, they snuggled together in the cool evening air, watching the lights come on in the windows of the apartment block across the dock, and their reflections wavering in the inky water.

This time their lovemaking was more considered. Sam watched, in the dim light of his cabin, enjoying the sight of her naked body as Julie folded first her clothes then his, before joining him on the bed. No stone was left unturned as they explored each other's body and wordlessly exchanged pleasures at what they found.

Chapter 18

The day started in an idealised dream of domestic bliss. Jodi woke at six, sleepily wandered into the aft cabin and crawled into bed between the two consenting adults. The sensation of a small body clambering over the duvet woke Sam with a start but he managed to stay immobile until the child settled, hugging his mother and forming an effective barrier between them.

Resignedly, Sam slipped out of bed, found his boxers on the pile and crept to the galley. Looking back, he saw Julie open one eye, smile serenely and wrap a comforting arm around her son. Avoiding his usual clatter and bang approach to domestic chores, so as not to disturb the somnolent Madonna and Child, he set the coffee to brew and took a shower.

Sipping his hot drink at the table on deck, he checked his emails on his smart-phone. At sometime Saturday afternoon, Higgins from SOCO had responded. He would be at Coleman St by nine a.m. Sam tapped out an acceptance and was adding instructions for Forest when Julie appeared at the wheelhouse door. Looking fresh and cool in one of his white work shirts, it looked better on her than it ever would on him, she came to join him

'Sorry about that, Sam, did Jodi disturb you this morning?'

'Well,' Sam waggled an open hand, 'I was hoping . . .'

She leaned over and kissed him gently on the lips. 'He usually gets into bed with me in the mornings. He's back asleep now but he's sure to wake if we,' she waggled her hand.

'In that case,' Sam grinned, 'coffee?'

'It's one of the joys of parenthood.' Julie slid a spare cup towards him.

'What, coffee?'

'That too, but small boys cramping your style goes with the territory I'm afraid.'

'I'll get used to it. If you'll let me.'

'I'll think about it,' she frowned in concentration, 'OK, I've thought,' she grinned, 'welcome on board.' They embraced again.

'Can you come with me to Welling tonight?'

'Sure, but I didn't think, you know, won't Tony Russell be there, won't it be a bit awkward after you cancelled . . .'

'Sam, I,' she hesitated, 'I didn't cancel.'

'What!'

'I was going to but his line was engaged and . . . anyway, he came round on Friday, no harm done.'

188

'After what I said.' Sam's voice was getting louder and reaching for the upper register.

'I can't believe he could do what you say. He may be a flirt and no doubt would try his luck but he's not a sadist. Anyway I can handle him.'

'Not under the influence of Rohypnol you can't.' Sam yelled his voice echoing off the stone dock walls.

'I'll be careful, Sam, promise,' by contrast, her voice was getting softer.

'Mummee,' Jodi was clambering up the companionway, clearly upset.

'It's alright, darling; mummy and Sam were just talking.' She held out her arms and the boy ran into them, just a trace of a tear on his cheek. Hugging the boy to her, she looked back at Sam. 'Anyway,' she said determinedly, 'I'm entering the National Championships with him.'

Sam knew when he was beaten, but only the skirmish not the battle.

Sam left Julie with a spare set of keys to the boat so that she could lock up after she had got Jodi ready for nursery school, and made his thoughtful way to the office. The incident room was abuzz by eight o'clock. The team were telephoning the list of attendees to the dance. Despite the baffles around each workstation, the voices filled the room.

Unprecedented in Sam's experience, the DCI walked in at twenty past. Forest was sitting on the edge of Sam's desk as Archer approached.

'That's what I like to see, a team in action.' Archer dismissed Forest with a wave of his hand. 'Sam, a word please,' he looked around, 'My office, I think.'

'I was just briefing DS Forest on a new line . . .' Sam said to the retreating back of his senior officer. He pulled a face at Forest and stood to follow. 'Have Kingy bring a car round the front. We have to be at Colman St by nine.'

DCI Archer was seated behind his desk, pretending to write something on an A4 pad, when Sam came in. 'Close the door Sam,' he said without looking up.

Sam complied and, having not been invited to sit, stood at attention fixing his gaze on the wall clock above his boss' head.

'That's the last time I cover up for you,' Archer snapped.

'I didn't ask you . . .'

'Do you think that by coming in here in your sharp suits and laundered shirts, I don't know what's going on?' He glared up at Sam. 'Your old DCI put up with it after your wife died but there is no excuse now.'

'But what . . .'

'I haven't finished.' Archer looked torn between anger and resignation. 'Oh for god sake sit down you're giving me a stiff neck.'

Sam pulled up a chair.

'Dr Fielding suggests that you are suffering from work related stress. This job in particular has got to you.'

'I don't think . . .'

'The fact that the first victim is similar in appearance to your wife has to have some bearing on that.' Archers tone softened. 'Drink may be your way of coping, Sam, but it is not acceptable in a modern police force.'

'I know.'

'Let me make it clear. One sniff of booze on duty and you'll be off the case and straight down to psychiatric evaluation. Got it?'

'Yes sir.'

'OK, so what's this new line of enquiry?'

'Well sir. These are particularly bloody types of killings. The perpetrator must have been covered in it. We know that they cleaned up the scene at Ealing and must have cleaned themselves up too. The fire scotched any trace at Colman St but SOCO will check the waste traps in the bathroom and kitchen. We might find traces we can get a DNA profile from.

'We can't test the DNA of all two hundred suspects. It'll take forever.'

'I know but if we can narrow the candidates down, we have a way of proving they were there.'

'All right, but don't order any tests without my say so . . . and. Sam, remember what I said.'

'OK, you're the boss.' Sam wondered if he had kept the irony out of his voice.

On the way down to where Forest and King were waiting, Sam pondered on only one thing the DCI had said. He broached it with his DS as they drove off.

'You met Andrea didn't you, Mike?'

'Yes, only once, at that Christmas do.'

'Would you say that Sheila Delaney looked like her?'

'You mean you didn't notice?'

'Well, if I did I must have blanked it out.' Sam brought up images of the two women in his mind's eye. Yes, there are superficial similarities I suppose but Andrea was special in a way that, despite their physical differences, only Julie could match. With that thought, he fell silent.

It was twenty past nine when the Scene of Crime officer arrived.

Sam opened the door of the van for him. 'Ah, Posthumous Higgins, I presume.'

The boffin blinked at him through the thick lenses of his oversized, wire rimmed glasses.

'He means you're late,' Forest tried to dispel the man's confusion. 'You're going to love this.'

192

Higgins had brought the key to the sheet metal replacement door and, once in the dim interior, Sam explained what he wanted.

'All the u-bends or bottle traps in the house to be removed and their contents analysed. Including washing machine and dishwasher filters. Anywhere that might hold a scrap of skin or hair that may not be baked into oblivion by the fire. Eliminate Dempsey's DNA and run any other against the suspects' and the CRO database.' Sam was pleased to see that someone had cleared a path through the musty detritus that had covered the floor on his last visit, what remained had set like concrete. He made one brief walk through the rooms then left the technician to it.

On the way back, he called Owen Jones and expanded on the brief conversation they had had on Saturday. Owen said he was on his way to meet his techs as they spoke and would keep him posted.

The team, now six strong, was ploughing through the two hundred telephone interviews. Any that could not put up a corroborated alibi for either of the crimes were passed to the Holmes receiver marked for further attention, before being passed on to Forest and Miller. Already five were on the list for the Greenwich killing and seven for Ealing, only one featured in both. Miller seized on the latter.

'Might as well follow it up,' Sam said to Forest, 'better than waiting here. The DNA results are probably days away and our Mr Archer likes to see "a team in action."' Sam looked at his watch. 'Where can we find him this time of day?'

'He's a Vet. Works over in Dagenham. Shall I call and let him know we're coming.'

'No, let's surprise him.'

The Blackwall Tunnel was still backed up to the Sun in the Sands roundabout and, although they approached via Tunnel Avenue, King had to resort to judicious whoops on the siren and the hard shoulder to get to the front where an over-height articulated lorry bearing Hungarian plates was being manoeuvred into the escape road. At least once it was gone they had a clear road through to the Bow Flyover where they turned right towards Essex. Sam wondered how he would get on in the Traffic Division. *Perhaps I'll find out soon enough,* he thought. *Would they put a borderline alcoholic behind the wheel of a "Jam Sandwich,"* he wondered. *It hadn't stopped them before.*

Robin Cooper's veterinary surgery was in the converted ground floor of an end-of-terrace house in a residential back street of what continues to be the largest housing estate in Europe. Uniform, brown brick, nineteen-thirties houses blanketed

194

over four square miles in an area known as The Becontree Estate. The three of them marched into the busy reception area.

In response to an intercom call from his receptionist, a galleon built, middle aged, woman with a jolly smile, he replied that he would be right out and, sure enough, he soon appeared at the open doorway to his surgery guiding a little girl cuddling the biggest ginger tom cat Sam had ever seen. Cooper was a mousy man with a pencil moustache. Sam estimated him to be in his late thirties but the Clark Gable look aged him.

'Keep Ginger in for a couple of nights and he will be back to normal, Lucy. Now off you go and be careful of the roads.' He looked up and smiled, 'Now gentlemen,' he swept his arm towards his inner sanctum, before turning to the half dozen clients waiting in the reception area. 'This won't take long.' He looked questioningly at Sam, 'will it Officer?'

'Just a few questions we hope you can help us with.' Sam led the way into the white tiled back room. Forest, showing his warrant card, did the introductions. They were offered a seat; brown moulded plastic on a tubular frame. Forest preferred to stand.

Facing each other across the examination table, Sam drew his chair closer. 'We are investigating the murder of Sheila Delaney on 30th March.'

'So I gather from your people who phoned yesterday. How can I help?'

'We'd like you to account for your movements that Friday night if you don't mind.'

'Well, like I said, I left the dance at about ten-thirty and went straight home.'

'Driving? That is your Volvo outside?'

'Yes. but I used public transport that night.'

'Why?'

'I knew I'd have a few drinks so didn't want to risk it.'

'Hmm. Very wise, I'm sure. Can you tell me your route?'

'I had to catch the last DLR, that's why I left early.'

'On your own?'

'Unfortunately yes.'

'Then what?'

'Oh it's a trek I admit. Change at Canary Wharf then again at Stratford and again at Witham. I didn't get to Braintree Station until half past twelve. My house is a fifteen minute walk from there.'

'So you're saying you were tucked up in bed by say one on Saturday morning.'

'About that, yes.'

'And can you tell me where you were on the night of, Saturday Night 13th / 14th'

'Why?'

'Just answer the question please, sir.'

'Like I said to your people, I work here Saturday mornings. After that, I had a pub lunch at the Green Dragon near where I live then home and a night in watching TV. Same as any Saturday unless there's a dance on somewhere.'

'And no one can corroborate that?'

'Not after I left the pub, They know me in there.'

'I see,' Sam paused for thought, 'one last thing. As a vet you have access to certain drugs.'

'Yes,' he replied cagily.

'Do you keep them here?'

'Yes, but they're locked away in a metal cabinet. There's never a large quantity of anything . . . contentious. What specifically did you have in mind?'

'Things that might be considered date rape drugs.'

'Oh, you're thinking of Ketamine. We use it from time to time as an anaesthetic.'

'Or Rohypnol?'

'No, not that, it has no vetinary use and I only keep a single dose of Ketamine for emergencies. If I'm planning an operation I buy it in specially. Would you like to see my drugs book?' He swivelled in his seat and opened a draw in the bank of units that occupied one wall of the room and drew out a blue hardbound notebook. 'Help yourself.' He handed it to Miller.

Sam flicked through the pages. It was neatly laid out in small but perfectly formed hand, complete with purchase and use dates.' He committed the most recent page to memory and handed it back. 'Thank you, sir, I don't think we need bother you anymore but you're not planning a trip in the near future are you?'

'No, nothing but a dance weekend next month and that's only at Camber Sands.'

'Well if you change your mind please let us know.'

PC King took circuitous route via the M25 and Queen Elizabeth II Bridge and heading back towards Greenwich on the A2. They passed so close to Bexley that Sam was tempted to call in on Julie and probably would have done if Forest was not with them.

They discussed Cooper's interview and came to the conclusion that he was probably telling the truth. Sam had always been of the opinion that those with a ready alibi were most worthy of further investigation. So far, every suspect fell outside of that category.

Back at the incident room, Sam discovered that two more candidates had come into the frame but they were in North West London and Owen Jones had them in hand. Sam stepped outside and, avoiding the pub, took on a Full English in a local cafe as an afternoon breakfast. On the way back, he called Julie on his mobile.

After almost a minute she answered with a curt, 'Sam.'

'Julie . . . I want to apologise for this morning.'

'So you should, Sam.'

'I was just worried about you . . . I couldn't bear it if anything . . .'

'You ruined a perfect weekend.'

'It's just that Russell is still a suspect and . . .'

'You're wrong about him. He wouldn't . . . couldn't do what you say.'

'Is there no way I can persuade you to drop it?'

'Don't start again, Sam.'

'But I don't trust him . . .'

'Neither do I, but not in the way you think. Look, the National Ceroc Championships is a big deal. If we crack it, apart from the prize money, the prestige would put our dance clubs on the map, a second venue would be in the offing and, to be honest, I could do with the income.'

'But why Russell?'

'Tony is the best partner I know. Possibly the best lead in the country.'

'Why isn't he entering with what's-her-name?'

'Stella? You've seen her dance.'

'OK does she know she's out?'

'No. He's going to tell her tonight.'

'Oh. Do you think you'll need a police presence?'

'If you're still up for it.'

'Of course . . .'

'Deal,' she said, 'as long as you don't keep on about Tony.'

'Fine . . . I'll pick you up about seven?' *At least I am still in with a shout,* he thought.

Chapter 19

Julie ran across the road and slid into the passenger seat of Sam's Saab. 'Let's go, she said urgently, 'I didn't let Jodi see me off in case he got too excited. He's been on about you and your "boat house" all day. Mum'll never get him off to sleep if he saw you.' She smiled and kissed him on the cheek as he put the car into drive.

'All forgiven?'

'Oh I don't know. I have been known to hold a grudge for years,' she grinned.

Russell glared at the couple as they walked in, arm in arm. *He's still looking daggers at me*, Sam thought, *but what do you expect from a knife killer, shotguns?* He allowed the humour to show on his face as he returned the look and was pleased to see it wound the man up.

The session followed the usual format with the same crowd at the same table. Tony and Stella did the demos. In the free dance session, Stella donned an oversized black T-shirt with Taxi Dancer emblazoned in white on it and asked the beginners if they needed any help with practicing what they had learned. Sam took her up on it while Julie was dancing a spectacular routine to

Amy Winehouse's "Back to Black" with Tony, mostly because he could not bear to watch them.

Both couples returned to the table at the change of record.

Sam took Julie's hand and said 'You'll have to teach me to do one of those dips,' referring to their elegant last move.

'Not to this, lover,' she replied. The DJ was playing Brown Eyed Girl, a Van Morrison classic. 'A bit too fast I think.' She saw his disappointed look and added, 'we'll try to the next slow one.' They were still chatting when "Sway," came on.

'This'll do,' She grabbed Russell's arm and said, 'come on Tony let's show him.'

Effortlessly they swung into a couple of basic moves that Sam knew then a simple dip. From her almost horizontal position, she grinned at Sam and said, 'got it?'

Sam was wishing he had not mentioned it but nodded. It went quite well until the last moment when he lost his balance, dumping Julie on the floor and followed down on top of her.

'Not as easy as it looks, is it?' Julie was laughing fit to bust, 'try again?'

Clambering to his feet, he helped her up to general applause and laughter. He took an ironic bow and murmured 'I think we should practice this at home before I try again.' *It would be more fun naked anyway*, he thought.

Having learned not to run before he could walk, Sam sat out the advanced class but continued to watch Tony and Stella intently. It was clear, even to his untrained eye, why Russell would prefer to have Julie as a partner for a competition.

As soon as they handed over to the DJ for the last half hour free dance session, Tony pulled off his headset microphone and guided Stella to the side of the stage. It was obvious by her reaction what he had said.

Raised voices carried over a loud and base driven instrumental, blasting from the elevated speakers but Sam could not make out any actual words. However, he did not need the help of a psychologist to read the body language.

Julie, who had ended up dancing with Maureen, glanced at the demo team then as she spun, gave Sam a knowing look. Stella gathered up her bag and coat from a chair near the stage and, with a face like a thunderhead, stormed out. On the way past she deliberately shouldered the unsighted Julie in the back. Julie, on one foot in the middle of a spin, careened off balance and ended up dumped hard on her back side. Sam rushed to her aid.

'That's the second time I've ended up on the floor tonight.' With barely any pressure on his outstretched hand, she regained her feet more elegantly than Sam would have thought possible.

'Want to go for the hat trick,' he grinned.

'Ooo, your place or mine,' she smiled back.

The music changed to Alison Moyet's version of "That Old Devil Called Love". Maureen had tactfully disappeared into the background and so they clung together gently swaying together with no pretentions at Jiving.

Russell was waiting when they returned to the table.

'That went well,' he said to Julie, deliberately ignoring Sam.

'Yes, we saw,' she replied.

The incident seemed to have precipitated an end to the meeting. Apart from a few stalwarts, who would dance through an earthquake as long as the music kept playing, people were changing their shoes, and getting ready to leave. Patrick and Gilda were on their way to the door. The others from their table had already left.

Outside it had started to rain; that fine drizzle that seeped through your clothes and into your bones. Sam drove Julie home and, although the parting kiss, sitting in the parked car, was full of passion, Sam's dream of making love on a blanket on the ground had to remain just that.

Monday 18th April

What a stroke of luck. Stella was stuck for a lift and she lives in Blackheath, just a few miles from me. I found her soaked through, shivering and still waiting for a taxi when I came out. There was no one about so I offered her a lift and let her cry on my shoulder all the way home. I went in with her, for coffee. When she unpacked her bag, she found she had gathered up Tony's sweaty shirt. I said I would return it for her and she accepted but not until she had ripped it into strips. We both laughed about that. Of course she did not realise how much grief that shirt is going to bring him. Both of them actually.

She even accepted the offer of one of my special tablets to help her sleep. I would have done it there and then but there was not a single decent knife in her kitchen. I have arranged to pick her up and take her to Ceroc Ealing on Thursday. Cannot wait.

Another two days, working late into the evenings, following up on weak alibis produced nothing but depression. By Wednesday afternoon, Sam, in a low number state of mind, had still not heard back from either forensic department. He chased up his local unit first.

'Higgins,' the chief technician had answered the phone after two rings.

'Sam Miller, here. Any luck with the stuff from the drains at Coleman Street?'

'I was just typing up the report . . .'

'I'll look forward to that but can you give me the gist?'

'I'd rather . . .'

'I know you'd rather. Did you find anything, what you might call, DNA-able?'

'The washing machine filter was knackered and full of bleach so no hope there I'm afraid.'

'What about the shower?'

'The kitchen sink was pretty much the same and the plastic pipes had melted in the fire too.'

'The bathroom?'

'Yes, more luck with the sink there, a lot of hair. Hard to separate but preliminary results indicate it is all the victims. We probed the shower trap and found a trace of the victim's blood among the hair in there.'

'What do you mean you probed the shower?'

'We couldn't get at the trap. The shower tray is concreted in over it. So we probed down the plug hole to get a sample.'

'Well, I suggest you go back with a plumber or a big hammer and break out that trap, and all the nearby waste pipes and find me some evidence.' Sam's raised voice hushed the incident room. He went on more quietly, 'if there's blood in the shower trap our killer put it there. Find me a stranger's hair in with it and we'll have our killer.'

'The blood could have been from shaving her legs or something. It'll take some time separating each hair and testing it.'

'Then you'd better get on with it then.' Sam was shouting again. He slammed the phone down. 'What?' he said, looking round the office. He took a swig of cold coffee, whilst waiting for the heads to lower again, then called Jones at Ealing.

There was something about the Welshman's singsong voice that mollified the anger that Sam carried forward from his previous call.

'Owen,' he said, 'any luck with the forensics.'

'They're still working on it, boy. Found blood in the shower and kitchen sink, definitely the victim's. There's an amount of hair in the shower and they are going through it now. I shouldn't hold your breath though.'

'Good. Keep them at it, mate. Anything else?'

'They did find a couple of pubes in the washing machine. Bleached to buggery though.'

'I knew there had to be. Nothing to be had from DNA?'

'Not really. Two different donors, both female but not enough to identify an individual.'

'OK, Owen, keep me posted.'

'Will do,' he let out a brief, soft chuckle, 'for the next week anyway, then I'm out of here.'

'Well good luck with that.'

'You too, boy.'

Hands behind his head, Sam sat back in his chair. *Whoever they are,* he thought, *they certainly know how to cover their tracks.* 'Bloody American CSI,' he said aloud.

He was swinging into the higher numbers of his personal mood register as he pulled up outside Julie's place. They had agreed that, if he was not tied up at work, he would arrive early and have tea with them. He was surprised how much the prospect of spending time with Jodi again buoyed him up.

Tea for Jodi consisted of a boiled egg and marmite soldiers. Sam opted for the same.

'Bit if a come down from Coquille St Jacques,' Julie's mother said, as she bustled about the kitchen.

'Especially with spaghetti hoops, Margret,' Sam replied. He had seated himself next to Jodi at the small melamine drop-leaf table that was only brought out for mealtimes. The boy was already tucking into his meal and most of it somehow made its way into his mouth. However, that did not stop him chatting away.

'Jodi told me about that . . . Jodi don't speak with your mouthful . . . We have some if you want.' She waved the familiar Heinz tin.

Sam laughed. 'Marmite on toast will be fine, thanks.'

Julie came in wearing another skimpy dance outfit, pink this time. 'How are my two favourite men getting on?'

'We're doing fine,' Sam made to stand but Julie put a restraining hand on his shoulder and kissed the top of his head. 'You look fabulous.' Sam said.

'You look obvious, more like,' her mother admonished her.

Laughing, Julie gave her son a similar kiss to Sam and pecked her mother on the cheek. 'Even you've worn smaller bikinis, mum.'

'Maybe but not around the house.'

Sam was on stage helping Julie and her DJ set up when Russell walked in. It was Sam's turn to offer a disparaging look across the hall. The session took the usual format and Sam found himself competent in half a dozen or so basic moves and getting there in as many more. He made sure he was near the stage at the end of the beginner's class and claimed the first dance in the middle free session. Julie seemed impressed with his progress but as Lou Rawls' "Fine Brown Frame" ended, she kissed him on the cheek and rushed off to assist one of the other beginners. He had little time to be disappointed as "Are You in it for

Love," a favourite among the dancers started he was claimed by Gilda and for half an hour did not get a chance to sit down. By the time Julie returned to the stage, he was exhausted and his shirt, like most of the other men was soaked in perspiration.

Outside, the light rain that had let up earlier in the evening resumed. It was pleasantly cooling as Sam dashed back to his car to retrieve a fresh polo shirt he, on Julie's advice, had brought with him. He did not expect to need it so left it, plastic wrapped, in the Saab's boot.

In the Gents he found he was not the only one in need of a freshen up. Tony Russell was just leaving, looking young and athletic in a stylish cheesecloth shirt that emphasised his broad shoulders and narrow waist and tight black trousers that did the same for his narrow hips. They nodded curtly as they passed.

Sam stripped off his soaked shirt and examined himself in the mirror above the line of sinks. Years of heavy drinking had taken its toll of his waistline and he suspected himself of developing man-boobs. As for his backside clad in sad and saggy jeans, he had to avert his gaze. *What does she see in me,* he thought.

The sight that met him as he returned to the hall exacerbated the downturn in his self-esteem. Russell had taken over the role of demo dancer.

Julie spotted him as he came through the door. 'Room for one more on the men's line Sam,' her cheery call booming through the speaker system, 'You can do this.'

Sam shook his head mouthed, "No way,' and, with a wan smile, skulked away to the bar.

He ordered a bottle of Peroni and moodily sipped it, leaning on the counter, while the class went on without him. It was the first alcohol to pass his lips since his run in with DCI Archer and it tasted so good. Watching from a distance, he had to admire the fluent way Tony and Julie moved together. Julie was right, he could have picked the intermediate moves up, no trouble. That realisation only deepened his depression. A second beer followed before the tutorial ended.

This time Julie sought him out. She took a big sip of his remaining beer then dragged him by the hand onto the dance floor. Still sulking, he went through the motions of what remained of, "Ladies Night," but the next selection struck a chord and he threw all he knew into "I Just Want to Make Love to You." By the time the Etta James track had finished Sam was ready to go but forced himself to stick it out for the final hour. Not much in the mood for dancing with anyone but Julie, he politely declined the requests by many of the women present. Only Gilda would not take no for an answer.

'You're a very popular man, Sam,' she said as she muscled him out of his seat.

'I don't know why.'

'It's your dancing. You've got natural rhythm.'

Sam shrugged, 'I don't know . . .'

'Believe me, you've got it, come on.' She threw herself into a spin and caught his unprepared hand. Encouraged, he smiled and danced on; with the slow realisation that, maybe he was being manipulated.

He managed to get the last dance with Julie, but only by tapping Tony on the shoulder. It was a song in French, that was gentle paced and easy to jive to, or not. They spent a lot of time in each other's arms. For once, the words did not matter.

At last, they were ready to leave.

'Mum's not expecting me home tonight.' Julie's coquettish smile, picked out in the pink glow of the dashboard lights, left Sam in no doubt in which direction to drive.

'How does that sit with her puritanical mindset?'

'Oh, that applies to men in general. You are now elevated to her approved list,' she giggled.

'Anyone else on the list?' *like Tony Russell,* Sam thought.

'Oh it's a very short list. Just you and Jodi.'

Sam could not hide the relief and drove all the way through Greenwich in silence before saying, 'Do you know anything about a dance weekend down in Camber Sands?'

'Yes, we're all going . . . you know; the whole crowd.'

'Oh,'

'Did you want to come too?'

'Well . . .'

'The tickets are sold out six months in advance, and there is a waiting list for cancellations. I could try if you like?'

'OK. He paused as the prospect sank in, 'where do you stay?'

'It's an old holiday camp. Three of the girls and I are sharing a chalet. I could get you in with the boys if you like.'

'Oh.'

'Don't worry, we'll think of something.' She kissed him on the cheek.

Thank god we're nearly home, Sam thought.

214

Chapter 20

The days that dragged by seemed to conspire against them. Despite desperately wanting to keep Russell in the frame, they could gather no concrete evidence against him. Sykes' DNA was found in, of all places, the u-bend of Delaney's toilet but, as he admitted being there and disposing of his condom that way, it did not help. There was the odd hit of strange male and female hair in both crime scenes but the samples were so cross contaminated it was a miracle the boffins could define the gender.

Julie called on Thursday afternoon. 'I've got good news and bad news,' she sounded buoyant.

'OK give me the bad news first. It'll match the atmosphere here.'

'There is no chance of getting an extra ticket from Jivetime.'

'Oh. And the good?'

'Tony said that, as he and Stella have split up, I could use his spare ticket. Of course it would mean sharing a double room.'

Sam almost choked on his coffee.

'Don't you see, Sam? Imagine you turning up to share his bed. It'll probably drive him out altogether.'

'And then?'

'You and me in a double bed,' she giggled, 'On dry land!'

'Hmm.' *Nice idea*, Sam thought. Although he was peeved that Julie was still seeing, or at least communicating with, Russell.

'Anyway, I said I'd take the ticket and meet him down there. Oh do say you'll come.'

'I'll think about it. When is it?'

'Oh it's a couple of weeks away yet. We go down after work on the Friday, that's the tenth May, and come back on Monday morning.'

'We'll see.' As it turned out, events would make the decision much simpler.

Although the investigation remained stalled, Sam was in the high numbers as he looked forward to a weekend on his boat with Julie and Jodi. He had even bought a couple of kids DVDs to keep the lad amused and reloaded his fridge with ice cream for him, and savoury snacks for the adults. By ten am, the day was already beginning to drag so when the DCI called for him into his office, Sam looked upon it as a way to pass the time and entered ready for a witty exchange.

'There's been another,' Archer's face was grim.

'Another what, Sir?'

'Another,' Archer looked at the header of the file on his desk, 'Another "Slow Hand" killing.'

'Who? Where?'

'Local this time. Black Heath . . . a Miss Stevens'

'Stella Stevens?'

'You know her?'

'Yes, well, I've interviewed her with regard to the first one.' Sam's heart was pounding. It took a force of will not to show how much the slaying of another beautiful young woman was driving his anger level through the roof.

'I think we need help now, Sam, don't you?'

'Let me get over there and assess the situation, Boss, I'll get back to you but I think our killer has over played his hand this time.'

'Russell?'

He has read my reports, Sam thought, 'Has to be. He was the girl's partner, well ex partner, and they had a big row on Monday.'

'Bring him in!'

'I'll send Forest and some uniforms. I'd better get to the scene.'

Thursday 21st April

It was delicious. Her skin, soft and white, parted so easily I was tempted to cut deeper. It opened

217

in such perfect lines; it seemed a shame to spoil the symmetry.

Even under the influence of the drugs, she did not much like the idea of the gag but as she was already handcuffed, she did not have much choice. The look in her eyes right from the start, like a hunted gazelle was worth it on its own.

Stella Stephens lived in a basement or, as the estate agents liked to call it a garden flat, in The Paragon, a private crescent of colonnade fronted, Georgian mansions facing the heath but screened by a row of deciduous trees from the public highway. A high-end residential area, popular as corporate and embassy residences.

For once, the forensic team had beaten him to it. Green coveralled technicians were appearing out the back of a van as if from a Tardis. Sam was greeted by young Henderson, who handed him a pair of surgeon's gloves and white cloth overshoes, for when he entered the building.

'Have you been inside yet?' Sam asked

'No, but the constable over there warned me it's not a pretty sight.' Henderson snapped the cuff of his plastic gloves to emphasise his resolve.

Sam turned to his trainee who was pulling on her own gloves. 'Wait here for the DP, and bring her through as soon as she arrives, Kingy.'

Two uniformed constables were busy rigging a screen along the railings to the basement.

218

'Who's in charge here?' Sam asked briskly.

'Sergeant Smith, Sir. He's in the flat.' The man cupped his hands and shouted, 'Sarge!' at the front window. Sam led Henderson down, his five-man team followed in single file.

Accessed to the apartment was by way of curved York Stone steps and its own front door the interior was a sharp contrast to the listed exterior. The flat was ultra modern with clean lines, concealed lighting and quality modern furnishing. The kitchen, with its gleaming red, high gloss units and built in appliances, appeared largely unused. Even the granite worktops were uncluttered by anything except an electric kettle and a tray laid out with a coffee pot and milk jug and two mugs.

Smith was leaning on an island unit. 'Sam,' he greeted him with a grim smile. 'It's through here.'

It was only the bedroom that showed any evidence that a young woman lived there and that was countered by the gory scene on the bed. Half a dozen dolls and teddy bears were lined up on the back of the dressing table innocent unseeing eyes, mute witnesses to the horror that had been enacted there.

If only you could talk, Sam thought.

They stood in the doorway, none ready to lead the way. Stella spread-eagled on the bed head back, throat like a toothless open mouth from where they stood. Dried blood streaks on her abdomen marked out the game the killer was playing. One more nought and one more cross were added to the previous position.

Will it end when one of us wins, Sam thought. *By the look of it, the most probable outcome would be a stalemate; will it all start again then?* He did not even know if he was playing the noughts or the crosses.

'Excuse me,' Melanie Gordon's voice broke his reverie.

The trio parted to allow the Home Office Pathologist to pass through. She put down her bag just inside the door and in a no nonsense way set about her work. Miller and Sergeant Smith left the technicians to it and wandered out into the fresh air.

'Is it me or was it hot in there?' Sam asked.

'You should have felt it when I first went in. Apparently, the heating was cranked up to maximum all night. The cleaner turned it off when she arrived.'

'Is that who found the body?'

'Yep. Shall we see if she's calmed down?' Smith led the way to a wooden bench on the swath of grass on the other side of the road, where PC King had taken over the job of calming the woman. 'Her name's Maria. That's all I could get so far.' Smith said by way of introduction. 'Italian, I think.'

'Spanish, Sarge, Maria Portales.' King turned to the thin, dusky woman seated beside her. 'Maria, this is Detective Inspector Miller, he needs to ask you some questions.'

'Si.' The woman was still visibly trembling. She dabbed at the rivulets of mascara stained tears that streaked her face. 'Who do this to my Miss Stephens?' she wailed.

'We are going to find out,' Sam said, grim determination in his voice, 'and you can help us.' He sat down on the other side of her.

'I try Inspectore. I try.'

'Good. Now can you tell me what time you arrived?'

'It was eight. I always at eight on Friday.'

'Do you remember, was the door locked?'

'Locked, yes. I have key, I always make coffee for my Miss Stephens. We drink together then she go . . . work.'

'And did you find her . . . straight away?'

'Not straight away. Soon.' She sighed, long and deep, suppressing her sobs. 'The apartment so hot. I fix heating, open windows and make coffee then go wake Miss Stephens and . . .' She broke down again.

'OK, Maria,' Sam felt helpless. 'Get her a cup of tea Jackie,'

'One on the way, Guv.' She nodded in the direction of a young constable who had just appeared at the corner of the street with a cardboard tray full of drinks containers.

Sam walked over to where the Sergeant was talking to one of his men. 'I don't suppose anyone saw or heard anything, Harry?' Sam was secretly pleased that at last Smith's first name had come to him. 'No cloaked figure running off into the night?'

'Not so far, Sam.' Smith dismissed his constable who hurried away. The place above is one of those grace and favour mansions for the American Embassy. As you can see it's a private road so no passing traffic. The main drag,' he waved a hand at the well-trafficked road beyond the line of trees, 'always full of parked cars. They come and go almost all the time but the flat is pretty much unsighted from there.'

'CCTV?'

'Nearest one is over on the old A2. It runs across the heath.'

'OK, I'll get it checked when I get back.'

'Tea, Sarge?' The young constable held a depleted tray of drinks. 'Your DC said you like black coffee, Sir.'

'I do,' Sam spotted the stylised "M" on the side of the last remaining container, 'but I think I'll give it a miss this time, son.' *How they've got*

222

the cheek to call that stuff coffee I don't know, Sam thought.

Impatient and desperate for a drink, Sam waited for Melanie Gordon to reappear. Before she did, a long blast on a motor-horn drew his attention. At the lifting barrier that kept the riffraff from parking in the exclusive crescent, a woman in a Jaguar sports car was arguing with the constable on duty.

Smith's radio crackled. 'There's a lady here, Sarge, says she's with DI Miller.'

'Do you know her, Sam?' Smith asked.

'Afraid so . . . Psych-witch.'

'DI Miller says let the wi-lady in, Kelly.'

Miller and Smith strolled across the road and stood at the sightscreen while the psychologist parked her XKR.

'What are you doing here?' Sam greeted her curtly.

'Mr Archer called me.'

'Might have guessed.' Sam did the introductions. As usual, Dr Fielding insisted Smith call her Liz. Smith declined and did not offer his first name.

Good on you, Harry, Sam thought. 'You can't go in.'

'Why not?' Fielding snapped back.

'The pathologist and SOCO are in there at the moment,' Smith stepped in to mediate, 'we're keeping out the way.'

'Melanie Gordon? She won't mind if I . . .'

'She would,' the woman in question was coming up the stairs, followed by Henderson. 'As a matter of fact I've finished here. You can remove the body when you're ready, Sergeant, I'll get to work on it as soon as they get it back to my lab.'

'Do you have a time of death for me, Mel?' Sam asked.

'Between nine and ten last night. There's a bit of a problem with the ambient temperature in there but that is a good approximation.'

'Is it the same as the others?' Fielding asked.

'Similar, yes.' Dr Gordon turned away from the psychologist. 'I'll email you my preliminary as soon as I get back, Sam.'

'Thanks, Mel. 'If you want a look, Miss, best do it now. My boys are about to start ripping out the drains.' Henderson grinned at Sam. One of his green clad team was coming out carrying a black plastic bin liner, 'Interesting contents of the washing machine, Sam.' He waved the man over and they all peered inside. On top of the expected bed sheets and pillowcases was Sam's dream come true. Henderson articulated it, 'Man's cheesecloth shirt, ripped to buggery but with definite organics still on it.'

'Brilliant, son, well done.' Sam could have jumped for joy. 'OK you know what to do, now let's get the body out of there. I'm going back to the office.'

'Wait, I haven't seen the crime scene yet,' Fielding demanded.

'Knock yourself out, Elizabeth. I'm off.' He strode away towards the car. 'Kingy; let's go.'

Well up in the high numbers, Sam tried to calm down as they drove across the open grassy expanse of Blackheath. The towers of Canary Wharf briefly appeared, misted by distance, heat haze and pollution, before the car plunged down Crooms Hill.

'Did you get anything more out of Miss Portales, Kingy?'

'Only background stuff, Guv. She's a student doing art and English at the Polly, cleans for Miss Stephens twice a week for a bit of beer money. Worried it's not on her permit, you know? I've got all her details.' King turned the unmarked Focus into Burnley Street and moments later dropped Sam off at the front entrance to the police station.

In the first floor squad room Forest was at the whiteboard, he had added a third panel and headed it "Stephens - Stella". He grinned at Sam. Didn't know if we'd need it, Guv, but we had a spare so.' he shrugged.

Sam grinned back as he strode to his desk.

Forest followed. 'We've got Russell on ice downstairs. Not a happy estate agent I can tell you. Screaming for a lawyer.'

'Then we'd better get him one,'

'I thought you might want a chat first.'

'Better not. By the book this time. Dr, bloody, Fielding will be coming through that door any minute now and she's worse than any shyster he might bring in.'

Right on cue the psychologist appeared in the doorway long enough to give Miller a withering look before disappearing again.

'I know where she's going,' Sam pointed at his desk phone then started a silent countdown on his fingers. When he got to nine, it rang. 'Miller,' he said, rolling his eyes at Forest. 'Yes Sir, we have him in custody now.' He put his hand over the mouthpiece and said, 'Get our friend a Brief, Mick.' He waved Forest away as he said into the phone. 'No, Sir, I haven't interviewed him yet. Waiting for his Lawyer.' When the call finished, Sam gathered up the primary files on the first two cases and, on his way out past their Civilian Secretary said, 'Have you made up a new file yet, Rosie?'

'Nothing to put in it yet, Guv,' she replied, waving an empty pink folder.

'OK, call it "Slow Hand Three"'

With a flick of her wrist, she turned the binder so that he could see the title box, "SLOW HAND III" they exchanged knowing smiles.

'I'll be in with His Nibs if anyone wants me.'

For once, they were in agreement. Fielding had Russell pegged as a sadistic sexual predator that got off on torturing the woman during intercourse. Physically the resultant spasms from their pain would no doubt add to the sensation. Mentally, having experienced it once with Sheila Delaney, probably a sex game that got out of hand, he had become addicted.

It was Miller that had the most reservations. 'There was no sign of his DNA at Colman Street.' He stroked the burgeoning bristles on his chin.

'He used a condom.' Fielding replied.

'Why?'

'In order to leave no evidence.'

'A bit calculating for the heat of the moment?'

'Well there's always contraception, of course or STDs'

'Well both the first two were on the pill and clean.'

'Are you saying you're not convinced, Sam?' Archer spoke for the first time in the exchange.

'No. I fancied him for it, at least for Gloria Wallace, and if that was to silence her it leads back to the first one. But this one . . . It's a bit too easy.'

'What do you mean too easy?' Fielding stared intently into Millers face.

'So far his cleanup operation has been almost perfect. He even cranked up the heating in an attempt to disguise the time of death. So why now does he leaves his shirt in the washing machine.'

'You'll have to ask him,' said Fielding, 'and I'll be there to watch his reaction.'

That's right claim your seat, Sam thought. 'Unless he didn't' he said, 'maybe it was already in there.'

'And he didn't notice?' Fielding was standing her ground.

'It's possible. I've often lost a sock only to find it reappear with the next wash.'

'But why would Miss Stephens wash his ripped up shirt.'

'You're the Psychologist, Elizabeth. You tell me.'

'Let's see what he has to say?'

'Let's wait for forensics and the pathologists report,' Sam replied.

Fielding looked at her watch. 'When will that be?' she said with impatience.

Sam felt the same but seeing her irritation gave him a certain satisfaction, 'Soon, maybe tomorrow, depends what's in the preliminary.'

Archer's desk phone rang. He answered it straight away. Grunted a couple of times then hung up. 'Russell's opted for the duty solicitor. He's with him now. You'd better see what he has to say, Sam.'

Glad to escape, Sam stood up to go.

'I'll come with you Sam.' Fielding uncrossed her legs and reached for her bag.

'I'll call you when I need you,' Sam put a restraining hand on her bony shoulder.

She looked at it as if it had leprosy. 'I must . . .'

'I'm only going to talk to his brief at the moment.' Sam turned and left before she could reply.

Chapter 21

Emanuel Okeke was waiting alone in the interview room.

'Good afternoon, Manny, nice day.' Sam greeted him. He was carrying two steaming mugs of coffee. Putting them on the table, he extended his hand.

'I would prefer if you call me by my given name, Detective inspector.' Half rising, Okeke shook hands briefly and without conviction.

Sam sat and pushed one of the mugs across the table. 'So Mr Okeke, what has your client got to say for himself?'

'I am instructed to demand that you release my client forthwith.'

Not an unexpected line from a lawyer, Sam thought. 'Why?'

'Because he is innocent of all wrong doing.'

'He is being held on suspicion of the brutal murder of three young women; do you expect me to take his word?'

'I have not seen any evidence of three murders.'

'It is coming, Emanuel, it is coming.'

'Until it is, you must release my client, or charge him and take him before a magistrate. That is the law.'

'I can hold him for thirty six hours pending enquiries.'

'You have already done that.'

'Not for this case.'

'I have to advise you that my client is considering bringing harassment charges against you DCI Miller.'

'Meanwhile I am considering bringing three counts of wrongful imprisonment, rape, torture and murder.'

'I suggest you go back to your client and advise him to confess, or give up any plans you might have for the weekend. I'll send the files to your office as soon as they are made up and advise you when we are ready to interview Mr Russell.' Sam stood up, 'Good day to you Mr Okeke.' Sam realised this had blown a hole in his weekend plans as well.

It was close to four o'clock when the pathologist's preliminary report came through. In the meantime, emailed crime scene photographs had been printed and were "decorating," if that is the right word, the third panel of whiteboard.

Sam gathered his team around it for a progress meeting. He wanted them to feel as angry as he did about the wanton waste of a young life.

'OK, Mick, tell us about Miss Stephens.' He felt self-conscious under the scrutiny of Dr Fielding watching the proceedings from the back of the room.

Forest stepped up to the board and gestured across the gory crime scene pictures to the single photograph of the woman smiling in happier days. Slim and shapely in tight, blue, jeans and grey, polo-necked, sweater, she looked vibrant and full of life. Her long, fair hair, despite being gathered in a ponytail cascaded around her head, halo like blown from behind by a strong breeze from the stark moorland scene that formed the backdrop.

'Stella Olivia Stephens,' he began, 'Parents have been contacted and are coming in from Wiltshire as we speak.' He checked his notes, 'Nicholas and Elaine, Due by about six,'

'We'll need a PC on hand when we take them down to the Mortuary,' Sam interrupted. 'Volunteers?' the room fell silent for a while then shyly a small hand was raised near the back. Sam spotted it. 'PC King, thank you. Sorry, Mike, carry on.'

'Miss Stephens was twenty three and worked as a researcher for the BBC,'

'This means,' Sam interrupted again, 'there's bound to be a mention on the news and we'll be up to our arses in reporters by morning. Everybody keep shtoom. Mr Archer will, no doubt, prepare a press release but until then not a word, especially the word "serial," got it? We do not want panic out there.' He stepped back.

'From the pathologist's preliminary report.' Fletcher held up the printout. 'Time of death between ten and ten-thirty last night. Cause of death, same as Gloria and Sheila.' He pointed across at the other two boards. 'Mutilation the same, but in this case, although the woman was sexually active, there was no evidence of sexual activity immediately prior to death.'

Sam shot a look at the psychologist. *How does that sit with your graphic account of the act, Elizabeth,* he thought. She did not meet his gaze.

Fletcher flipped over the page. 'Forensics: Clean up using bleach and washing machine full of bed linen the same as Gloria but there are plenty of biological traces all over the place. DNA will take time. Priority is being given to this. He added a picture of the tattered shirt. Despite being washed, this shirt still retains blood and sweat stains. It is believed to belong to this suspect. He pinned up Russell's picture. We're waiting for confirmation before charging him . . . Sam?'

'Right, people.' Miller stood with his back to the board. 'It may appear that Russell is a shoe in for this but we cannot afford to be complacent. The presence of the shirt only proves the presence of the shirt, right? The fact that he knew all three victims is purely circumstantial. We searched his residence and office and turned up nothing. We need the knife. Where would he stash it? Also, we need a witness; someone who saw him in the area at least. Follow up the door to door and canvas the local bars and shops. Search the CCTV for his blue BMW, you have the number, and one more thing keep an open mind. Anyone who might have known Stella and was in the area on Thursday needs to be interviewed. OK. Off you go.'

Friday 22nd April

We made it onto the nine o'clock news, at least Stella did. The police statement said that they expected an arrest within twenty-four-hours. So, Tony Russell, serves you right for being such an arrogant bastard.

The painful task of conducting Mr and Mrs Stephens to the mortuary left Sam deep in the low numbers. PC King had been brilliant with them, calming the overwrought Elaine and reassuring them both that we were close to finding the killer. Nick, as Mr Stephens insisted to be called, was grim and stoic, but Sam felt a larva build up in him that could quickly precipitate another Pompeii.

There was nothing he could say to mitigate their grief except that he shared their pain, which, although it was true, he did not actually express, for fear of appearing trite. Resorting instead to the clichéd, "Sorry for your loss," he wished it did not sound as insincere as its repeated use on television had made it. He booked them into the nearby Ibis Hotel for the night. Unable to tell them when they might be able to take their daughters body home, he promised to contact them in the morning. Feeling a hundred years old he drove slowly home.

The lights were on in the wheelhouse of the Andrea when he slid his Saab to a halt beside Julie's Fiat. He looked at the dashboard clock as he switched off his engine. 21:58. Julie had probably been here since seven.

She slid open the wheelhouse door as he crossed the gangplank. Even her radiant smile failed to raise his mood. He needed to drink enough to obliterate the day. He let her kiss him and tried his best to respond but there was no fooling her.

'Sam. What's wrong?' She took his hand and led him inside, 'you need coffee,'

'Whisky,' he said, his voice hoarse with pent up emotion.

'Bushmills?' she asked.

'I'm out.'

'I bought some today, a present.' She poured a pub-sized tot into a tumbler. He took it from her, downed it in one, grabbed the bottle and poured a large one.

'Sam, please don't.'

He took another swig. The delicious burn in his throat was matched by the stinging in his eyes. 'Sorry,' he croaked, and felt a tear escape onto his cheek. He'd not let his guard down with anyone since Andrea. He sniffed. 'Sorry, bad day.'

'Do you want to tell me about it?'

He shrugged. Pull yourself together man 'Have you seen the news?' he said, looking down through the amber liquid at the pattern in the bottom of his glass. He took another sip.

'Yes,' she put two and two together, 'The BBC researcher . . . Stella?'

He nodded.

As if her legs had failed her, she sat down heavily beside him. 'Was it the same as Sheila and Gloria?'

'Worse.'

Julie choked on her next word and gave up trying to speak. He could feel her chest heaving against him and put a comforting arm around her.

Somehow, it made him feel better. He wanted to blurt out the terrible details but at the same time wanted to protect her from that horror. For a long time they sat quietly sobbing together.

It was Julie that got it together first. 'Come on Detective Inspector Samuel Miller, this won't do.' She stood up and pulled him to his feet. 'Go and get a shower, you'll feel better.'

He nodded and turned but she pulled him back.

'Kiss first,' she said, so he did, automatically. 'Have you eaten today?' she demanded as they broke the clinch.

He shook his head.

'I thought not, I'll make you something. Go on get changed and put on a better face. I don't want Jodi to see his hero in this state.'

Jodi, 'I forgot. Where is he?'

'He's asleep in the "captain's cabin". Tried to stay awake but . . . Want to take a peep?'

Sam nodded and wiped his face on the sleeve of his mohair jacket.

Together they eased open the door to the small berth. Curled up under the sheet only his bronze, curly haired, head showing the boy slept, totally innocent and peaceful. The calm was contagious.

On deck, they ate omelettes and sipped dry white wine. With gentle coaxing from Julie, Sam told her of his day, leaving out the graphic details but ending with the arrest of her dancing partner.

'Do you really think he killed all those women, Sam?' it sounded like she still did not.

'All the evidence points to it. We're waiting for the DNA report. That should seal it.'

'How long does DNA last, I mean could his DNA be still be in the flat from when they went out together?'

'Yes but his shirt was in with the washing. It looked to me to be the same one he wore that night at Welling when they broke up. The white cheesecloth one, you know?'

'I think he may have more than one of those, he wears one almost every dance session. He had one on when I saw him on Thursday.'

Sam frowned at the thought of Julie meeting up with Russell. *How easily she could have been the one on the mortuary slab.*

'By the way I've got his spare ticket in my bag . . . will he be kept locked up now?'

'I expect so. He'll go before a magistrate on Monday I doubt if he'll be given bail. You're quite safe now.'

'I always feel safe with you around, Sam.' She slid along the bench and snuggled into his shoulder. 'But that's not what I meant, don't you see, his double room at Camber is all ours.' She laughed. That thought in mind they fell silent the gentle lapping of water on the hull lulled them to sleep.

Mentally and physically exhausted and wrapped in the arms of the woman he now realised he loved, Sam had barely noticed when she woke him and they transferred to the warmth of his bed. He remembered no more until Jodi, pyjamas emblazoned with brightly coloured clown fish, landed on his chest.

'Sam, Sam, I slept in the Captain's cabin all night.'

'Wha' . . . yes I saw you.' Sam looked at his watch; it was the only thing he was wearing apart from his boxers, under the duvet. Half past five?

'You had to work very late last night.' A grave look on his face, the boy crawled in between them and commenced to name all the characters on his new pyjamas. Julie raised her head to see over her son and grinned at Sam. He had no alternative but to grin back. However, another grim day ahead threatened to spoil their weekend; if he let it.

The press were already gathering outside Greenwich police station when Sam arrived. Despite it being nine am on a bright and sunny morning cameras flashed in his face as he ran the gauntlet. He knew there would be a feeding frenzy but was still annoyed at being snapped in his weekend casuals, jeans and a polo shirt. However, formalities required he interview the parents and investigate any leads that they might throw up.

Someone had spread a sheet over the white boards in the incident room. It was always possible that an enterprising newspaperman might sneak in for a look.

'Anything from SOCO, Jackie?'

'Nothing new, Guv,' PC King was the only other person in the room.

Sam looked at his watch, 'Right, we'll give it until half past then go down and talk to the parents again.'

'Right Guv. DCI Archer has called a press conference for ten.'

'Is there anyone else about?'

'DS Forest is on his way in,' she glanced at the clock on the wall, 'any time now.'

'Good we'll use him as a decoy; I don't want those vultures finding out where I've stashed the Stephens'. With any luck, we can shield them until they've had time to compose themselves.'

It seemed to have worked, Forest made a big show of leaving by the front steps, causing a gaggle of reporters from the nationals to trail after him towards Deptford. His real mission was to get the bacon sandwiches in. Meanwhile Miller and King slipped out the back and made a clean getaway in the unmarked Focus, up Royal Hill then back down to the Ibis via King George St and Crooms Hill. Unobserved, PC King tucked the car into the pay and display not two hundred yard from where they had just left.

Feeling satisfied, Sam led the way through the rear entrance and having established from reception that they were still in their room, took the lift to the third floor.

'I hope we're not intruding,' Sam said as Mr Stephens opened the door, 'but the press are all over the police station and I wanted to talk to you before they found you. May we come in?'

'It's Detective inspector Miller, dear,' he said over his shoulder as he stepped back from the entrance. Although freshly shaved and smartly dressed, the dark patches under his eyes told of a sleepless night. Mrs Stephens, dressed in a dark skirt and white blouse, had not yet managed to fix her hair or makeup. She sat on a stool in front of the dressing table Mascara brush held in a shaky hand and a pile of smudged tissues in front of her. It looked as if she had not stopped crying all night.

Jackie King went straight to her, 'Here, Elaine, let me help.'

Sam took the husband by the arm and guided him to a chair alongside a small round table where

242

an array of breakfast things lay, untouched and now cold.

'You know the newspaper people will want an interview,' Sam said softly, 'It would be best if you prepared a statement and held a press conference to get it out of the way. They might leave you alone after that.'

'I know how it works, Inspector, my daughter was in journalism,' He stifled a sob. 'She was about to go on her first assignment in front of the cameras.' He sighed long and deep. 'You will catch the bastard, won't you?'

'We already have someone in custody.' I shouldn't have told him that yet, Sam realised.

'Where is he? At the police station? I want to see him . . .'

'For the moment he is just a suspect. We are gathering the evidence as we speak.'

'Let me see him, I'll get your evidence.' Stephens snarled. Fists clenched he started to rise.

'Mr Stephens, Nick . . . Nick, sit down,' Sam glanced across the room; Mrs Stephens had spun on her stool and was being gently restrained by PC King.

'Nick, listen to me. The best thing you can do now is to help us fill in Stella's background.'

With calm restored, the grieving parents poured out their daughter's story. Although they had not actually met him, their daughter had told them about her boyfriend, Tony. They met when he was the agent that rented her flat. They hit it off and had been going out for about a year. She seemed quite smitten until last week, when she called her mother to say they had broken up. She was quite upset at the time but a couple of days later the good news from work raised her spirits and she had, jokingly, sworn off men and set herself to concentrate on her career.

Miller and King had successfully smuggled the Stephens' into the police station and carefully skirted past both the cells and the incident room to deposit them in Archer's office. On the way, Sam had managed to dissuade Mr Stephens from mentioning that they had a suspect in custody. Instead, they would simply express their grief and appeal for anyone who could shed some light on their daughter's death to come forward.

Archer stated that their enquiries were rapidly drawing to a conclusion and he expected the culprit to be charged in the very near future.

Despite persistent thrusting of microphones and voice recorders, Mick Forest with the aid of Jackie King managed to extract the Stephens', leaving Archer and Miller to bat away at the barrage of questions.

Forest was updating the whiteboards when Sam stepped wearily into the incident room.

'For God's sake cover that up the parents might . . .'

'It's OK, Guv, Kingy's taken them back to their hotel.'

'Good, what's new?'

'DNA on the shirt is definitely Russell's, pit stains mostly, and Stella's blood is deposited over it,' he grinned. 'We've got him, Guv!'

How convenient, Sam thought, *is he getting slapdash or over confident. The washing machine in the other case could barely throw up any readable DNA.*

'Anything else?'

'CCTV picked up his Beamer crossing Blackheath on the Thursday afternoon.'

'What times?'

'Eastbound at 16.30 and westbound at 20.35'

'A bit early. We'll have to have another word with Melanie about her time of death.' Could she be two hours out? Sam shrugged 'OK I think we can now take this to the boss.'

'D'you want to talk to Russell first?'

'Do you think he'll confess?'

Forest shrugged, 'Not likely.'

'Then let him sweat. We've got all day.'

DCI Archer agreed that there was enough evidence against Russell to formally charge him and scheduled a meeting with the CPS lawyer for first thing Monday morning followed by a Magistrate's hearing.

It was the middle of the afternoon when Miller and Forest finally confronted their suspect in the interview room.

Russell and his solicitor sat impassively while Forest formally read out the charges. Murder, torture and wrongful imprisonment of Stella Stephens. They had decided to hold back on the previous murders, as a second bite of the cherry should there be a problem with this one.

'So,' said Sam, 'is there anything you want to tell us, Mr Russell?'

'Only that I am not guilty.'

'Then how come your sweat stained shirt was found in her washing machine, along with her bloody sheets.'

'She must have put it there.'

'After she was dead? It was soaked in her blood too.'

'Maybe whoever killed her was wearing it.'

'Only you and Stella's DNA were found on it and how did it get there in the first place?'

'Stella often used to take my dance shirts home to wash for me.'

'Even after you broke up?' Sam shouted.

'She must have kept it from when she grabbed her things and stormed out of Welling . . . I haven't seen her since that night.'

'Look, son,' Sam's voice softened, 'why don't you tell us all about it.

'Are you are asking my client to confess to being a serial killer?' Okeke stepped in, 'I must advise you to say nothing more on the matter, Mr Russell.'

'Confession is good for the soul,' Sam smiled.

'I never went near her after we had that row,' Russell was shouting now.

'In that case what were you doing in Blackheath on the night of the murder?'

'I wasn't.'

'Well your car was! Mike.'

Forest read out the CCTV record, sliding the photographs across the table.

'I had an appointment for a survey at five-o'clock in Brigade Street.'

'And that took almost three hours did it?'

'Yes, well no . . . I'

'OK give us the details and we'll talk to them.'

'I can't. They didn't turn up and it was an empty property.'

'Oh yes?'

'Honest, I hung about for half an hour; the phone number they gave me was unobtainable. I expect it was a hoax. We get them sometimes.'

'So what did you do from half-five to eight-thirty; walk round the corner to collect your shirt from your ex girlfriend? Is that it? And while you were there, you had a row and killed her. Is that what happened?'

'No! I didn't . . . I wouldn't . . . not like that.'

'So what did you do?'

'I went for a drink and something to eat in O'Neal's Pub. I kept trying the number and went back to the house to see if they had turned up. And then I went home.'

'Did you speak to anyone in O'Neal's?'

'The barman.'

'Do you think he'd remember you?'

'He might.'

'We'll check it out but it doesn't get you off the hook in any case.'

'I think my client has said enough,' Emanuel Okeke started to stack his papers in order. 'We will present our defence to the Magistrate on Monday. As there is little more than circumstantial evidence against him, I request my client be released on Police Bail until the hearing.'

'No chance,' said Sam with an air of finality, 'Take him back to his Cell, Mike.'

Okeke turned to Russell, shrugged and said, 'Do not worry. We will obtain your freedom as soon as we are before a judge.'

Forest agreed to check out O'Neill's bar on his way home and phone Sam if there was anything in it. Back in the incident room, Sam flicked through the stack of reports that had accumulated on his desk. With Russell charged, there was a chance to get the remainder of his weekend back on track. These could wait until Monday.

Chapter 22

Sam arrived back at the marina, a sense of regret that Julie's car was not there. He knew it wouldn't be. They had agreed that, as he had to work, Julie would take Jodi out for the day. He tried phoning her as he drove home but the call went straight to voicemail.

Inside, the barge had been returned to its usual orderly show house condition. A page from a notebook, trapped in the polished brass cover of the compass binnacle, displayed a brightly coloured drawing of a boat with three smiling stick people on it holding hands, small one in the middle. The future as Jodi saw it. Sam picked it up. On the other side, in Julie's neat hand, the word "Love". That was all he needed to know.

Ignoring his drinks cupboard, that had been his original first port of call, Sam took to the shower and had successfully hosed the events of the previous few days down the plughole by the time he heard the creak of the gangplank, followed by footsteps on deck. Wrapping a towel around his waist, he stepped out and made it through to the main salon to witness Julie's tight, denim clad posterior as she backed down the steep companionway from the wheelhouse. His hands flew to her hips, to help her.

'Thank you kind sir,' she giggled, 'steady now Captain, your losing something.'

His towel was unravelling and sliding to the deck. 'Oops.' He made a grab for it.

'Let it go, Lover,' she whispered as she turned to face him.

'Is Jodi . . .'

'I left him with mum for the night. I figured my man needed my undivided attention.' Undoing her blouse with one hand, she pulled him towards the master cabin. He helped by undoing her belt, the towel lay forgotten on the deck, a trail of Julie's clothing soon joined it.

Their lovemaking had been all-consuming, followed by a full hour of deep and dreamless sleep. Somehow, they woke at exactly the same time.

Was this a measure of their compatibility, Sam thought. His watch was propped up on a bulkhead shelf beside the bed. 'It's only half-eight, shall we go out for dinner?' Sam was starving

'Luckily I brought a frock with me,' she kissed him lightly on the lips and slid out from under the covers. 'Give me ten minutes to get ready.'

Entranced, Sam watched her gather her clothes, not moving himself until she had disappeared into the bathroom. 'There's a pretty good Italian on the High Street,' he called through the half open door.

'Great,' she replied, 'I'm famished.'

Compatibility indeed. Sam unwrapped a newly laundered pale blue shirt to go with a pair of grey slacks. Julie returned wearing only her underwear and a big smile. Seeing his open shirtfront, she sidled over to him and started work on the buttons.

'We could always go out for supper,' Sam murmured.

'Discipline, man,' she said, 'we've got all night.'

They munched through all the complementary garlic bread and took a gladiatorial approach to the main course pasta, Vongole for him, Carbonara for her. They barely spoke until contemplating the desert menu over the last glass of Pino Grigio.

'That should top the energy levels up,' Julie sat back and smoothed the front of her pale cream, summer, dress. 'Tiramisu to round it off?'

'Sam patted his stomach, 'I'm not sure I can.' Where does she put it all?

'Share one?'

'OK.'

They skipped coffee, Sam preferred his own, and the leisurely stroll back to the marina settled the food nicely.

Julie watched as Sam carried out his coffee making ritual. 'I see you found Jodi's picture.' Sam had pinned it on the bulkhead. 'Did you get my note on the back?'

'I couldn't have put it better myself.'

'You could try.'

He took her in his arms; her light perfume only slightly tinged with garlic, nuzzled her ear and murmured, 'I love you.'

'Good job,' she whispered, 'now come to bed.'

Sunday morning was an anticlimax waking without Jodi bouncing around the room; but it had its compensations. They did not emerge into the bright new day until close to ten o'clock. They took both cars over to Bexley, and leaving Julie's outside her house, took Jodi and Margret to Greenwich.

The centre of Greenwich lies on the south bank of the Thames where attractions like The Cutty Sark and the nearby Maritime Museum keep the place lively, even on a Sunday. They made a cursory circuit of the dry docked ship during which Jodi craned his neck to peer up past Sam, who's hand he was holding, to see the tall masts of the tea clipper and barrage his new best friend with questions.

Julie then guided them to a specialist shoe shop and, with all of her powers of persuasion, cajoled Sam into purchasing a pair of dancing pumps. Inside the wrought iron and glass-covered market, they wandered among the stalls, pausing to taste exotic foods here and admire handmade crafts there among the merry jostle of the crowds. Snatches of music, aromas of spices, not all legal substances, Sam noticed and a general buzz of good-natured banter engulfed them. Sam insisted on buying Jodi a brightly coloured kite and, after lunch in a bespoke burger restaurant, they took him up the hill of Greenwich Park to fly it.

A call from Mick Forest, to tell him that no one in O'Neill's bar recognised Russell's mug shot, had Sam's mind replaying the scene of carnage. Not half a mile from there, across the heath, a young woman had been brutally murdered. However, the boy's enthusiasm and frantic running about, quickly brought him back.

Apart from that, the afternoon passed quickly, with only one curly head-butt to Sam's groin. The quartet tired and happy finally made their way back to Bexley. Margaret, in a thinly disguised act of diplomacy, asked to be dropped off home, leaving them to enjoy another night together, like a proper family.

Julie had not mentioned the case all weekend, concentrating on taking his mind to a much happier place. Next morning, as she saw him off at her front door, she asked the question she had successfully suppressed all that time.

'Is there no doubt that Tony Russell did those horrible things, Sam.'

'The evidence is very strong,' Sam replied while thinking, though mostly circumstantial, 'we charged him on Saturday. It'll be in the news tonight.'

'I still can't . . .' she broke off and kissed him on the lips. 'Off you go, I'll be thinking of you.'

Sunday 24th April

Stella's parents were on the news last night. County Set. Full of phony remorse. Pathetic. Bound to be expected at the funeral, better practice crying. Not too much though. As long as it does not clash with Camber weekend. I have big plans for that event.

The incident room was full, everyone keen to wrap the case up. Cardboard boxes of evidence and documents that had already been entered in the Holmes system were being filed. However, Sam noticed that the stack of data yet to be entered was almost as big. The team seemed to

256

have lost all sense of urgency about it. A general sense of finality, almost to the point of celebration filled the place.

Sam stepped up to the white boards and dramatically threw back the covers on each one in turn. Silence descended over them like a parachute after landing.

When he was sure all eyes were on him, he said, 'It is not, as you seem to assume, all over bar the shouting. Before we can get a diva to waggle her tonsils, there is the little matter of the murder weapon.'

'We can get a conviction without it though, can't we, Guv?' a voice from the back sang out.

'It's a lot more likely with it. So let's trace every move he made over the last month, search everywhere he stopped more than once. He has to have a hidey-hole somewhere.'

'The last month, Guv?' Forest spoke up, 'not just since Thursday?'

'We have these others to bring in yet,' Sam waved his hand at boards one and two, 'and no let up on the CCTV searches either.

At Archer's insistence, they took their files to the CPS solicitor to sanction charging Russell with three counts of murder. It didn't go well.

'You have nothing here that definitively places Russell at any of the crime scenes at the requisite time.' Billings, a barrel of a man in his mid thirties leaned back in the standard swivel chair he swamped, eliciting a resigned groan from its mechanism. 'We'd never even get him remanded if this is all you have.' He hooked his thumbs into the broad braces that were the only way a man of his girth could ever hope to keep his grey pinstriped trousers up. 'Find me a weapon, or a witness and I'll back you all the way. In the meantime let him go on police bail.'

No amount of profiling logic From Dr Fielding or Sam's passionate concern for public safety could change his mind.

'I can't believe that,' Sam raved as they made their way back from the CPS office in Greenwich Magistrates court. 'How could he release that maniac back into society? He could do half a dozen more women before it comes to trial. Russell's Lawyer is already piling up paper to negate his bail conditions.' They had decided to walk the three quarters of a mile back to the office and, to his surprise, Elizabeth Fielding had fallen into step with him and Mick Forest.

'I couldn't agree more,' she said, and seemed almost as angry as he was.

'Innocent until proven guilty,' Forest mimicked the plumb in the Churchillian voice Billings. 'For a while there I thought he was going to throw the whole case out.'

258

'I think he would have if it had not have been for Liz's analysis,' Sam smiled at the psychologist. It was the first time he had used her preferred abbreviated name. Clearly, it had not gone unnoticed. *A victory for her,* Sam thought. But he didn't care anymore. She had come down firmly on his side, even if he did not entirely agree with her version of the motive. On autopilot, he turned into the little courtyard seating area of Davey's Wine Vaults. The other two followed him in.

Realising what he had done he grinned sheepishly at Elizabeth and said, 'Lunch?'

'It's about time you bought me a meal, Sam Miller,' she replied as she ducked her head to clear the low doorway into the dim interior.

Established as a restaurant and wine bar in the early nineteen-seventies Davey's had retained the atmosphere and some of the decor of the wine warehouse from where it was developed. Low beamed ceilings with candles on tables gave it an intimate, almost claustrophobic, atmosphere. This was mitigated by the warm shade of varnish on the panelled walls and fresh bright paint where the old rough plaster was still visible.

Lunch service had just started and the place was already filling up with the young professional set that found it still trendy. The prices usually excluded the local students and general lunchtime drinkers that Sam had joined in the bad old days when he first arrived in the area.

They found a small round table in the corner and ordered club sandwiches and wines by the glass for Sam and Elizabeth. Mick Forest preferred a bottle of real ale.

'I hate to say this,' said Sam, 'but it is true what that solicitor said. Our evidence does fall short of, "beyond reasonable doubt". With a good lawyer, which he seems to have found, and Russell's personal charm, he could easily sway a jury.'

'Well Russell certainly has the necessary charm,' said Forest.

'I thought he'd got you going too at first, Liz,' Sam managed a non-condescending smile.

'I don't go for the oily types,' she replied, 'but that is one of his weapons. Charm and seduce a vulnerable woman into an intimate situation and-'

'It's a shame he has chosen to prey on such an innocent group of people,' Sam sipped his glass of Burgundy. It was good, but if it was not for the constraints of having the psychologist with him, he would be on his second or third bottle of five percent ale by now.

'What do you mean?' Elizabeth had chosen a light, crisp white and had added a bottle of mineral water; she sipped them each in turn.

The sandwiches arrived; Sam and Mick had gone for the Steak and Dijon Mayo while Elizabeth had chosen Chicken and Avocado. Unlike the egg-banjos the police officers normally favoured, these could not be tackled without a knife and fork.

Sam waited for the waiter to go before he replied. 'I've got to know a lot more about the modern Jive clubs. It is generally one of the safest environments that women can go to dance in. Misbehaviour on the dance floor is frowned on by general consent. Dancing partners are selected for their dancing prowess, irrespective of gender considerations. Although it is still officially a male - female partnering pursuit.'

'Are you saying there is no sexual motivation among any of them?' Elizabeth frowned.

'Certainly not; but say for instance a woman asks a man to dance, a more frequent occurrence than the other way round. It is not to be considered an invitation to anything more.'

'So no romances?'

'Oh there are, as can always be expected in any social situation, but you can feel safe from being hit on, just because you agree to dance with someone.'

'Even so, Russell used that so called innocent activity to get into the pants of these girls,' said Forest.

'Yes, but what I don't understand is why. If he is such a charmer, why did he need to tackle such easy prey?' Sam looked to Elizabeth for an answer.

'For that we have to look back to his childhood for a root cause. Something back then may have left him with an inability to break the ice. You say he is a good dancer, Sam?'

'I have to say he is, yes.'

'Perhaps he developed his expertise in order to fill this need for initial contact.'

'So now he's out there, free to dance his way into some other girls bedroom.' Forest speared a chunk of his steak and conveyed it to his mouth. Sam looked down at his food, still untouched. Now, for some reason, his appetite returned.

'I do not think he will continue with his dance activities now,' said Elizabeth.

'At least he has to report to his local nick every day.' *So if we can get through this week Julie will be safe down in Camber with her friends while he has to be in Dartford,* Sam thought. 'I'd still be happier if he was locked up,' he said.

They ate in silence brooding on the prospect.

On his return to the incident room, Sam spent an hour skimming the forensic reports. Fogged by lunch and two glasses of red wine, his brain was not prepared to analyse even the conclusions. The team had done what he had asked and the result was too much information. As the afternoon wore on, he realised that, although he turned the pages, nothing was going in. A quest for fresh air brought him out into a now overcast late afternoon. Being rush hour, all he encountered was vehicle fumes rolling up from Greenwich High Street. A walk by the river was needed and where better than South Dock. He booked himself out and drove home.

Without bothering to go on board, Sam left his car in its usual slot and sauntered around to the lock. It was close to high tide and the swirling grey water of the Thames was the same height as the turgid, litter spattered stillness of the basin where the Andrea was moored. A light breeze off the river smelled vaguely of seaweed. It was beginning to have the required affect. Supplemented by mug or two of Blue Mountain his full faculties would soon be restored. Quickly completing his circuit, he soon had the kettle on and the cafetiere primed.

Big, sporadic spots of rain precluded his preferred place of contemplation on deck, so he sat in the wheelhouse with the door open watching the droplets bounce off the teak decking. Sipping his favourite brew, he reviewed his afternoon's work. There was something that demanded more attention but he could not pin it down.

Halfway through his second cup his mobile began to buzz. He had set it to silent for the hearing and forgotten to switch it back. He snatched it off of the compass binnacle, against which it vibrated annoyingly and, irritated at the intrusion into his reverie, spat, 'Miller,' into the mouthpiece.

'Sam?' Julies voice almost reproachful, 'Are you coming?'

Sam looked at his watch, a quarter to seven. 'Oh sorry, Julie. I got held up.' He had forgotten that they had planned to have a meal together then go to Welling, 'I'm just leaving,' he lied.

'I can meet you there if you like. Have you eaten?'

'I had a late lunch.' He was unbuttoning his shirt as he spoke. 'Be there in fifteen minutes.'

'I'll wait here. Be careful, Sam.'

No time to shower. A swill with mouthwash, top up on deodorant and clean polo shirt would have to do. Stuffing a spare shirt into his sports bag with his gleaming new dance shoes, he was outside in the rain within five minutes. A light windcheater kept the worst of the rain off as he dashed to the car.

The traffic was a nightmare. Although his predominant thought was that, with Russell back at large, Julie could be in danger. Wishing he had a siren and Jackie King behind the wheel, he broke plenty of traffic laws on the way. How could I forget about Julie just because something in the reports was bugging me, he admonished himself.

Julie was sheltering in her doorway as he turned into her mews. Sam slewed the Saab across the road so that she did not need her umbrella.

She slid in beside him. 'Shocking weather,' she said as she leaned over to kiss his cheek.

He wanted more.

'Come on,' she slammed the door. 'I promised to take the class for Tony until he gets things sorted.'

'You spoke to him?' Sam gunned the engine.

'Yes. He's very upset. Thinks he ought to brazen it out but just can't face everyone until he's cleared.'

'Two of his ex-girlfriends are dead and you still think he's innocent?'

'He sounded sincere to me.' She gave him a defiant look.

Sam gave up.

The venue was packed. Bill, Tony Russell's DJ, was playing the ever popular "Dance the Night Away" and the floor was crowded with gyrating jivers. Almost all stopped and heads turned towards the door as Sam and Julie walked in.

Normal dancing resumed as Julie pecked Sam on the lips and said, 'see you in a minute, Lover; I have to go to work.'

Sam dumped his bag on a table, next to a graffiti covered canvas sack that he recognised as belonging to Gilda, and made his way to the bar for a beer. When he returned, "Up and Down," by Scent was playing and the usual suspects had all seated around with one spare chair for him. They looked him up and down expectantly.

'Evening,' he said with a cheesy grin.

'Is that right you arrested Tony?' Gilda demanded from the opposite diagonal of the table.

'Sorry, I can't comment on it,'

'Why not?' Maureen said, leaning in to see along the table from behind the bulk of Carol O'Connor; her head almost touching Gilda's weird deep red quiff opposite. Their hair colours exactly matched.

'Sub-Judice.' Sam tried to change the subject, 'Are you all going to Camber this weekend?'

'Wouldn't miss it,' said Ted.

'Are you going?' Roger pushed his pebble glasses back up to the bridge of his nose.

'Work permitting,' Sam continued to smile.

'So you're satisfied you've caught the killer?' said Maureen with a smile.

'Still plenty of work to do,' Sam said, 'anyone dancing?' Time to escape.

266

'Come on then, big boy,' Carol jumped to her feet. They were playing "Titanic," by Ingrid. The music was alternately frenetic and slow but Sam seemed to be able to follow the rhythm easily and despite her size, his partner spun and dipped with frenzied ease. He was breathing heavily by the time the track changed and was relieved to hand over to Patrick who was hovering nearby. There was barely time to sip his beer at the now vacated table before Julie called them into line for the beginner's class.

The session followed the usual format and, with a change of shirt put off to just before the end, Sam felt good as he drove home. The last tune of the night was, Nat King Cole's, "Let there be Love", and there was.

Monday 25th April

So, Policeman Sam is going to Camber. Perhaps I need to arrange something to keep him busy in London. I'll enjoy that. But who?

Chapter 23

Sam was rereading the lab reports. He had the feeling there was something he was missing but could not pin it down. Monday had the team tracking back and forth along the route Russell had claimed to use to get to and from Blackheath and any other areas through which he might have diverted. All the unoccupied premises he had on his books at the estate agency were searched, to no avail.

Eventually Mick Forest found time, late on Tuesday afternoon, to go back and interview the staff at O'Neill's bar. The result was fruitless. No one could say categorically if he was or was not there that fateful evening. However, he had come away with the footage from their internal CCTV. On Wednesday morning, he was diligently going through the grainy black and white images.

'Guv, I think I've got him,' he called across the room. News that usually meant success but in this case, it was quite the opposite.

Sam dropped the folder he was scanning and ambled across. The freeze frame image on Forest's screen showed a crowded bar, customers jostling to be served waved banknotes at the bar staff, others easing away from the counter carrying drinks. Russell was one of the latter. Forest, his left hand on a computer mouse flicked back and forth a few frames at a time to show their subject emerging from behind a huge man in overalls who, sipped a pint of Guinness with elbows out, occupying about twice his share of the counter. They tracked Russell's progress as he carefully carried his brimming glass of lager through the throng, until he disappeared out the door.

Forest pointed out the time display (21:04:05 - 20:03:22.) 'It fits his story, Guv.'

'OK keep going. Let's see if he brings his glass back or anything.' Sam replied, 'it still doesn't rule him out. If anything it proves he was in the area.'

'Yes, Guv.' Forest started the tape rolling again.

Sam turned to go, then spun around again. 'Hang on a minute, take it back a bit . . . back to where he goes out the door.' He watched the screen intently. 'There, can you zoom in on that bit.' The image got bigger but with each increment, the quality diminished. Is that the best you can do?'

'It's VHS, Guv. We could get it digitalised. That might make more sense of it. What is it you've spotted?'

'That girl there, the one in the hoody. She looks familiar. It's probably nothing.'

'You can't see much of her face and what you can is a blur.'

'It's more the way she moves, reminds me of someone, I don't know who. See if you can follow her back for a better shot of her face.'

'It'll be easier in digital. I'll have to give it to technical support to convert. They've got the kit.'

'Do it but, before you go, see if you can track her movements . . . and his; times and directions, OK.' Eyes barely in focus and deep in thought, Sam wandered back to his desk. He could always recall anything he had seen but, with such a welter of information, it made it difficult for him to sieve the wheat from the chaff. His mental cross-referencing software was close to overload.

Half an hour later Forest slipped into the chair alongside Sam's desk. He was holding the VHS cassette and a hand written piece of paper. 'I've got all their movements written down, did you want to go through the tape before I send it off.

'Is there a better shot of the woman?'

'Not really, Guv. For all I can tell it might even be a bloke.'

'OK, send it off. Are they the movements?' Sam took the note and flattened it on top of the file he had been reading.

'Yes, Guv. She, if it's a she, might have been following him. She enters five minutes after he does and leaves just after he does. No sign of her buying a drink or anything. She just merges into the crowd and does not show up again.' Forest pointed to the last two entries. 'He reappears briefly, heads off towards the loo then, a few minutes later, goes back out the door at half past eight.

'OK, send that over by courier and then I think we should take another trip to Blackheath Village. Let's see if we can find any other shops with CCTV. We might get lucky.'

'Guv,' Forest paused pensively, are you thinking we might have charged the wrong man?'

'Something's wrong here. I can feel it in my water.' Julie's assessment of Russell's mood echoed in Sam's Head, "He's very upset. Thinks he ought to brazen it out but just can't face everyone until he's cleared."'

Sam restacked his folders and pocketed the movement record. 'Right, let's go. Kingy can come with us too.'

Blackheath village centre consists of a short main street; with retail frontages, converted from Victorian residential villas either side. Too small for major stores, it is sprinkled with local convenience stores, bakers, butchers and the like. This stretches from the railway station, with an adjacent pub, to a triangular one-way system. The island it creates has outer faces lined with similar commercial premises. One side faces out to the grassy expanse of the heath, the view obstructed only by a large church near the apex. The two other sides face further shops. As a trendy meeting place, seven days a week, it has attracted designer and specialists retailers, wedging in among the coffee shops, bars, restaurants and pubs.

The triangle is bifurcated by a zigzag of alleyways providing access to rear entrances and occasional small commercial enterprises. It was there that they made their start.

'According to Russell, it's this place he was called to survey.' Forest gestured at a narrow brick building that was clearly vacant.

'OK, we'll split up,' Sam said, 'You two take the alley up towards the heath then one go left and the other right. I'll go back to Tranquil Vale side and we'll meet at O'Neill's. If anyone has a CCTV, that gives even a glimpse of the street, pull the tapes.'

It was a full hour before they gathered in the bar. Sam was last to arrive. Having completed his short leg of the triangle he had wandered down the High Street as far as the station then returned on the other side. Rewarded by collecting two tapes from the main search area, he had also obtained one from a specialist perfumery shop, along with a large bottle of "Coco" by Chanel. The shop had gift wrapped his purchase and provided a paper carrier bag of distinctive quality that was large enough to accommodate his video collection as well. He placed it on the table alongside the two cheap plastic sacks his colleagues had brought in.

PC King giggled at the sight and hastily sipped her soda water. Forest just grinned and pushed the pint of larger he had bought for his boss forward.

'How many tapes d'you get?' Sam asked.

'Three, Guv,' Forest patted his bag; 'I went clockwise and got one from this side of the road and two from the other.'

'Kingy?'

Jackie King was peering into Sam's bag. She looked up with a jolt, 'Sorry, Guv, I was wondering,' she fished out the tissue wrapped and beribboned box, 'what . . .'

Sam held out his arm wrist up so that she could sniff where they had insisted on spraying a sample.

'Ooo, gorgeous, she'll love it.' Julie smiled.

'So, if your satisfied,' Sam's countenance turned serious, 'your tapes?'

'Oh, yes . . . I went along the top and picked up two tapes, then down Royal Parade but no joy there. But a thought occurred, what about the busses. Some of them have cameras.'

'Good idea. Have a word with Transport for London when we get back.' Sam downed his beer in one. 'Come on then, let's get going. We've got eight tapes to review.'

Back in the incident room, TFL had put PC King onto someone at British Transport Police, while she waited for a call back, she tee'd up one of her tapes. 'What're we looking for, Guv?'

'Russell, in the first place, and any sign of someone following him,' Sam replied, 'possibly someone in a hoody. If you spot anything like that call me over. We're only interested in Thursday late afternoon to Friday morning.'

Unlike the system used by O'Neill's, which was probably the first to be installed in the area and never upgraded, several of the tapes were in colour but, being located inside the premises, gave only a limited view through the windows outside. Sam ran through the tape from the perfumery. It was the least likely to be significant but the shop had big, clear windows with a good view of the pedestrians and road traffic passing outside. Besides, the shop interior and the faint aroma from his wrist, evoked pleasant anticipation of Julie's reaction when he handed her his gift.

The tape was near the end of its thirty-one day cycle. Sam allowed it to run its stop motion record at high speed. Images flickered hypnotically in front of his eyes as he waited for it to reach the twenty-first of April. What he saw was processed in arrears, so he was on the twenty-fifth before he stopped the tape and ran it back. Not however, to the day of the crime but to something he had spotted earlier. After another overrun, he settled on an image he recognized. Dateline 19:04:2005 - 13:32, two people peering at the display in the shop window. He knew them straight away.

Sam rummaged in his drawer and came out with a notebook filled with rough diagrams and random notes he had made in his various attempts at piecing together the facts of the three crimes. He flicked through until he found a list of known associates of the victims.

It was a table he had formulated, trying to assign them in order of intimacy, but abandoned when Julie's name kept coming to the top. That was, however, before Russell's second girlfriend was found dead. He added a column headed Stella Stephens and entered Russell's name below it. The next one he was compelled to enter was Julie Button. She had been the person who befriended Stella when she first came to modern Jive classes. Below that were the other members of the usual suspects. *All right*, Sam thought, *Julie was a common factor, as was Gilda and Maureen, but he was looking for a male perpetrator wasn't he?*

Was it pure coincidence that the two women that were staring out of the monitor at him were in the area two days before Stella's slaying. His eyes flicked back from the list to his screen. Could one of them be involved somehow? Was that the same coat he had spotted in the other tape? Gilda was wearing a bright red zip up jacket. The hood was down but he could imagine it pulled up, shading her face. If only the O'Neill's tape had been in colour.

'Kingy,' he called before looking over to her. PC King was talking on the phone; she peered over the monitor back at him.

He waved her back to what she was doing and walked down the room to their civilian aid instead. 'Rosie, could you chase up the IT guys about our tape?'

'Right Guv . . . er, there's someone to see you,' she nodded towards the open door. Elizabeth Fielding was standing there, briefcase in hand.

'Just the woman I want to see,' Sam's greeting had the whole room taken aback.

Smiling naturally, for the first time in Sam's experience, she followed him back to his desk where he directed her into the vacant chair alongside his.

'How can I help you, Sam,' she asked in a breathy voice that bordered on the seductive.

'Is it possible that Russell had an accomplice?'

'What makes you ask that?' she edged forward on her seat her skirt falling away from her thighs to reveal the tops of holdup stockings, 'Is there something you think he could not have managed on his own?'

'No, nothing like that, Liz, I was just wondering if we could be sure this would be a solo activity.'

'In my opinion, due to the slow and deliberate execution of the cuts, it is unlikely that he would share the experience with another man.'

'What about another woman?'

'Hm, I see what you mean . . . There have been quite a few cases where a female has participated in depraved acts, paedophilia in particular but also rape and torture. Sometimes they were even the instigator.'

'It would explain why, in Stella's case there was no evidence of sexual activity, wouldn't it?'

'You mean he indulged with his partner to consummate the act, rather than the victim?'

'That is what I was considering, yes.'

'It is certainly possible . . . do you have someone in mind?

'Look here.' Sam moved his mouse to dismiss the Metropolitan Police Roundel screen saver, to reveal the two women looking in the shop window.

Liz shuffled her chair round to face the screen her thigh hard up against his. 'And they are?'

'Two women, known to Russell and, to some extent, all three victims.'

'And where exactly do they fit in?'

'This was taken by CCTV in a shop close to the third victim's house.'

'Blackheath,'

'Yes.'

'On the day she was killed?'

'No. A couple of days before.'

'Not empirical evidence then?'

'Not in itself, no but someone in a similar top to that one was seen in the proximity of Russell on the day of the crime. We're waiting for an enhanced video to compare.'

'Do you know who they are?'

'The one on the left is Gilda, and on the right is Maureen they both go to the same dance group.'

'Have you spoken to them yet?'

'Not yet. I had only just spotted them when you came in.'

'Well, perhaps we should.'

They were interrupted by Rosie who, appearing alongside the desk, appraised the proximity of Fielding in Sam's personal space before saying, 'this just arrived by courier from IT.' She handed over the DVD and left, fanning her face with her hand and grinning at everyone in the office.

Sam quickly inserted the disk into his computer and searched through until he found the image he had seen earlier. 'See here,' he pointed at the screen, 'and here, I reckon that's her,' he switched images, 'Maureen.'

'Elizabeth put her hand over Sam's and moved the mouse to guide the cursor on the screen. He did not resist. Expertly, she brought the images up side by side and used the pointer as she said. 'The face here is too shadowed by the hood to tell but it could be the same jacket as worn by the other one . . . Gilda, is it?'

'Yes but body wise it looks to me more like Maureen.'

'You can only see the top half, Sam. And above the waist they are about the same size.'

'It's more about the posture . . . this bloody enhanced version is hardly any better than the original.' Sam was getting frustrated. He pulled his hand out from under Fielding's. 'Maybe I'm reading too much into it but I know where they'll be tonight. A few discreet questions will sort it out.'

'Would you like me to come with you?' she moved her hand to his knee.

No, it's probably nothing, I don't want to waste your time, Liz. Blackheath is a popular area and reasonably local to both girls,' *That's the first time she's asked rather than demanded to be in on an interview,* he thought.

'Oh no, Sam, your theory has merit. If I could have another word with Russell I have a few questions which might reveal his raison d'être.'

Sam looked at his watch, 'I know where he will be in half an hour, too.'

'Dartford police station?'

'Yes, his check in time is five-thirty.'

'Well what are we waiting for?' Fielding got up to go, leaving Sam suddenly aware of the absence of heat from her hand on his upper thigh. Hardened policeman that he was, he felt himself blush.

Wednesday 28th April

I thought I would have to wait for Tony to leave his office, but he was already in his car when I arrived. I watched from across the street until his BMW turned off into Westgate Road. The last girl in the office, whoever that was, would do. My story was simple. Tony promised me a quick look inside a show house on a new-build estate but I had been held up. I was a cash buyer but had to leave the area on business the next day so this was my, or more importantly their, only chance to secure the deal.

She was delighted to steal his client, bloody ruthless bitch, so she grabbed her bag and was ready to go within minutes. While she was looking for her keys, it was easy to slip a Roofie into her half finished coffee. She was so keen I had to persuade her to finish it before we left and there was a bit of a sticky moment when we turned off the dual carriageway. She was already driving like the worst kind of drunk driver. I hate drunk drivers. I persuaded her to pull over and let me drive.

The show house was fully furnished and, once I got her on the bed, she was no trouble. She was quite fleshy, almost as nice to cut as I imagine Julie will be. Lovely. The building site was deserted so, with no neighbours to worry about, I let her scream for a while but the noise was doing my head in so I used my gag.

Clean up was a problem because the washing machine and dishwasher were not connected. But the shower worked. I used the coverlet off the bed to wipe everything I had touched then found a bin liner and took everything outside with me. In the backyard of an incomplete house further along the road I found where the builders had been burning rubbish so I was able to burn the linen and with it all the evidence.

It was almost dark by the time I came back to clean inside the car. I used petrol from its tank. I thought about torching that too but the smoke might have attracted attention. Then it was just a long walk to the main road and home by public transport. A quick change and off to Charlton. I will get there late but that is not

282

unusual and at least I can avoid the beginner's lesson.

My tools are in the dishwasher again. Perhaps I should get some nice new handcuffs for the weekend, pink fur I think.

Sam let Fielding drive, at least it kept her hands occupied, and they covered the ground through the evening rush quicker than even King could manage with the twos going.

I really ought to write her a ticket, he thought as, white knuckled, he involuntarily gripped the stitched leather seat squab between his legs. Even so, the journey took best part of an hour due to a total standstill on the A2, just before the Dartford turn off.

Russell's BMW was parked outside as they swung into the station yard, but Sam had phoned ahead to ask the desk sergeant to detain the man for questioning.

They were shown to an interview room where Russell was pacing up and down. Before he could protest Sam said, 'Please sit down, Mr Russell. This won't take long.' His no nonsense tone left the suspect without an option. 'Miss Fielding here has a few more questions, that's all.'

Elisabeth Fielding sat across the table from Russell with Sam in the chair alongside her. Without taking her eyes off her subject, she slowly opened her briefcase and extracted a notebook, flipped a few pages over and made a brief note, before she spoke.

'Mr Russell . . . Tony . . . May I call you Tony?'

Russell shrugged.

'Tony . . .'

'Hang on,' Russell said indignantly, 'shouldn't this be recorded.'

'This is just an informal interview, she replied, do you want it recorded?'

'What about my lawyer?'

Sam stepped in, 'We can send for your brief if you like but it could be hours before he gets here, do you want to wait and make it formal? Doctor Fielding here has just a few questions, off the record, and you can be on your way.'

Russell calmed down, 'OK,' he smiled his most charming smile at Elisabeth and said 'OK shoot.' On this occasion it did not work.

What followed went far over Sam's head. She asked about his childhood his parents, siblings and stupid things like, did he prefer boxer shorts to briefs and where did he usually go on his holidays.

Sam glazed over, happy to wait for the psychobabble of expert analysis that would surely follow.

Forty-five-minutes later, they were back on the road streaking against the flow of traffic on the A2.

Eventually Sam said, 'Why don't you slow down and tell me what that was all about.'

'Oh, I was waiting for you to tell me.'

'Speed cameras coming up,' he warned. They had just passed a fifty limit sign.

'Thanks,' Elizabeth took her foot off the gas and allowed her speed to drop to fifty-four. 'Well he's pretty much a loner,' she said 'and for all his flirting he's actually afraid of women, so I do not think he would allow another female to be with him in such a vulnerable situation.'

'Vulnerable?'

'Yes. To him the difference between total domination and his fear of even a slight loss of control is finely balanced.'

'So, no female accomplice?'

'No.'

'Male?'

'Again, no.'

'Oh well, it was worth a try. Thanks Liz.'

'Is that another dinner you owe me, Sam?'

'Probably. But not tonight. I have a . . . date.

'Your little dancing friend . . . I should be careful there. If he was up for an accomplice, she could be one he'd choose.' Without slackening speed, she swung the Jaguar onto the off ramp and minutes later dropped him outside his police station.

He had not responded to her last remark and, from the way she roared off as soon as he had closed the passenger door, he felt she must be a bit peeved at him. It made him smile.

Chapter 24

Sam missed the beginner's lesson again. But he knew he would and had phoned and told Julie he would see her there when he could. "This is The World we Live In" came wafting out as he opened the door to the hall. Weaving deftly through the dancers, he reached Julie as the music changed to "I Like The Way You Move". Sam took over the lead, from a guy he did not recognise, with minimal resistance. Julie immediately manoeuvred him into a half dip and they managed a brief kiss to the plaintive strains of Kenny G's saxophone.

It was the last dance before Julie had to take to the stage for the intermediate lesson. As soon as they separated, Sam joined the usual suspects at their usual table. Seizing the opportunity he confronted Maureen and Gilda who were sat together opposite him.

'I saw you two the other day,' he said with a cheery smile.

'Oh, where?' Maureen look up from where she had been doing something to her shoe under the table.

'Blackheath, you were looking in the window of a perfume shop.'

'I know the one you mean . . . That must have been on a Tuesday,' said Gilda, 'we usually meet for lunch on Tuesdays.'

'We go to Pizza Express,' Maureen put in.

'We often look at that shop. It's too expensive for us though, I get mine from Boots.' Gilda leaned forward and presented her neck 'Do you like it?'

'Hm,' he sniffed, yes . . . very nice, Gilda,' Sam replied. *Smells like Toilet Duck*, he thought.

They were interrupted by Julie, calling the students into two lines.

'Come on, Sam, you can do this,' Gilda took his hand and led him onto the floor.

'So why Blackheath?' Sam asked, as other dancers were shuffling into position. Maureen was one of the small pool of women without partners waiting their turn on the sidelines.

'It's halfway between us. Maureen works in Lewisham Hospital and I'm a receptionist for a building firm in Greenwich.'

Julie, with Patrick as her co-demonstrator, was running through new moves for the night. It looked complicated to Sam but with the aid of a succession of helpful partners, including Maureen, he pretty much got them down. Pleased with himself, he found himself dancing the session out with the formidable bulk of Carol, the light glinting off her abundant piercings that turned a basically pleasant face into a glorified scrap-yard. However, she had been the best partner to learn from. As the "Mambo Crazy" faded into the next track they, by mutual consent, made their way back to the table where Julie was applauding his efforts.

'You're coming along nicely, Lover,' she murmured as he came up to her.

Sam felt his face form a cheek aching grin. 'Thank you kindly, fair damsel,' he replied with a deep bow and flourish.

Thursday 28th April

He was there again last night asking questions. I think he suspects Gilda is involved he was certainly pumping her for information. Luckily, I was already there when he arrived so now he can be my alibi too.

The wind down song to end the night was "Stuck on You." Sam sang it in his head as he drove to work straight from Bexley. One day to tie up the remaining loose ends then a dance weekend at the holiday camp with Julie in Russell's double room. He could not disguise his pleasure at the thought.

'Good night?' Forest asked as he fell into step crossing the station yard.

'Not bad,' Sam grinned. 'There was nothing in the presence of those two women. They go there for lunch every Tuesday. For once he was

289

not wearing a shirt and tie. However, the pale blue polo shirt he wore with his jacket and chinos, received an approving raised eyebrow from PC King and a big smile from Rosie as he breezed through the office.

A new geek had appeared in the incident room. He was seated next to Sam's desk, laptop on his knee. As they approached he sprang up and clutching his laptop in his left hand he extended his right. 'DI Miller?'

Sam nodded and gripped the pale thin hand that responded surprisingly firmly. 'And you are?'

'Wiltshire, Steve Wiltshire, Geographic profiler.' He peered at Sam earnestly through the upper half of a pair of wire rimmed bifocal spectacles. 'DCI Archer brought me in to assist in finding the murder weapon.'

'Welcome aboard,' Sam made the introductions, 'this is DS Mick Forest my number two. He'll give you all the data we have.'

'No need sir,' Wiltshire patted his laptop like it was a lapdog, 'I'm fully linked in.'

'Yes well I wish Holmes was.' Sam looked disparagingly at the stack of unprocessed reports. 'It will be quicker if we do it the old way, I think.'

They found room for the profiler in a corner of the incident room, near one of the few bare spaces on the wall. It was quickly opened filled with a large map. Miller and Wiltshire spent the morning collating the results of the searches they had instigated tracing Russell's movements on a map of the area trying to spot any hidey-hole he might have used to stash the knife. The team had been thorough. It had to be somewhere easily accessible.

Thinking back to what the psychologist had said about an accomplice it occurred to Sam that, although Fielding ruled out anyone, male or female being present at the killings, what about someone covering for him by hiding the weapon, not only the weapon but also the restraints that had left those marks on poor Stella's wrists. A friend that lived locally, someone he saw frequently; possibly one of the dance club members.

'Mick,' He waved Forest over, 'do we have a list of names and addresses of the dance club members that we interviewed after Sheila's murder?'

'Not a list as such, but the details are in the file.'

'Look them out, will you.' Sam looked across the room for someone to lend a hand. 'Kingy, bring an A to Z over here please.'

PC King had just hung up the phone. She looked around the office, quickly spotting Rosie who, having heard the call, was waving a telephone directory sized tome. With Forest calling out the names and addresses and King looking them up, Sam was able to mark the locations with little red stickers on the map. Simultaneously Wiltshire updated his computer.

They were scattered all over Southeast London and Kent; from Bermondsey in the west, to Gravesend in the East and as far south of the river as Bromley.

'Of course, we do not have all the members from Russell's own dance class at Welling,' Sam said, as he put a yellow star at Russell's residence.

'Do you think we should go back and collect them?' Forest was looking dubious.

'Can't do that until Monday.' Sam was placing black stickers at each of the crime scenes, except the one at Ealing, which was off the map.

'And that's a Bank Holiday,' said Forest.

Miller gave him a withering look.

'May I,' Wiltshire swivelled his laptop around then clutching a handful of magic markers approached the wall map. He drew, in red marker pen, Russell's claimed route home from Blackheath. Notional routes were added for the other two locations. The A2 was the most natural conduit in all cases. It ran through Blackheath and close by Greenwich and Dartford. Joining between the two was the South Circular, which was, via the Blackwall tunnel, one of two most likely routes from Ealing. The other way would pick up the A2 earlier anyway. One other thing leapt out at him at the centre of the web of activity, Bexley.

Sam realised he was avoiding an obvious conclusion. Julie's home was right in the middle of the crosshairs on the map. Not only that, she had, against his advice, met with Russell on the day after Gloria's death but she was planning to join up with him as a dance team before that. Sheila's death had made that possible. She had even spoken to Russell after Stella's murder and defended him or at least seemed sympathetic. *Surely she's not covering for him*, he thought. *Perhaps she unwittingly is hiding the weapon. No, she's too bright for that. There was an alternative he had to talk to her about.*

Wilson was pointing right to the spot that denoted Julie's home. King was looking worried and shaking her head at Forest.

'I know,' Sam said, 'I'll talk to her first . . . assemble a search team but don't move until I call in, right.' Mick, see about getting a warrant, just in case.

Heart pounding at the prospect of seeing Julie and dreading the thought of how he could broach the subject with her, Sam gunned the Saab through the back streets to Bexley. He could have phoned to let her know he was coming but did not know what to say; therefore it was no surprise when there was no answer when he rang her doorbell. Her car was not parked in its usual spot in the resident's bay either.

He tried her mobile. It rang the full course before switching to voicemail. He hung up, and dialled again with the same result. This time he left a message, 'Julie, it's Sam. Give me a call when you get this. It's important.'

He had no sooner hung up when their unmarked Focus, with King at the wheel and Forest by her side, rounded the corner and glided to a stop alongside his car, effectively blocking the street. It was followed moments later by a Transit crew bus and the forensic team's van, bringing up the rear. Uniformed officers poured from the bus and Higgins emerged from the van with one of his boffin buddies.

'I thought I told you to hold off until I called.' Sam glared at Forest through the open car window. 'Who gave the ordered for this bloody circus?'

Forest, his face full of sympathy, jerked a thumb towards the end of the street. DCI Archer's Mondeo was just pulling up. Sam's reaction was immediate and not unexpected. He strode towards his line commander, fury all over his face. Forest and King hastened after him in the hopes of prevent him from doing something irrevocable.

'What the bloody hell do you think you're doing?' Sam screamed at Archer as he reached the car.

The DCI was in the act of clambering out. Sam grabbed him by the shoulder and swung him round inevitably causing the senior officer's head to hit the doorframe, a glancing blow.

'Get a hold of yourself, Miller,' Archer growled, rubbing his head. 'You ordered this search.'

'Not until I was ready.' Miller was still shouting now nose to nose with Archer. 'Anyway she's not in, so you can all fuck off again.'

With a sweep of his arm, Archer brushed past Miller and addressed the uniformed sergeant. 'Robinson, break down the door.' Sam lunged at his CO but Forest leapt between them. Archer turned back to Miller, 'You're too close to this, Sam. Go back to the station. I'll talk to you there.'

Sam took a deep breath. If ever he needed self-control, it was now. 'Sir . . . Sir this is my case, at least let me supervise the search.'

Archer ignored him. There was a dull thud and a creak of splintered wood from Julie's front door.

'Hold up there, lads, this is a search not a raid.' Miller ran in front of the men stealing themselves to charge into the house. 'We haven't even got a warrant.' Archer strode up to Miller and slapped the document into his hand.

'Well at least stand down the riot squad. Let SOCO do the honours, we don't want to be trampling all over the evidence if there is any.' Sam positioned himself in the doorway facing out. A small group of bystanders had gathered at the end of the lane. 'And move the rubberneckers on, someone, will you. The uniformed squad looked from Miller to Archer.

'DI Miller is quite right,' he frowned, 'Sergeant; you had better do something about those.' He waved an arm at the gathering crowd. 'You two,' he waved the white clad forensic team forward. 'Get on with it.' He leaned in close to Miller and said, 'My office as soon as you've finished,' then strode back to his car.

'What we looking for Sam?' Higgins asked.

'Murder weapon, the knife and possibly bondage gear.'

'We'll start in the bedroom then, shall we?' Higgins grinned.

'You start in the kitchen; I'll take care of the bedroom.'

'You'd better suit up first.'

'No need, my DNA's all over it . . . through there and don't make a mess.'

While the forensic team went to work, Miller examined the damage to the door. It had been quite weakly secured, the striking plate had been broken straight out of the jamb. Apart from the damaged paint on the front door, there was no structural damage. He detailed PC King off to find a local locksmith and left Fletcher on door duty.

Upstairs, he sat on the edge of the bed, his mind in turmoil. Would he ever be allowed in this room again after this? What could he say to Julie? I could have explained the problem and searched the place without all this but now . . . His phone rang, he flipped it open, Julie's name was on the screen.

He answered it on the fifth ring. 'Julie,'

'No . . . I'm Julie, you're Sam,' her voice was perky and bright.

'I know . . .'

'Sam are you alright?'

'Where are you?'

'Bluewater. You called me but I was getting my hair done.'

'When are you coming home?'

'I'm just getting in the car now but I have to pick Jodi up from kindergarten, first.'

'How long?'

'About an hour, I suppose. Sam you sound serious, has something happened.'

'It's alright; I'll see you when you get home. Drive carefully.' Sam had no sooner closed the connection than Higgins called from the foot of the stairs.

'Guv, we've got something.'

Miller's mood dropped to sub zero. He slumped forward, head in his hands. Eventually he managed to say, 'I'll be right down.' With legs that felt like they were walking in treacle, he stomped down the stairs.

'In here, Guv.' Higgins' voice full of triumph, he led the way to the kitchen. Haven't moved it yet, he pointed to the washing up bowl. An inch of cloudy water remained and visible through it a large kitchen knife. 'We did a quick test on the water, there's blood present.' Higgins held up a vial.

'That's ridiculous. Who would keep a murder weapon a whole week before washing it?'

'Unless there's been another one we don't know about yet?' Higgins grinned.

'Enough blood for DNA?'

'No problem.'

'OK, get it back to the lab and give it the full Monty. Top priority, right?' Sam left them to it and went back to the bedroom. He had not intended to search up there originally; it was an invasion into her privacy beyond where he was prepared to go. Now, better him than some other clown rummaging through her underwear. If that was the knife, where were the restraints? He could not help thinking like a policeman.

He was quick and thorough but left everything exactly as he found it. Nothing more incriminating than a pair of unwashed tights. The bathroom was the same, nothing hidden in the cistern for the loo, nothing behind the panel of the bath. More laundry but no blood. He even trawled through Jodi's room, before he heard car doors slamming in the street outside.

Unable to get in the resident's bay because of the two remaining vehicles, Julie parked fifteen metres further along and, leaving Jodi strapped in his car seat, she ran back to her house. 'What's going on?'

PC King ran from the end of the street to intercept her.

'I'm sorry madam you can't go in there.' Forest put out an arm to block the entrance.

'It's my house,' Julie looked frantically back and forth between Forest and her car. 'I live here . . . Where's Sam?'

Forest said nothing.

'DI Miller . . . your Boss.'

'Julie,' PC King stepped in front and firmly took her by the elbows, 'Julie, it's me, Jackie King. Calm down, Sam will be out in a minute.'

'Guv.' Forest shouted over his shoulder, 'she's here.'

Miller had just made it to the foot of the stairs. 'All right Mick, let her in.' He came to the door.

Julie looked confused. 'Sam,' she looked back towards her car. 'Jodi . . . I . . .'

'Come in and sit down, Julie. Jackie will take care of Jodi.' Miller nodded King away.

'What is it . . . my God, is it mum?' she stumbled forward.

'It's alright, it's not your mum.' Sam put a supporting arm around her and guided her into the sitting room.

'What is it then, Sam? My door is broken. Have I been burgled?' She looked frantically around the room as he gently sat her down on the sofa and squatted in front of her.

'It was me. Well, my fault.' Sam took her hand in his.

'Why, Sam. I would have given you a key.' Julie smiled but it did not reach her eyes.

'Let me explain.' He moved to sit alongside her.

She slid to the end away from him, turned and folding her arms said, 'It had better be good,' she sounded fierce.

Sam tried to explain about the missing knife, the map and the Geographic Profiler and the forensic evidence, it did not go down well.

'So you let a bunch of nosey coppers search my house. I bet they had fun going through my knickers draw.'

'Well no, actually, that was me.' He tried a risky grin. It did not help.

'So did you find a secret torture chamber behind the fireplace?' There was fury in her voice. 'Did you find anything?'

'Forensic found blood in the washing up bowl and took away your big knife.'

'Are you stupid? Why would I keep a murder weapon in my sink?'

'That's what I said, but they found it and had to take it for testing. It could have been Stella's blood. Maybe Russell left the knife with you for safe keeping.'

'And I didn't wash the blood off for a week!'

'That's what I said.' Sam put out a comforting hand. She shied away. 'Anyway, they need to test it for DNA.'

'All they had to do is look in the fridge. The blood is from some fillet steak. I sliced it up and put it in a marinade before I went out this morning. It was for your dinner tonight.'

Sam laughed.

'It's not funny. Anyway, you can forget it now I'll give it to the dog.'

'You haven't got a dog.'

'I'll get one . . . More loyal than a man anyway.'

'Sorry Julie. It just got out of hand.'

'Are you done?' Tears were rolling down her cheeks dragging mascara with it.

Sam nodded.

'Well get out of my house, then.' She stood up arms still folded across her chest. If she was at all inclined to make physical contact with him, it would probably be only to frog march him off the premises. She was right behind him as he left.

Outside, Jackie King was holding Jodi in her arms. As they emerged from the house she put the toddler down and with a joyous yell of 'Saaaam,' he ran at his friend, scoring a direct hit with his head.

Wincing and crossing his legs, Sam hoisted the boy up and was rewarded with a wet kiss on the cheek.

'Come here babe,' Julie held out her arms to her son. 'Sam can't play today. He's here on business.' She shot her former lover a withering look. Sam tipped the boy gently into his mother's arms and turned to go.

'Hoi!' Julie shouted at his back, 'What about my door?'

'We've got a locksmith coming.' Sam did not turn round knowing that the tears welling up in his eyes were not entirely from the pain in his crotch. 'I like your hair by the way.' He got into the car and, still with his back to everyone, wiped his face as best he could with the back of his hands. They still smelled of Julie from his search. 'Kingy, stay here until the door is fixed,' he said through the window, 'Mick, you had better come with me.'

He drove back to Greenwich in silence.

Sam's mood could not get any lower but it tried for negative numbers. I'll jack it all in and go to the pub, Drinking himself to death was a definite option. But he did not.

He dropped Forest off at the front entrance to the police station with instructions to tell Archer he would be in later.

He needed to think and he needed a drink, but which first? Driving aimlessly and without paying any conscious attention to the roads, he found himself drifting back towards Bexley. Arresting the subconscious desire to chase a lost cause, he turned back across Blackheath and drove into Greenwich Park. The Royal Observatory was located on the top of the hill, close to where he had flown the kite with Jodi. It had the advantage of being the furthest point from any pubs in the area. Sam, of course, knew exactly where they all

303

were. The nearest, directly north, exactly on the meridian line, a seven or eight minute walk across the park ,was a one room nautical themed bar, quiet and comfortable. He was tempted but, deterred by the uphill walk back, he stayed in the car and closed his eyes. Images of Julie screaming, being dragged away to jail and Jodi, bewildered, tearful and alone, chased others of Tony Russell taking Sam's place in her bed. He felt sick. This was not right.

Occasional rational thoughts had him reviewing the files, forensic, interview reports, crime scene photographs, DNA. There was something about the forensics. Archer, forcing the search, and their public row. A blur of data from the files. Julie. Jodi. Russell. Numbers, something about numbers. His head whirled. The sun was low and bright, shining through the windscreen heating the car. Stifling, he needed a drink.

His phone vibrated against his chest. Julie. He flipped it open and looked at the screen "Office" it stated. He answered on reflex and wished he had not.

'Guv, where are you?' it was Rosie's voice. 'The DCI's going ballistic.'

'Tell him to get . . . Tell him I'm on my way.' I need to go through the files, find the number that's bugging me. To do that, first I have to face the Ayatollah. He started the engine and cruised down to the park gate then on past the Greenwich Tavern, left at the "Kings Arms", past the "Coach and Horses", left again opposite "O'Sullivan's Bar", right at "Ye Olde Rose and Crown," then left up Royal Hill towards the "Richard I" and immediately left into the police station yard.

His phone buzzed again as he heaved himself out of the car. He flipped it out ready to reject the call. The caller ID said "Julie" but he saw it too late. He sat on the front wing of the Saab and called her back. Engaged. He tried again. Engaged. He started to walk in through the back door. The phone still in his hand buzzed again. 'Julie?'

'Guv?' it was PC King. 'Guv, I have Julie Button here for you.'

'Sam?'

The both said "Sorry," at once, followed by simultaneous nervous laughs.

'Let me go first, Sam.'

'Always ladies first,' he said with relief.

'Jackie told me all about it. It was Mr Archer who forced the issue, I understand. She said you never believed I would willingly help a killer. That is right isn't it Sam?'

'Of course . . . the only thing . . .'

'What only thing?' she sounded spiky again.

'Well, he might have conned you into looking after a bag, or something, for him.'

'He didn't, Sam, he gave me nothing.'

'I know . . . so are we OK now?'

'Do you want to come round for Steak Florentine tonight?'

'You haven't given it to the dog, then?'

'I haven't got a dog,' she giggled.

'I know.'

'Love you . . . here's Jackie for you.'

'Did you hear about the knife, Guv?' he could hear Kingy's grin over the phone.

'No. What?'

'Animal blood. Beef.'

'My dinner.'

'So I heard. The locksmith's here, Guv. says it won't take long, shall I come back now.'

'Yes fine, Kingy, see you in the IR. Oh, and thanks.'

Sam bounced into the incident room. 'Is the old man in his office, Rosie?'

'He's gone home, Guv. As soon as he got the news about the knife he took off. Rosie was in the act of putting her coat on. 'You know about the blood?'

'Kingy told me.' Sam looked at his watch, Ten past Five. Start again tomorrow.

It was been a night of domestic bliss; helping get Jodi ready for bed, sitting either side of him on his "Finding Nemo" quilt cover while Julie told him a bedtime story then downstairs for a great meal. Followed by a night of gentle lovemaking and dreamless sleep, what more could a man want.

308

Chapter 25

DCI Archer appeared at the incident room door before Sam could reach his desk. 'Sam!' The expected roasting was long overdue. However, what replaced it was worse. 'There's been another one.'

Sam's mood plunged from nine to Three quicker than he could count backwards. 'I knew we should have kept him locked up!' he exclaimed. 'Mick, go drag him in here.' He snatched the printout from his boss's hand and scanned the details. 'Kingy, you're with me.'

'Another dancer?' Forest asked, as they retraced their steps to the car park.

'No! His bloody co-worker! Tell you what, we'll pick him up on the way. He can confront what he's done first hand.'

'I'll get some back up and meet you at his office.'

'Good . . . No noise until we're sure we've got him then unleash the blues and twos.'

Russell was standing anxiously at the door to his estate agency shop when King brought the Focus to a stop outside. Recognising Sam, he took a halting step forward. Simultaneously two Panda Cars skidded to a halt either side of him. Both released a warning peep from their sirens. He froze.

Sam sprang out onto the pavement and spun Russell round so fast he lost his footing. Pinning him to the floor, Sam slapped on the handcuffs, crushing them as hard as he could eliciting a satisfying cry of pain from his prisoner. Two burley constables arrived and gripping Russell's arms, dragged him back upright.

'Anthony John Russell, I am arresting you on suspicion of the murder of Marcia Williams.' DS Forest arrived at Sam's elbow. 'Read him his rights, Mick then dump him in Dartford Nick. You'd better come on down to the new scene after that.'

Sam sat back alongside his driver unconsciously brushing the dust off the knees of his Chino's, 'Let's go Kingy.'

On the way, Sam called Julie to let her know he was not going to be able to drive her down to Camber.

'That's alright, Sam, Ted is driving everyone else down in a minibus this afternoon. I'll bunk in with them,' Julie said, 'will you be able to make it at all?'

'I'll get there when I can, can't tell for sure when though.'

'OK, Lover. I'll keep your place warm.'

310

Sam lapsed into silence as he closed the connection. He contemplated the prospect of Julie travelling down to the Sussex seaside resort with Ted.

Ted's a sound enough guy Sam thought. *Married man whose wife had lost interest in dancing but he continued alone one or two nights a week, because he was good at it. What about the other "Usual Subjects"?* He'd already checked out their files. Patrick, a super fit and handsome, black man. No shortage of admirers but lives with his, air stewardess, girlfriend who was often away on long haul flight but had been with him at the Town Hall Dance. She'd confirmed his alibi before jetting off to Australia or somewhere. Then there's Roger, Sam laughed to himself, Skinny kid, probably in his twenties, late to lose his teenage acne and still living with his mum. Solid alibi and I doubt that he would have the confidence let alone the strength to commit the crimes. Then there's the girls. But this was a sexual act motivated by some kind of sadistic perversion. No as long as we have Russell locked up Julie would be quite safe at Camber . . .

'Coming up on the building site, Guv,' Jackie King broke Sam's reverie.

Blue and white tape fixed to iron road pins surrounded the entire plot where the show-house stood. A pale faced uniformed constable lifted the tape to allow Sam and King to duck under.

'Stay here, Jackie. See if you can find the person who found the body,' Sam did not want to subject the young woman to any more sights of carnage. *She'll resent that,* he thought and she obviously did as she turned away.

'Site canteen, Guv,' the constable volunteered.

'Go talk to him, Kingy.' Sam took a deep breath and strode to the show-house door.

The crime scene was exactly like the others, the body spread-eagled on the bed. This time swarms of flies infesting the noughts and crosses game etched in blood on a soft and rounded abdomen, added to the revulsion. With only one square available, the game was inevitably a draw. Sam still did not know if he was playing the nought or the crosses. Unable to look at it any more he left the SOCO team to their grim task and told the sergeant in charge to let the pathologist know, when she arrived, that he would be at Dartford police station if she wanted him.

He used the short walk to the site canteen to suppress the nausea that was building up inside him. Another young woman mutilated and killed. This time it could have been prevented. They had had the perpetrator in custody and had let him go. If only they had pushed the issue of the first two murders with the CPS solicitor. It was Archer's decision but Sam knew he should have argued the point more forcefully. All my fault.

He went to join PC King in the double Portacabin that provided deliciously greasy, fried breakfasts for the small army of construction workers, most of whom were crowded inside discussing the topic of the day over egg-banjos and mugs of tea. Some sombre and others laughing and joking. Sam wanted desperately to take a truncheon to the latter. He spotted King in the corner; she had evidently cleared some space around her table and was sitting facing the room, occasionally glaring at eavesdroppers. Across from her was a huge donkey jacketed man, his white hard hat pushed back on his head. He was constantly crossing himself as he spoke.

King patted the man's hand and nodded in Sam's direction as he approached.

'Detective Inspector Miller this is Tom Doyle, he found the body,' she said by way of introduction.

'I didn't touch anything, sir; I just came out and told the boss.'

'That's good, Tom,' Sam said. 'Have you got all his details, Jackie? You can fill me in on the way back.' I want, no, need, to get to grips with Russell. Now! He was shouting inside his head. Sam walked out.

Pausing only to thank Mr Doyle, Jackie King ran after her boss, catching up as he reached their car. She handed him a paper cup that smelt vaguely of coffee. Sam took a sip through the slot in its plastic cap. The contents bore more resemblance to the muddy puddles that spotted the unmade roads of the site. Ferociously, he slung it away.

Two more vehicles had arrived, Forest was getting out of one and Melanie Gordon was rummaging in the back of her estate car alongside him.

Melanie looked at Sam around the tailgate of her Volvo, 'I know, "time of death,"' she quoted with a thin smile.

'Tell it to Forest. He's in charge here now. I'll get it out of Russell.' Sam looked at his DS and nodded towards the house, 'In there.' Stating the obvious. 'It's not pretty,' he warned. 'Come on Jackie, Dartford.'

Jackie King put the Focus into gear. 'You don't have to protect me, you know,' she said.

'I know.' Sam was almost contrite. 'What did you find out from your friend, Tom?'

'It's his job to do the rounds of finished properties, from time to time, checking the doors and stuff. There's a night security firm that drives around but the manager doesn't trust them so Tom

314

does a quick check before he gets on with his work, he's a general labourer. Dogsbody he calls himself. Anyway, he found the front door unlocked and had a quick look round to see if anything had been nicked. Found her upstairs, unfortunately by the time he got back with the site manager, half the men on the site were in the room having an ogle.'

'Typical. Anything for a flash of fanny that lot . . . Sorry Kingy.'

'That won't help SOCO. Will it Guv?'

'No it bloody well won't.' They were turning onto the dual carriageway. 'Come on Kingy, step on it. I want a word with our Mr Anthony John Russell.'

King accelerated out into the fast moving traffic. Morning rush hour was over and the road was relatively clear so less than a minute later they were at the Dartford off-ramp.

'I see your friend Doc Fielding is here,' King remarked as she parked alongside the psychologist's Jaguar.

'Oh that's alright, as long as she keeps her hands to herself,' Sam's expression belied the flippancy of the remark. *There goes my chance of beating a confession out of him.* He thought.

In fact, Elizabeth had persuaded the custody sergeant to let her sit in the interview room with Russell. A constable was standing just inside the door to keep order, but it appeared Fielding had calmed the suspect down. At least he was sitting down and talking quietly to her.

'I'm not saying anything until my lawyer gets here' Russell barked at Sam as he entered the room.

'Fine by me.' Sam took to the only vacant chair as PC King took up a position, standing parade-at-ease, against the wall. 'Could you rustle up a couple more chairs please constable?' Sam said to the local PC, 'and maybe some coffee.' Sam returned his attention to the prisoner fixing him with a gaze that could no way be interpreted as anything other than malice.

King whispered important instructions on how her boss liked his coffee to the constable and, as soon as he left, resumed her stance in his place. Silence descended crushing the life out of the room. Sam's glare never wavered but not once was it met by Russell.

The air in the room was still and hot. Sam could detect Russell's perspiration in its battle with his aftershave. The sweat was winning. Elizabeth's perfume, on the other hand, was light and full of pheromones of a different nature. All this was brushed aside by the arrival of the coffee. Its welcome pungency sweeping through the room, cleansing and adding energy.

King took them at the door and distributed the cups, cream and sugar for Fielding, black and unsweetened for Sam. She looked at Russell and back to her boss. Sam dismissed her querying look with an almost imperceptible shake of his head. The constable returned with two more chairs.

Sam directed him where they were to go. One for the lawyer, alongside his client, and one against the back wall.

'Would you mind Elizabeth?' He indicated the chair by the wall. 'My constable will need to take notes.' The reshuffle accomplished, King took out her pocket book and a pen and sat at the ready. 'Is there anything you would like to tell me while we are waiting?' Sam wanted to smile at the prisoner but could not bring himself to do it, so sipped his coffee instead. It was hot and good, not Blue Mountain but better than the stuff they served at Greenwich. Perhaps I should put in for a transfer here. Now he managed a smile, 'I can turn the tape on if you like.'

'I didn't do anything,' Russell growled through gritted teeth, 'I did not kill any of those women.' Tears of frustration rolled down his cheeks.

'Then where were you last night?'

'Nowhere,'

'Nowhere? Everyone has to be somewhere.'

'I mean I didn't go out. After work I came straight here then went home. You know I was here. I was talking to you and her.' Russell nodded at Fielding, all thoughts of charming her gone.

Sam fished in his jacket pocket and produced a crumpled photograph. It was a print out from the perfume shop video. 'How well do you know these two women?'

Before Russell could reply there was a tap at the door and it opened without waiting for a response. Emanuel Okeke, briefcase in one hand and a bundle of files under the other arm, strode in.

'Do not say another word, Mr Russell,' was his predictable opening phrase.

'Mr Okeke, glad you could make it. At last.'

'You have no right to interview my client without my presence.'

'We were just having a friendly chat over a cup of coffee,' Sam forced another smile and sipped. 'Oh did you want one? It's very good.'

'I require a private conversation with my client.'

'You can have five minutes, and then we can get down to discussing the brutal murder of another of his friends.' Sam snatched back the picture and stormed out. PC King and Elizabeth Fielding trailed after him.

Sam, still carrying his almost empty mug, set out to find the source of the coffee. The small canteen was on the top floor, presided over by a one-woman team of caterers. A large glass jug of freshly made Arabica was keeping warm on a hotplate by the till. Sam zeroed in. He had just drained his mug and put down for a refill when his mobile phone vibrated against his chest.

'Miller' he answered. It was Forest with bad news.

Chapter 26

Sam finished the call and snatched up his mug, which had been refilled for him, spilling scalding coffee over his fingers. Swapping hands, he sucked his stinging fingers, at the same time savouring the brew. He joined Fielding and King who had taken a table close to a window that framed extensive views of the rooftops of old Dartford and the elevated railway line that sliced between the residential and industrial sectors of the town.

'We've got to let him go.' Sam sighed, as he sank into the plastic bucket of the chair they had left out for him.

'Why?' the two women asked simultaneously.

'He's got an alibi . . . cast iron.'

'Have you checked?' Elizabeth asked.

'Don't have to. It's us.'

'What?' The psychologist's face was a picture of incredulity.

According to Melanie Gordon, time of death was thirty-five to thirty-seven hours ago. That puts it between six and eight the night before last. Also, the GPS in the victim's car puts her at the scene at that same time. We were with Russell

321

from just before six to almost eight. No way could he have done this one.'

'No chance of a mistake about the time of death?'

'Mel doesn't make that kind of mistake. It was definitely within those parameters.'

'A copycat, maybe?'

'No. The noughts and crosses game progresses perfectly, two moves per killing. It has to be someone at least present at the previous two.' Sam, elbows on the table held his head in his hands over his steaming mug.

'Perhaps his accomplice has stepped up to the plate.' Elizabeth's head also needed support. She rested her pointy chin on one hand.

'Does that mean we're back to square one, Guv?' King's normally cheerful outlook was equally down.

'I think he may have been set up for this right from the start . . . Russell that is.' Sam sipped his coffee, his only salvation.

'Maybe not for the first one though.' Fielding reached out a hand to touch Sam's. 'I said that one was inconsistent.'

'Does that bring us back to Sykes?' King asked.

'No, Kingy. His alibi panned out. His lawyer even found the black cab driver that drove him home that night. I think our killer learned as he went along.'

'Or she,' King added.

'Or she, right. What do you think Elizabeth?'

'Possible,' Fielding thought long and hard. 'In that case we'd be looking for someone with some kind of perversion, perhaps repressed homosexual tendencies.'

'Someone who might mutilate their own body too, say with piercings or tattoos?'

'Possibly . . . do you have someone in mind?'

'Yes.' Sam downed his coffee and said, 'right, let's give Russell the good news. He stood up. 'We need to ask a couple of questions before we let him in on it. Follow my lead and read what you can, Liz. He may still be involved.'

As soon as they entered the interview room, Okeke jumped up to lodge his protest. He had barely got to "Harassment", his forth word, when Miller snapped, 'Sit down and shut up, Manny.'

They assembled in the previous seats, King with her notebook and Fielding leaning forward watching Russell's every nervous movement.

'Mr Russell . . .'

'Just a minute,' Okeke interrupted, 'are you not going to switch on the tape recorder.'

Sam sighed, flipped the switch and waited for the tone. He then looked at his watch and recited the standard interview opening. 'Satisfied?'

Okeke, nodded.

'For the tape please Mr Okeke.'

'Yes.'

'Mr Russell,' Sam started again, 'do you know either of these women?' He flattened out the print, now folded in quarters, slid across the table.'

'They go to my dance class sometimes.'

'Do you know their names?'

'The one on the left is Maureen Duffy and the other one's Gilda something. Like I said they are in my group.'

'Have you ever had an affair with either of them?'

Russell snorted. 'You've got to be joking,'

'How about,' Sam dredged his memory, 'Carol O'Connor?'

Russell laughed out loud. 'That one with all the ironwork and tats? Hardly my type.'

'Mr Russell,' Elizabeth put in, 'sorry to interrupt, Sam. Can I ask, did any of them ever have a crush on you?'

Russell grinned, 'All of them, probably.'

'But any one more than the others?'

Russell shrugged.

'Mr Russell, we have reason to believe that you have been set up. Framed if you like, and the possible motive is that it's someone you've slighted recently.' Sam crossed his arms and watched his words sink in.

'Could it be one of the three women we've mentioned?'

Russell sat back and relaxed, probably for the first time in days. 'I, I never gave any of them reason to think they were anything more than dancing partners. Carol was the best, I suppose, despite her size. Better than Sheila really, but she was never a candidate for competition. Not a good image for Ceroc.

'What about the others?'

'They both demo'd for me, from time to time, nothing more.'

Sam took the picture back, put it away and produced a card, 'Thank you Mr Russell. Sorry you have been put to so much trouble, he pressed his card into Russell's hand, 'If you think of anything . . .' Sam was already rising. 'That will be all for now, you are free to go.'

Okeke was on his feet, ready with a tirade about claiming for compensation, but Russell put out a restraining hand. 'Let them get on with finding whoever did this, Emanuel, that can be sorted out later.' He nodded at Sam and flashed his ever winning, Anton Du Beke, smile at

Elizabeth then with his hand on his lawyer's shoulder ushered him out.

'Smarmy sod,' Jackie King muttered as soon as the door closed.

'Yuk,' said Fielding getting up from her chair. 'But in the clear.'

'Only for this one. Did you pick up on anything, Liz,' Sam asked.

'I think he was a bit more than a partner to all of them at some time but didn't want to admit it.'

'Assuming it's a frame up, which one would be most aggrieved about it?'

'He was very disparaging about one with the "Iron Work".'

'Carol?'

'Carol.'

'OK let's see if we can find her.' Sam used his phone to get an address as they left.

Carol O'Connor lived with her disabled mother on the twelfth floor of a tower block in Woolwich. The kind of place where the lifts were forever being vandalised and you stood a good chance of being mugged if you used the stairs. In this case, the lift was actually working although the light in it was not and it smelt strongly of stale urine.

Sam tried to hold his breath for as long as possible and ended up panting in God knows what, well before it made its groaning and ponderous way to twelve. I wonder how Liz is coping. He tried to make out her face in the brief flicker of light when the cracked, wired glass in the slit window coincided with that of the outer doors.

Eyes watering slightly, they stepped out into the only marginally less ammonia-tinged air of the lobby and marched along the balcony.

'We're walking down, right?' Sam stated flatly.

'Agreed,' said Elizabeth.

'Oh good,' said Jackie.

O'Connor opened the door in response to a single peal from her, "Westminster Chimes", doorbell. She quickly invited them in, poking her head out to look left and right along the balcony, before closing the door.

'This looks official,' Sam, she said glancing from Fielding to King and back to him.

'Just some questions, you might be able to help us with.' Sam's smile felt tired and phony.

'You'd better come through and sit down.' Fresh pine and furniture wax displaced the pungency of the lift still hanging in their nostrils as they crossed the threshold and had them wiping their feet on the square of coir matting, before stepping out onto the spotless laminate flooring of the hall.

Carol led the way into a bright and pleasant sitting room. 'I haven't got long, I have to get mother settled before I go out. I'm meeting Ted at half-four.'

'You're going to Camber?' Sam asked.

'Yes, big treat, my sister's coming to collect mum for the weekend. I'd offer you tea but, like I said, time's tight. What is it you want?'

'Carol,' a weak voice carried in through the door.

'Coming mum,' Carol stepped through the door, turning to whisper, 'she's in the loo.'

During an awkward wait of ten minutes, Sam wandered around the spacious but sparsely furnished room. Apart from the twenty-four inch television mounted low on the wall, there was a small bookcase containing several crime novels on its lower shelves, some displaying Dewey Decimal codes on their spines, indicating they were from a public library. The top shelves were packed with history textbooks and, arranged on the shelves in between, a fine collection of gleaming Capo Di Monte porcelain figures. He joined the others arranging themselves on the old but still smart Chesterfield sofa.

Carol returned, pushing a smartly dressed, white haired woman of about sixty, in a wheelchair. 'Mum, this is Sam.' She started to make the introductions, 'I don't know . . .'

'Elizabeth Fielding, I'm working with the police.' Fielding extended a hand to Carol's mother.

The woman ignored it. 'So you're Sam, I've heard a lot about you.' She smiled revealing a full set of gleaming teeth. 'Are you taking my Carol away for the weekend?'

'No mum, I'm going with Ted. Sam just wants to ask some questions . . . Go on, Sam, what do you want to know.'

'OK. First, can you tell me where you were on Wednesday, before going to Charlton, that is.'

'I was here . . . wasn't I mum?' Her mother nodded.

Carol squeezed herself into a large, leather wing chair facing him. 'Why, did something happen?' she looked concerned but not worried.

'So what time did you leave here?'

''bout half past six. I got there at ten to seven. Julie can tell you that. I helped to bring in some of her stuff.'

Miller shot a frustrated glance at Fielding. 'That's what I thought.'

'How well do you know Tony Russell?' Fielding took over the questioning.

'Quite well I suppose. I used to go to his class every week before I switched to Charlton. Now though, I only go to Welling when I feel like it.'

'Oh, why did you switch classes?'

'Don't know really. I got friendly with Julie and I like the crowd there.'

'Did Tony do anything to . . . put you off in any way?'

'No nothing like that . . . he can be a bit of a sleaze-ball sometimes, but I can't believe he killed anyone.'

'How did you get on with Sheila Delaney?'

Carol shrugged, 'Alright, I suppose. She was a good dancer . . . I don't really socialise with any of the crowd outside of dancing. It's my only thing, what with work and Mum, I don't have time for anything else.'

'One last question,' Miller cut in, 'did Tony Russell ever leave something here with you for safekeeping, A bag or anything?'

'You are joking; Tony Russell wouldn't be seen dead in this area, let alone climb all the way up here.'

'OK, thanks Carol. We'll see ourselves out.' Sam got up to go. From the window, the vista was spectacular; out past the Thames barrier to the hazy outline of the Queen Elizabeth II Bridge to the east and the loftier towers of Canary Wharf to the west with the river winding between. *The only asset to this shabby relic of the Fifties,* Sam thought. 'Quite a view,' he said.

'Yes, we'll miss it. We're on the council list for a bungalow. Not holding our breath though, eh

Mum?' Carol led the way to the front door and peered out, left and right, before letting them past. 'Are you coming down to Camber, Sam?'

'Hopefully . . . when I can.'

'See you there.'

The descent of the stairs was less traumatic than the lift but the sights and smells were, if anything, more disturbing. Broken toys, discarded lollipop sticks and sweet wrappers lay cheek by jowl with fish and chips wrappers, used condoms and broken hypodermic needles.

'Bloody place needs pulling down,' Sam growled, as they emerged into the street.

'But to some it is home,' Elizabeth replied, 'their place was a little palace.'

They had taken the precaution of leaving their cars in the public car park adjacent to the Magistrate's Court. The normality of exhaust fumes and fast food outlets was like a breath of fresh air as they walked back to them.

'What now?' Elizabeth looked at her watch.

Cartier, Sam noted, miracle she still had it, Sam felt to reassure himself his was still on his wrist. I think you might call it a day, Liz. We'll go back to the Nick and see if SOCO have come up with anything.'

'Fine, I can cross on the ferry from here,' Fielding extended a hand for Sam to shake. *It's a tough job but someone has to do it,* Sam thought as he took it.

'Let me know if there's anything . . . anything at all I can do.' Elizabeth clicked the remote in her other hand and the Jaguar chirruped in reply.

King had the Focus started and was grinning as Sam got in.

'What?' Sam said.

'She fancies you rotten,' she laughed.

'Nonsense,' Sam looked away*, can't imagine why.*

It took an hour to bring DCI Archer fully up to speed on the case. Mick Forest returned and set up another board. They occupied the whole end of the incident room, no space for any more. While they waited for forensic and post mortem results, Miller and Forest posted what they could and compared the facts.

'The only connecting factor is Tony Russell. He knew them all but could not have been at the last scene.' Forest had stuck another tragic crime scene portrait on the wall of death.

'That doesn't actually rule him out of any of the others,' Sam walked along the line studying the jumble of pictures and written notes. 'It only confirms someone else is involved.'

'Let's hope forensics come up with something.'

'Not a lot of hope there, at least quickly, the scene was badly disturbed. Elimination will take forever. Anyway, before that it had been wiped clean. When we opened her car, it stank of petrol. Miracle it didn't blow up when the light came on. It was swabbed with the stuff.'

'So that proves the murderer had been in the car, probably travelled with her. CCTV again. Everything we have on the route from the estate agent's office to the building site.'

'Already on it, Guv.'

It was gone five pm and his team were splitting up for the night. Sam gathered the stack of files off his desk, humped them down the stairs and stacked them in the boot of his Saab.

A little light reading overnight and sleeping on it might resolve the nagging suspicion he had missed something. He ran back in, to sign out, when his mobile phone chirruped. A text message. He waited until he was back in the car before opening it. "All we are missing is you" it was from Julie and there was a picture attached. It showed a group picture of all the usual suspects. Julie was in the front row, sitting on a low, stone wall, between Roger and Ted then Carol and Patrick. Standing at the back of them, Tony

Russell, grinning, with his arms around Gilda and Maureen. If they stayed together like that they'd all be safe. Julie told him that the music started at nine and often went on until four in the morning.

He tried to call her back as he started the car. Unobtainable. *I'll be happier with Julie in my arms where I can look after her.* He decided to go home and grab a bag then drive on down and join them. No more than a two hour drive, even at this time of day. An hour later, he was on the M20, still choked with the last of the Friday rush. He had to revise his journey time and now did not expect to arrive until close to nine. *Still we have all night,* he thought.

Friday 28th April

It was a good trip down, six of us in a minibus all jolly with good music from the CD player. We are all looking forward to dancing tonight.

Tony turned up out of the blue, told us about his friend being killed. Said he had been cleared because he was with the cops at the time. Ooops. I do not believe it.

Ah well A policeman is my alibi too. As long as no one tells him I was late that night.

Better move my schedule up.

Chapter 27

It started to rain as Sam left the A20 at Ashford. He immediately encountered road works at Kingsnorth. He nosed forward through the contra-flow feeling frustrated and excited. ETA. now nine-fifteen. The rain became a full on storm. Lightening slashed the sky ahead with blinding streaks; he counted seventeen before the thunder followed. Clear of the road works he tried to make up time. His reliable, Saab passing more timid drivers, on the rain-lashed tarmac. Headlights in his face dazzled, lightening sizzled only a nine count now to the increasingly loud roll from the heavens.

He was quite enjoying himself. Concentrating hard, scanning the road ahead. He almost missed his phone jangling, in its hands free cradle, below his central armrest. He hit the pick up button as he swerved back onto his own side of the road as a giant articulated lorry roared towards him. 'Hello, Miller here,' he shouted, over the outraged motor horn of the truck he had cut up behind.

It was Higgins' familiar voice, 'Just going off now, Sam, just thought I'd give you a quick update.'

Sam gunned the throttle to put some distance between himself and the irate driver. The road was completely awash as he made the curve. Another flash and loud crack, like artillery fire from the storm, almost simultaneous now. Even the Saab drifted, under-steering to the edge of the blacktop.

'Sam, are you alright?' the phone crackled and hissed.

'Hang on I'm driving,' Sam spotted a turnoff and, breaking as hard as he dare, just made it into the slip road and onto an empty minor road. He snatched up the handset as he skittered to a halt on the loose gravel of the splayed driveway of someone's house, 'Sorry, 'bout that. There's a hell of a storm going on here.' To emphasise the point, another flash illuminated the car's interior; the thunder a second later. 'What did you say?'

'We found some remains in a bonfire two houses along. Probably the woman's clothes and the bedding from the show-house. Among the debris was a watch. Blackened and cracked, it had stopped at eight o-five, so that confirms time of death to be before eight at night or eight am.'

'Anything else?'

'Nothing conclusive, odd scraps of hair, not the victims but could be any old ginger paddy from the site. We're processing it now but won't have any results before tomorrow.'

'Ginger?'

'Well more like red actually.'

'Could it be dyed?'

'Possibly,' a touch of hesitation crept in to the technician's reply, 'do you want me to check?'

'Could you . . . I know it's Friday night but...'

'OK, Sam, if you think it's important.'

'How long?'

'Give me an hour.'

'Good Man.' Sam hung up and leaving the engine running braved the lashing rain to retrieve the stack of files from the boot. In the narrow beam from the overhead map reading light, he went through the files one by one. Now he knew what had been bothering him.

There it was in file "SLOW HAND I" second addendum to the forensic report. Fragments of hair found in shower drain. Dyed red. Hair dye code 4/75. No DNA present. He dumped the folder in his lap and took up the next one.

"SLOW HAND II" no reference to hair dyes there.

"SLOW HAND III" Dyed burgundy, Hair dye code 4/75. Limited DNA present.

Red hair, Accomplice or perpetrator. It had to be Gilda or Maureen. Or Both. The car was steaming up inside, he turned on the screen demister. No, it can't be, I saw them myself at Charlton Wednesday night. Is this another red herring? He laughed aloud at the pun. Come on Higgins, is it red or burgundy.

Sam restacked the files on the passenger seat, trapped them behind the seatbelt to prevent them tipping into the foot well, threw the car into gear and made a wheel spinning u-turn to rejoin the A2070. Seeing a road sign to Hamstreet and gunned it, about fifteen miles to Rye and Camber. He was leaving the storm behind; it was going north while he headed south. The highway was narrower now, lined with plenty of residential buildings. He made the best progress he could through the twisting minor roads. Forty-five minutes later, he swung into the welcoming entrance to Pontins Holiday Park.

Sodden flags of all nations fluttered limply from tall poles in front of the main reception. Sam dumped his car at the foot of a flight of wide concrete steps and strode, three at a time, up to the check-in. The Bluecoat at the desk glanced at his Warrant Card and picked up the phone to call the manager.

'I need to find Miss Julie Button, urgently,' Sam demanded before he could finish dialling.

'Mr Turner can help you there.' He pressed the last digit and clearly got a swift response. 'Mr Turner . . . but there's a policeman here to see you . . . he's looking for . . .' he looked up at Sam. 'He'll be right out.'

338

'Tell him to bring his pass keys with him.'

The man looked at the phone as if it had personally offended him. 'He hung up already.'

A door behind the reception desk opened and a tall man in his mid thirties stepped smartly through. 'Do we have a problem, officer?' He looked Sam up and down as if suspecting a hoax.

Sam flipped out his ID again, 'Detective Inspector Miller.' Sam said, 'I need to find one of your guests. Miss Julie Button. Can you tell me her room number?'

Turner spun a small computer screen on its pedestal so that Sam could see and started to input the name. A list appeared. 'There we are "Button - party of seven - Chalets 209 and 210." They are over here.' He pointed to a large, wall mounted, site map, 'that's the far side of the complex.'

'Do you have a pass key?' Sam was already turning towards the door.

'Yes, but, what is the problem?'

'Come on. I'll tell you on the way.'

Sam told the man nothing on the way, he was too busy chivvying the man along. They ended up running between the chalet lines. 209 and 210 were on opposite sides of the service road single storey double fronted structures with windows either side of a central door. Both were in darkness.

'Which one first?' Turner asked between gasps for breath.

'That one.' 209 portrayed ladies in residence by the bikini drying on the washing line in the sideway.

'You're wasting your time, there's no one in,' Turner fumbled with keys on a long chain clipped to his waistband.

Once inside, Sam quickly opened each of the two bedroom doors, flipping on the lights and peered in. Both were in a certain level of disarray consistent with incomplete unpacking and a hasty change of clothes. There were three open bags in evidence none was Julie's.

'They'll all be in the ballroom by now,' Turner followed Sam around switching lights off again, 'they dump their gear and start dancing as soon as they arrive, this lot.'

'OK, we'll check the other side then go there next.'

The other chalet told the same story.

'What's the quickest way to the ballroom?'

'Follow me.' Turner seemed to be caught up in the urgency of the matter. He had dropped his need for an explanation and now led off at a trot. Cutting down grassy, side alleyways rather than following the tarmac roads they came out alongside a large, aluminium clad, two-storey building.

340

'The ballroom is up there.' He pointed to a line of windows that extended almost the whole length of the top floor. They blazed in ever changing, coloured light and the strains of "Come Up and See Me" by Cockney Rebel defeated the double glazing enough to be clearly audible from where they were. 'There's a fire escape stair on the corner.'

Sam took the lead, bounding up each of the three flights of iron stairs in two strides. In the hall, the music was all pervading, muffled only by the three hundred or so dancers gyrating to fill the dance floor; all different but all in perfect synchronicity, like migrating starlings on an autumn evening. Sam threaded his way between the swarm and the tables that lined the sides of the hall, making for the stage at the far end, where a DJ was set up. A stack of giant speakers made their presence felt, physically resisting his progress like a head wind.

'Sam,' Carol lunged out of the crowd, You made it. Have you . . .' The rest of the sentence was drowned out by the strident trumpet opening of "Salamone," a fast Latin number, as the music changed.

'Have you seen Julie,' Sam bellowed in her multi-ringed ear, as she first hugged him and then tried to drag him into the masses.

'That's what I said.' She threw an impromptu, and remarkably fast, spin returning to grab his hand, 'She went down stairs to the Blues Room.'

'Where's Tony?'

'He went too. There's only me, Gilda and Roger up here.'

Sam noticed Roger over her shoulder, dancing on his own as if to keep his engine running until Carol returned. He could not see Gilda but in that crowd, even her fire coloured quiff would be easily swallowed up. 'Which way?' was the best he could do. She pointed diagonally across the hall. The direct path was like swimming through a snake pit. Sam reversed his course, taking the perimeter route. The manager tagged along behind.

A broad, curved and carpeted internal staircase, with ornate balustrades, led down to a spacious atrium lit by a glittering multi-tiered chandelier. Sam was attracted by the sound of Louis Armstrong singing "Dancing Cheek to Cheek." He approved. In a few moments he would be doing just that with Julie, he hoped. Through double doors was a similar, if smaller, scene to above. The difference here was that the stage was draped and more theatrical in style and located on the long side. It was marginally less crowded and no tables cluttered the space just a single line of red velour flip up, cinema type seats lined one wall. Apparently, these were only used as an impromptu cloakroom.

Ella Fitzgerald took over the vocals as Sam waded into the centre of the room. He had spotted Russell dancing and blatantly showing off, to a tall, shapely brunette.

Sam tapped him on the shoulder, timing it as the woman arched backwards into a dramatic dip. 'Where's Julie?' Sam demanded.

Russell struggled to recover his partner without dropping on to her curvaceous behind. He apologised to her before replying. 'What is it with you?'

'Where's Julie?' Sam repeated.

'She was here earlier, but went off to move her things into my room.' He grinned, but not without a smidgen of malice. 'I said she could have it if you were coming down.' His partner had lost interest and was dancing with someone else now. 'Wish I hadn't now.'

'Was she on her own?'

'No . . . Maureen went to give her a hand.'

'Oh no! Where's your room?'

'C-Fifty-four, two rows over.' Russell saw Sam's expression and changed his own.

Sam ran to the door where the manager was leaning against the jamb.

'Come on,' Sam shouted as he ran past, 'C-fifty-four.' Outside he looked back and forth. Which way?

Before he could ask, Russell reached his elbow and pointed.

Together, they ran flat out, crossing between blocks of two storey studio rooms.

'Up there!' Russell pointed to the only lit window in the row.

They clattered up the stairs to a long, cantilevered balcony that served the upper apartments. Fifty-Four was six along. The manager was still puffing his way out of one of the cross paths below when they reached it.

'Julie!' Sam did not wait for a reply and shoulder barged the door. The flimsy frame splintered on impact and he stumbled in, only to be brought up short at what he saw.

Chapter 28

The double bed stuck out from the centre of the far wall. On it, secured by pink furred handcuffs to the four corners of it, was Julie. Naked and bleeding from the crisscross pattern carved on her stomach she stared back at Sam, eyes wide and full of panic.

Perched behind her, jammed between Julie's head and the wall, was Maureen, also naked. She sneered at Sam. 'So you've caught me, Detective Inspector Miller,' she almost spat his name. 'But the game's not over yet.' She had the fingers of her left hand entwined in Julie's fringe. She pulled it back hard. Julie's lips parted, in response to the newly imposed pain, but all she could do was gurgle, due to the large rubber gag jammed between her teeth.

The bloodstained fingers of Maureen's other hand were wrapped round the handle of a hollow ground butchers knife. She touched it to the underside of Julies chin causing a small trickle of blood to run down the already reddened blade.

'It's over Maureen. No need to hurt her anymore.' Sam edged into the room, still a yard away from the foot of the bed.

'We haven't finished playing yet.'

'But the games a draw . . . no one wins.' Sam watched as Maureen brought the tip of the blade up towards Julie's earlobe.

'There's still one square left. Fill it in for me will you, there's a dear.' Her voice was all mock sweetness.

'OK . . . give me the knife.' Sam took a step forward.

'Oh no you don't.' The blade nicked Julie's ear, another tiny drop of blood. 'Use your own.'

'I don't have a knife.'

'In that case,' her elbow came forward prepared to cut.

'Wait . . . would a pen be satisfactory?'

'A red pen?'

'I think I have one,' Sam fished in his jacket pocket and brought out two. He let the blue one fall to the floor. 'OK?' he held up the other.

'Go ahead, but no tricks.' She shuffled her legs further up under her. 'Look Julie, your lover is finishing our game for us.'

Carefully, Sam approached the side of the bed. The pattern of cuts was deep and bleeding continuously onto the pale blue coverlet. Her beautiful body would be defiled forever. 'I don't know if I am noughts or crosses,' Sam looked into the insane, green eyes of the serial killer.

You will have to guess then won't you.' she smiled almost sympathetically.

346

Sam hesitated, listening to the sound of heavy boots running along the balcony. There was nothing any amount of reinforcements could do.

'Come on, I haven't got all night.' Her elbow lifted again.

Sam leaned over to the vacant square and drew a circle.

'Wrong!' the blade swept down from Julie's ear cutting a swathe half way across her throat.

'No!' Sam threw himself across the bed, elbowing Maureen out of the way and clutching at Julies neck as blood sprayed out of the wound, splattering the scene right up to the ceiling. His fingers pressed deep into the wound and found the half severed carotid artery, there was just a chance he could stem the flow until help arrived. He pinched hard, harder. Gradually the blood flow reduced from a pulsing spray to a steady ooze. It was working.

He felt the blow like a punch rather than the sharpness of a stab, but the grinding of eight inches of steel against his shoulder blade left him in no doubt. His own blood now mixed with that of the woman he loved, offered no solace. All he knew was that he had two things to hang onto, Julie's artery and consciousness. The second blow dissolved the latter.

Chapter 29

Sunday 1st May 2005; May Day, celebrating spring's new bounty and a new beginning, but not for Sam Miller. True he emerged from the anaesthetic that day with the prospect of a full recovery subject to one or two further operations. However, the answer to the question that formed his first words would leave him with a wound that would never heal.

Julie had not made it. Paramedics arrived within minutes but she bled out before they could do anything. As it turned out Tony Russell had saved Sam's life. He stepped in, to deflect Maureen's second blow away from his heart and was rewarded with a slash across the face for his efforts. The security guards had restrained the woman, despite her sudden frenzy and she ended up confessing to all of the Slow Hand killings.

Mick forest found Maureen O'Connor's diary when he searched her room in the girl's chalet. It made for horrific reading. According to Dr Elizabeth Fielding, it told all. She planned to write a paper on it once she had finished her psychological evaluation for the trial.

The Jivers at Camber carried on jiving all weekend, skirting the, taped off, crime scene block. All that is except for the "Usual Suspects," every one of them elected to go home, once the police had collected their statements. Some of them declared they would never dance again.

Epilogue

The day of Julie's funeral dawned bright and clear. To Sam Miller it was totally out of keeping with his mood. He breakfasted on Blue Mountain coffee, Co-Codamol and Bushmills then pulled on the trousers of the black, mohair suit that he reserved for such occasions. It was impossible for him to get into a normal shirt and do up the buttons with his arm strapped across his chest. He struggled into a black cotton polo shirt leaving the empty right sleeve dangling and an incongruous lump under fabric. It was the best he could manage.

The first blow, Maureen Duffy had struck him with, fractured his scapula so badly it had to be pinned back together and the tendons to his shoulder had been severed. The second snapped his clavicle.

Pocketing a fresh strip of pain killers and with a last, long swig from the bottle of Irish Whisky; he made his way on to the deck of the Andrea in time to see Jackie King swing DCI Archer's Mondeo into place alongside Sam's Saab.

The tall frame of Elizabeth Fielding emerged from the rear door and strode, towards him.

351

Elegantly turned out in a black version of her trademark business suit and with the wrap around skirt parting to reveal sheer black stocking clad legs she swiftly covered the ground intent on helping him down the gangplank.

Determined to avoid that ignominy, Sam almost ended up in the dock as he hurried to make it to the quayside on his own.

'Sam, are you alright?' Fielding took his good arm in her claw like hand.

'I'm fine.' He snatched his arm away. 'Thanks,' he added grudgingly.

King was standing by the car, looking smart and trim in her dress uniform, in the front seat Archer looked uncomfortable as he toyed with his cap.

'How are you, Sam?' Jackie enquired as she opened the door for him.

I'm so fed up with being asked how I am, was the thought that Sam harboured, but realized that Jackie was one of the few who really cared so replied in as kindly way as he could muster, 'I've been better, Kingy, but I'll manage.'

'Morning, Sam,' Archer said over his shoulder as Sam eased himself into the back seat. 'Sad day.'

'Yes, Sir,' Sam muttered.

The chapel at Falconwood Crematorium was already full when they arrived. Mick Forest was occupying the aisle seat in the back row of pews. He stood to offer Sam the place but Julie's mother spotted them from the front row and waved for Sam to join her. As he walked slowly forward he recognised many of the dancers from Welling and Greenwich watched him pass with a mixture of grim smiles and sympathetic looks. Tony Russell offered a cursory nod which Miller returned. The front rows were reserved for family. As Sam arrived, Margret greeted him tearfully with a kiss on each cheek. She ushered him into the front row where Jodi sat, hidden by the back of the pew until that point. The lad turned, his big rheumy eyes to implore Sam to make his mummy come back. In the background was a recording of Roberta Flack singing "The First Time." Sam felt his throat close up. All he could do was smile sadly back.

When it came to the eulogies Tony Russell was first to speak. The scar still livid on his unshaved cheek he started by praising, Julie for her kindness, noting how she always saw the good in people. The Modern Jive community had lost an outstanding teacher and to all of those who knew her a stalwart friend. Finally, he begged the indulgence of the family and other non dancers if, when they left the chapel, they played one of her favourite tunes and danced in the style of a New Orleans funeral.

In a hoarse whisper Margret asked Sam if he wanted to say something. All he could do was shake his head. Already tearful, she walked unsteadily to the lectern. She spread out the piece of paper she was carrying and put on her glasses only to remove them again and spoke ignoring her notes.

She thanked everyone for coming and told them of her daughter's life. A good, if at times difficult, one. A life filled with love, hope and determination. Margret spoke of her daughter's one pleasure outside the home, dancing. A pleasure only surpassed by the delight she had in bringing up her son. Julie had been a devoted mother, a task she carried out alone until recently when in such traumatic times Sam Miller came on the scene. 'At last,' Margret said, 'my Julie had found a man she could trust. Someone she wanted to include into the life of her little family.' Margret turned to look directly at Sam. 'She loved you, Sam, and she'd want you to know that her last few weeks were the happiest of her life. Thank you for that.'

Weeping copiously she returned to her place next to Jodi who reached up and hugged her saying, 'Don't cry Nanny. Mummy has gone to live with Granddad now in heaven.'

To the strains of Sarah Brightman & Andrea Bocelli singing, "Time to Say Goodbye" the coffin passed from sight leaving the community to file slowly out. The remaining "Usual Suspects," offered their condolences to Margret and moved on to do the same to Sam as if he were here widower. They walked slowly past the mound of floral tributes to the car park where "Sway" her favourite dance tune played and all the jivers danced their own homage to their lost friend.

THE END

Discography

Wish I Didn't Miss You	by	Angie Stone
Hero	by	Enrique Iglesias
Regular Joe	by	Indigo Swing
How Lucky can one Guy Be	by	Indigo Swing
Back to Black	by	Amy Winehouse
Brown Eyed Girl	by	Van Morison
Sway	by	Pussycat Dolls
That old Devil Called Love	by	Alison Moyet
Fine Brown Frame	by	Lou Rawls
Are you in it for Love	by	Ricky Martin
Ladies Night	by	Cool and the Gang
I Just Want to Make Love	by	Eta James
Le Plus du Quartier	by	Carla Bruni
Dance the Night Away	by	The Mavericks
Up and Down	by	Scent
Titanic	by	Ingrid
I Like the Way You Move Fire	by	Kenny G/Earth Wind &
This is the Crazy World	by	Alcazar
Mambo Crazy	by	De-Phazz
Stuck on You	by	3 T
Come Up and See Me	by	Cockney Rebel
Salamone	by	Chayanne
Cheek to Cheek Armstrong	by	Ella Fitzgerald & Lois
The First Time	by	Roberta Flack
Time to Say Goodbye	by	Sarah Brightman & Andrea Bocelli

About the Author

In 2004 John Goodwin retired from his directorship of a Construction Industry PLC based in London. His aim: to pursue the good life in sunny Cyprus and indulge his passion for writing. Along with successful publication of many short stories, poems and essays in local English language periodicals and a regular column for a magazine in Dubai he has written two novels to date. A third is in development. An early version of his first 'The Last Olympiad' was long listed in the UK Authors Opening Pages competition and his Poem 'Monochrome Monday' was runner up in an international poetry competition.

John is currently developing Anixe Publishing Ltd to accommodate his own writing ambitions and to help other writers obtain the recognition they deserve. To date Anixe have published five books:

Nico's Whispers from Cyprus. (Short Stories by Nicolas Protopapas) **Raft of life.** (A Collaborative Novel by Members of the PWG) **Maggie's Secret.** (A Novel by Beryl Lowe) and of course his own **Slow Hand** and **The Last Olympiad.** All are available from Anixe publishing.co.uk and through all good online publishers.

If you have not read The Last Olympiad a synopsis follows.

THE LAST OLYMPIAD

By John Goodwin

Even before the British Olympic Committee won the right to stage the 2012 games they confidently displayed a 'Countdown to London' banner on their website. Little did they know that it was also a simultaneous countdown to events that could make London 2012: *__The Last Olympiad.__*

When Gavinder, a disaffected British born Moslem helped install an explosive device in the concrete undercroft of London's new Olympic Stadium he thought it was set to destroy the structure and cause the cancellation of the games. But other forces are at work and the consequences are far more than his conscience can reconcile.

How did the son of a peace loving, law abiding family find himself involved in terrorism? A remarkable athlete wasted when unwitting prejudice left him rejected and disillusioned. The well-intentioned attempts to turn him from the street-crime he was slipping into dropped him into the clutches of those who would capitalize on his troubled mental state for their own purposes.

Menaced by Shakir, a murderous munitions expert, he is torn between revenge, his innate

361

humanity and his duty to the Jihad. He is involved in love, hate, murder, rape and retribution. Can he keep his faith? If he tells the authorities will they believe him? Can he recover the computerized key that is the only way of disarming the device? Aided in London by a young Islamic student and complicated by a team of mercenaries with dubious loyalties, his adventures take him across Europe, into North Africa and back to London in time for the doomed opening ceremony. Fate, right wing extremists and Anglo-American confusion all play a vital part in the outcome.

www.ingramcontent.com/pod-product-compliance
Lightning Source LLC
Chambersburg PA
CBHW071238170626
46809CB00001B/I